The Predator Steps Softly

— A Novel —

By

Fred Dickey

 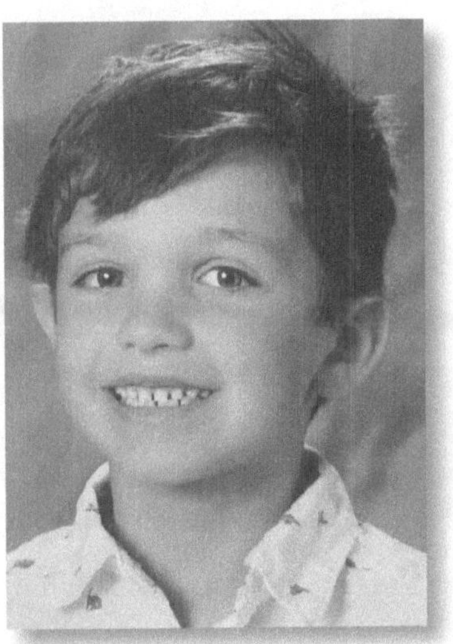

*Dedicated to Zoey and Hunter and all the
other family rascals to follow. Keep growing
in all the good ways.*

Early Reader Comments

Reviewed By Viga Boland for Readers' Favorite 5 STARS
This crime thriller, in many ways, is so much more than just another "whodunit." Several themes are explored through interesting and colorful characters. Readers will enjoy the profiling, coupled with the methods used by the police to narrow down the suspect list. This is an entertaining read that offers suspense relieved by humorous cop banter, along with a little sex and romance and plenty of other issues to think about after you close the book. Enjoy!

Legendary crime writer Joseph Wambaugh:
This is a suspenseful, authentic, and well-researched manhunt for a serial killer. It introduces rookie homicide detective Jaye Peoria, a young woman determined to prove herself and stop an elusive killer. It's a good book."

Maura Parga, San Diego P.D. cold case detective (ret.):
Fred Dickey is a brilliant writer. I love the way the detectives interact with each other, so right on target. It's just like I'm working the case myself. The investigation methods and procedures are accurate. The descriptions of the homeless and their struggles-- perfect. I LOVE THIS BOOK!

Anonymous:
Great job of bringing his characters to life. A must read start to finish. I would highly recommend this to all who love a good suspense story.

Anonymous:
Dickey is a master of metaphor and simile. Good detective mystery flavored with a hint of philosophy and wit.

Carolyn Bertussi:
Warning! Don't start this book if you have a busy schedule. You will not want to put it down! Very well written with an excellent idea of what it's like to be searching for a killer in the life of a detective. The characters are well drawn out and hopefully they will be seen again in a sequel.

Anonymous:
A novel with "page turners" that you'd best read undisturbed for the full effect, and the people law-enforcement come in contact with daily, in every configuration and situation.

Robert Conrad:
As a retired police officer, I can say this book could have been written by a cop. Dickey obviously did his research and got it right. Liked the accurate portrayal of the investigative techniques and the interaction amongst the cops. Suspenseful plot keeps your attention.

Anonymous:
I enjoyed following the investigation of the various suspects, also that it was the first serious crime the lady detective was involved in, I liked the romantic dalliances, showing her having a bit of fun in off duty moments. I have recommended it to my brother in law.

E. DeWan:
This was a fun book to read. The characters were very well developed. I would like to read more stories starring Jaye Peoria and her fellow cops. Highly recommend.

Anonymous:
Fred Dickey takes us into the world of a rookie homicide detective fighting to get her suspect while serving on an all-male detective force. Lots of research makes for a credible read with plenty of twists and turns.

Scott Coyle:
The story was very well written, the characters were believable, the suspense and build up to conclusion was riveting. It is a page turner for sure. Very easy read and being a San Diego boy made the story come alive!

Hub Rushing:
This is a book that holds your attention from start to finish. Clever, intriguing plot and realistic. Identifiable characters make it difficult to put down. I would look forward to reading anything by Fred Dickey.

Kenneth Eichner:
You won't be disappointed reading this book. Fred Dickey brings you in; Right alongside the detectives, you feel the energy as they unravel the mystery. This is a classic.

Anonymous:
I enjoyed following the investigation of the various suspects, also that it was the first serious crime the lady detective was involved in. I Liked the romantic dalliances showing her to have a bit of fun in off duty moments. I recommend.

Redimp:
I enjoyed following the investigation of The various suspects, also that it was the first serious crime the lady detective was involved in, Liked the romantic dalliances, showing her to have a bit of fun in off duty moments. Have recommended it.

Chapter One

She thought she was safe.

The dark alley was her home for the night. She laid down her cardboard mattress and then curled up in thin blankets beneath an old quilt. Her life's possessions were inside trash bags in a nearby grocery cart stolen two owners ago from Safeway.

She slept in clothes she had worn for a week—a flannel shirt with buttons missing and dirt-streaked slacks with puckered threads. Her hair was matted and stringy. Somewhere along the years, her brain had revolted against memories now locked away.

This was Imperial Avenue in the East Village, a part of San Diego where thrown-away people found refuge. Homeless men and women were wraithlike silhouettes along littered streets. They bedded down in empty lots, huddled in doorways, or loitered hopefully outside liquor stores. A Southern California November chill is like a Chicago April chill. After thirty minutes out in it, it's cold.

Occasional headlights penetrated the darkness, then turned away as the gloom washed back over the moody canyons between high rises.

In the slow pulse of after-midnight, evil was free to wander.

The pavement sounded the approach of footsteps. She had heard steps before in her confused mind, but these were different—these were real. But her delusions sedated fear.

The footsteps grew closer, but she only nestled deeper in her blankets. Then, silence. She became aware of a presence and opened her eyes. A pair of man's shoes pointed directly at her from a foot away.

The man grabbed her arm. She braced her feet and gripped her blankets. Feeble resistance was brushed aside. He jerked her upward so hard her head snapped back. He dragged her like a child deeper into the alley. The darkness deepened, and the only sounds to emerge were her gasps, scuffling, and the clatter of a garbage can overturning...the hands-on noise of murder.

The man's grip closed over her throat and slowly compressed. Her mouth parted, and her tongue slid forward. Her eyes grew wide, and her face reddened. A hoarse chicken-like squawk squeezed from her lips. Her face was only a foot from his. Her hands flailed wildly and grabbed at his.

After four minutes, her face turned blue, and her protruding eyes glassed over. Her arms fell limply with a soft slap to her sides. The man felt her carotid artery, was satisfied, lowered her body to the grease-spotted concrete, and hid it behind some trash barrels. He opened a half-gallon bottle and poured the contents on her neck and hands. He then emptied it all over the body. Finally, he stood and briefly examined his work.

He retreated to the alley opening, looked both ways cautiously, and then disappeared.

Patrol officer Norm Wilsey yawned. The streets lay silent as a deep forest this Sunday morning. The first rays of sunlight inched over the bay, fresh and orange, as the night briskness faded.

It was the hour of the graveyard shift when a police officer's blood seemed to thicken, and he yawned in a weak struggle against the urging for rest. The criminals were in the shadows, and the homeless had retreated to wherever. Even the neon seemed anemic.

Wilsey blinked hard to keep his eyes open and looked at his watch. Ten after six. Fifty minutes to go. He decided to make one more swing through the East Village district.

As Wilsey's black and white passed through trendy Fifth Avenue, touristy restaurants, clubs, and boutiques gave way to the sadness of Imperial Avenue.

Wilsey stared fixedly down the street. He almost overlooked a man in work clothes standing next to a truck, frantically waving and shouting for his attention. He snapped to full alert, spun the squad car into a tight U-turn, flicked on the lights, and pulled to a stop. He reached for his radio before exiting the car: "One sixty-four. Out on a citizen's flag. South side of Imperial and Fifteenth."

"Officer, in there!" The man rushed at him, shouting and gesturing toward an alley.

"What is it?"

"A—a body."

Wilsey followed the man into the alley. There, half-hidden behind some barrels, was a body. Wilsey shouldered his way past three workers and knelt beside it.

He saw a woman on her back in the death position of a discarded doll. She was in her fifties or sixties and dressed shabbily. Wilsey looked into the eyes for the unfocused stare of death: it was there. He touched the skin: cold. He tried for a pulse: none. He rose and asked the workers, "Did any of you touch anything?"

"No," they mumbled in ragged unison, shaking their heads.

Wilsey lifted his radio. "This is 164. I have a possible 11-44. Imperial Avenue at Fifteenth Street, south side."

The word "possible" gave urgency to the dispatcher, and she alerted a medical emergency.

Wilsey turned again to the bystanders and wrote down names and contact information from their IDs. "Okay, stand outside the alley, but don't leave." He went to the trunk of his car and grabbed a roll of yellow plastic tape. He crisscrossed it several times across both ends of the short alley identifying it as a crime scene and barring entry.

In about five minutes, two patrol cars in the area rolled up to where Wilsey stood. Patrol officers, "uniforms" as they're called, milled about, waiting to see if they were needed.

A moment later, an ambulance with a paramedic arrived with lights flashing. She immediately went under the tape, careful not to disturb a possible crime scene. She hurried to the body and started her dead-or-alive checklist. The paramedic put her finger on a carotid artery. No pulse. She felt the skin. Cold. Cyanosis had set in, making the skin a blue-marble-white color. Next, she tested the jaw, shoulders, and arms. There was the beginning of stiffening, most noticeable in the jaw. That meant rigor mortis had begun, normally about two hours after death.

She stood up, turned to the police, and said what everyone knew: "This person is dead."

A patrol sergeant arrived, stooped under the yellow tape, and approached the body. Satisfying himself that the subject was indeed dead, the sergeant turned to Wilsey. A quick exchange told him the patrolman knew no more than he.

What had been a bleak scene minutes before was now animated with flashing red and blue lights reflecting on the concrete with carnival color. Static blurts from police radios boomed across the sidewalk. Had this been the suburbs, residents would already be gathering across the street with housecoats bundled tightly against the chill. But in this neighborhood, the few pedestrians hurried on after curious glances.

Making the assumption they were dealing with a crime, although it was only an experienced guess, the sergeant dispatched two officers to search for witnesses. It was Wilsey's duty as discovering officer to guard the scene, protecting against anyone who might try to tamper with or destroy evidence, including blundering cops.

Back at the station, a dispatcher activated a message that made telephones erupt on nightstands next to the beds of five sleeping people. They were the on-call homicide squad. Within seconds, bleary eyes fluttered open, and hands groped for phones. They each listened for a few seconds, grunted, scribbled down a few notes, and regretfully threw the bed covers back.

Almost like a rehearsed drill, the detectives of Sergeant Dave Potter's team stared into bathroom mirrors, reached for toothbrushes and combs, and were out the door carrying steaming cups of coffee and swiping at the condensation on windshields.

An hour after Wilsey's first call, the squad began arriving. Jaye Peoria was first by a couple of minutes because she wouldn't allow it to be otherwise. She had skipped coffee, but she was first.

Shortly behind Jaye was Sergeant Potter, fifty-three. He was one of those ex-Marines who never get the corps out of their system, a by-the-book guy. He was a big, beefy man whose face, when angry or drunk, could resemble a robin's belly. His voice could be a scratchy bullhorn if he felt a situation called for fire and smoke.

Arriving at the same time from different directions were Drew Tatum and Ignacio Almaguer. Tatum was always just Tatum, never Drew. He was a handsome bachelor, not far from forty, who lusted after women in his red Mustang like a starving man reaching for stale bread. He once said he looked for women with "no no-no's."

Tatum spent his money on the ladies and car payments, unfortunately in that order, which meant the finance company and he spent more time in each other's company than either would have preferred.

Ignacio Almaguer was a fifty-ish Mexican-American who had crossed into Mexico only twice in his life and then briefly. The Spanish he spoke would amuse Mexicans across the border sixteen miles south.

Last was Art, lost somewhere in middle-age. His personality was as pastel as his name. He was a bit of a prude who tended to speak in blurts, but not too often, which was probably a good thing. He was the master of the non sequitur. Things would pop out of his mouth from left field. The problem would be his audience might be in the right field. Potter enjoyed ragging on Baker by sometimes calling him Ned Flanders after the pious nerd on the Simpsons TV show.

As the only woman detective in homicide, Jaye naturally attracted interest. And for those getting to know her, the curiosity was rewarded.

At thirty-two, she was the youngest and greenest of the team, having been promoted just three months earlier after six years on patrol. Her five-year-old Honda Civic and a two-bedroom rental were in the groove of a woman playing catch-up with the cost of living.

With his squad assembled, Potter clapped his hands and said, "Okay, let's go to work." The detectives stood near their sergeant as he examined the body. The three men seemed unaware of death's presence at their feet as they chatted. Jaye was quiet. Potter got down on one knee to take a closer look.

"At least I got a good night's sleep," Almaguer said, watching. "It's like an hour added to my life."

"You'll lose it again in the spring, so spend the hour wisely," Tatum said.

The men were not unaware of the tragedy at their feet, and they were not insensitive to tragedy, but one can attend to only so many bodies in alleys before developing callouses to protect one's peace of mind.

Jaye, however, couldn't refrain from glancing at the corpse uncomfortably. She had not been in homicide long enough to view dead bodies like office furniture.

"What kind of rat would do this?" she said with a head shake.

"A two-legged one," Almaguer said.

"A four-legged one would have better morals," Tatum said and looked up to make sure his humor was appreciated. "But, on the other hand, our four-legged cousins caused the Black Death. That in itself was a negative moral statement."

"Those were fleas that caused the Black Death, not the rats," Almaguer corrected him.

"Yeah, but fleas don't have the persona to be bad guys. They're only ugly under a microscope," Tatum said. "How would you say to a scumbag, 'You dirty flea!'"

Jaye was ignoring the banter. She looked up. "I smell bleach. I've scrubbed enough floors. Look at her clothes; they're bleached white like she was doused with it."

Baker said, "Bleach can erase evidence, both DNA and fingerprints."

"Thank you, Flanders," Potter said dryly as he raised himself and dusted off his pants. "She might have been strangled." He reached down and pointed to slightly purplish spots on the sides of the throat, careful not to touch the skin. "Those might be thumb bruises. For now, I'm going to call this a homicide. The bleach cinches it. But even with the bleach, we might be able to lift some prints. Maybe."

He turned to Jaye. "I checked the case rotation Friday, Peoria, and you're up. This one is yours." As lead detective, the crime scene, indeed, the crime itself, became her responsibility.

Potter grinned. "You're first as lead. I'm throwing you into deep water because I know you can swim."

Jaye returned the grin. However, she knew he was giving her a "minor league" murder. Fine. She could handle it—both her case and his doubts.

Jaye was now in charge of finding and organizing evidence and making sure everyone did their jobs. Of course, Potter was still there making observations, but he would be leaving, which Jaye hoped would happen quite soon.

The crime scene investigator from the lab arrived. The first thing she did was take photos of the **body**, including close-ups of the neck bruises. She then pulled paper bags over the hands and head. Then she started photographing the overall scene and doing an inch-by-inch search for physical evidence.

Jaye knelt and peered closely at the dead woman's throat, acutely conscious that the removal of fingerprints from human flesh was a delicate procedure and a race against time, and the clock had been ticking for a while. It might be futile, but they would try.

Jaye spoke to the investigator. "This is going to be dicey if we can get anything at all. Please ask print and DNA techs to meet the body at the morgue." The investigator nodded and took out her radio to make the request.

Jaye turned toward her three partners, but they had already started to fan out to conduct the outer-perimeter search. They looked for any evidence possibly lost or discarded in an escape or any material that didn't seem to belong, though they knew it was a long-shot.

Jaye went to her car to get a camera to record the overall crime scene and shoot extreme close-ups where needed. It was her personal back-up to what the CSI had already done. She and Potter walked the area, leaning over like hunchbacks. They found nothing suspicious.

"I'm going to call patrol and ask for several uniforms to help canvass and interview the area," she said and then asked one of the officers who first arrived to approach businesses for any video surveillance and to make certain no tapes would be erased. "Probably have to call the owners at home," she said.

The last to arrive was the medical examiner's investigator, who took his own notes of the scene. He was accompanied by a pathologist, and a staff medical doctor who came to observe the body prior to removal. The primary reason was to determine the condition of the corpse and to make note of anything at the scene that might have affected its condition. The question yet to be answered was whether this woman was a crime victim, or a casualty of living on the street, a far more common cause of death.

The pathologist did a rectal thermometer check for body temperature. It was 89.3. He calculated the woman had been dead for about five hours, based on an hourly reduction of 1.5 degrees on a cool morning.

He pulled up the torn shirt and got down low to the ground to examine the back. The flesh there was darker, where blood had drained to the lowest point. Lividity, it's called. He could also determine by the position of the pooled blood if the body had been moved. It hadn't.

The pathologist examined the whites of the eyes and took note of the presence of petechiae, which are tiny blood spots from broken capillaries, a common indicator of strangulation because it shows a cut-off of oxygen. There was also bruising in the area of the carotid arteries, another indicator. He observed scratch marks on the victim's neck. He attributed those to a defensive struggling to remove the killer's hands.

When the pathologist finished, and Jaye released the corpse, it was placed in a body bag with a seal over the zipper and then removed to the morgue for forensic testing and autopsy.

At 8:00 A.M., the streets were beginning to stir. Patiently but without success, the detectives and uniforms questioned everyone nearby and knocked on all doors. At the apartments, which were mainly tenements, they rang bells until someone answered

and could give them entry. Many people responded in bathrobes wiping the sleep from their eyes. The cops couldn't care less.

Jaye reached down and shook an old man sleeping a few doors distant in the entryway of a closed thrift store, oblivious to the commotion. He smelled like damp laundry left in a hamper for a week. Beside him was an empty bottle of cheap wine, and clutched tightly in his hand were two thirty-five-gallon black trash bags of his earthly possessions. His clothing was a ripped windbreaker over a grimy plaid shirt, equally dirty work pants, and sockless feet in torn running shoes.

His eyes popped open, and he grunted.

"Hey, mister, wake up." Jaye waited for him to shove himself into a sitting position against a display window. She flashed her badge. "Police officer."

The old man didn't react.

"Have you been here all night?"

Nothing.

She pointed in the direction of the scene. "Did you see anything happening in the alley over there late last night?"

Nothing.

"A woman might have been murdered in the alley over there during the night. Can you help us?"

The old man raised a bony finger to her face. The long nail was jagged and black with encrusted dirt. "All manner of men shall bear false witness against ye; they shall revile ye."

"Sorry to bother you, sir," Jaye muttered with a sigh as she turned toward the next pair of legs protruding from another doorway.

When the detectives rejoined Potter, the ME's van had already departed. Potter waved them over to his car. He rubbed his face to chase away drowsiness and, after hearing their empty reports, said, "Look, people, I don't see where this is going."

He looked forlornly at the now-empty spot in the alley as though some clue might suddenly appear. "Just a homeless woman found dead: probably a loner, no identification, no nothing. We don't even know she was murdered. She could have died of terminal halitosis. Who knows all the germs these derelicts have?"

Jaye winced inwardly at his slur. She had sympathy for these people who had fallen through society's net. She'd spent too much of her youth tight-rope-walking the rim of that pit not to.

Potter took out his car keys. "Let's see if we can find out who the hell she is and wait for the autopsy. It's all yours, Peoria,"

"Thanks, Sarge," Jaye said, trying to keep the relief of his leaving out of her voice. Either she was in charge, or she wasn't.

The four detectives and the borrowed cops fanned out to widen the search. No calls had been placed to 911 at the time of the assault on the woman, but that didn't mean nothing had been seen. Many in this neighborhood were as likely to be at ease with criminals as with cops.

As people answered the knocks, the cops tried to keep the conversations going long enough to observe reactions. They watched eyes, mannerisms, and the carotid arteries in the neck for stress indicators.

After two hours of canvassing, the result was unchanged—nothing. People were either ignorant of what had happened or pretended to be.

Chapter Two

ike Palmer yawned and blinked hard to force his eyes into focus as he reached for the glowing face of the cell phone alongside the bed. He rubbed his forehead as though to purge the sound of the jangling phone, pushed himself to his feet, and started for the kitchen. His wife, Dolores, mumbled, "What time is it?"

"Too early," he said, not wanting to renew the argument that had kept them awake well past midnight. It had been over his job and money, as usual, and didn't get resolved, also as usual.

"Will you start the coffee?" she mumbled.

"Okay. I've got to hurry to get some prints."

"It's Sunday morning, for God's sake! Whose?"

"I don't know, but I'm meeting her at the morgue."

Dolores raised herself to one elbow and squinted sleepily. "That's so depressing. I wish you'd quit and go to work for my father, honey."

"Go back to sleep, Dee." He went into the bathroom and closed the door.

Palmer reached the medical examiner's headquarters just as attendants were wheeling in the sheet-covered body. Also arriving was Marilyn Noguchi, the lab tech who would do the DNA search of the body when Palmer was finished. She went second because a fingerprint exam will normally not erase DNA, but the swabbing for DNA can erase fingerprints.

Jaye wrapped up the crime scene and joined Palmer and Noguchi to observe. She said, "The ME on scene said she was probably killed a couple of hours after midnight. Cause of death is probably strangulation. It looks like we've got bruises on the throat." She also told them about the bleach.

"Oh, this is going to be a walk in the park," Palmer said sardonically as the body was shifted onto a flat steel table. The clothes had been removed and bagged to send back to the lab with Noguchi for further examination, which would include using a luminol spray and also a UV "black light" to scan for trace evidence, especially blood.

Palmer looked at the body: A haggard, late-middle-age woman, gray hair falling in matted twists, skin as white as the laboratory walls. He took fingerprints on the corpse, but that was the easy part. Now, he would look for fingerprints on her body belonging to the killer. What he looked at most carefully was the condition of the skin: almost no hair, that was good; quite a few wrinkles, that was bad.

The bleach troubled him the most. Did the caustic cleaner wipe the body clean? Under the best of circumstances, removing fingerprints from the skin is difficult. In the back of his mind was the question: Is this a waste of time?

The clock was also a problem. With each passing hour, the chance of recovering a serviceable print grew dimmer.

Palmer tried the standard, most reliable methods to detect a fingerprint on the woman's skin, but to no avail. He even employed a laser to search the neck, inch by inch. Nothing.

He was about to quit but decided to try the only procedure left, the Magna-trace method. Though it had a lower success rate, he'd give it a shot, but with little expectation.

Palmer reached into a bag and removed a thick jar and a black wand that looked like a thick pencil. He flicked a small switch on the wand, turning it into a powerful magnet, and lowered it into a jar containing a mixture of iron filings and black carbon powder. Instantly, the mixture clung fast to the magnet, bristling like a hairbrush. Palmer slowly moved the wand across the skin, a fraction of an inch above the surface. If there were any residue of oil or grease from a human finger, such as is accumulated from touching one's hair or face, the powder might stick to it, forming the outline of a fingerprint.

He was about to accept failure when he noticed a small amount of powder had stuck to the skin on the left side of the neck, the marking so thin it was barely visible. Palmer moved quickly, almost holding his breath in fear of disturbing the black smudge. He placed a small ruler next to the mark and set up a thirty-five-millimeter camera on a tripod, and connected a portable floodlight. After snapping several pictures, he pulled the plug on the lamp and sagged into a chair, tired from lack of sleep and drained from the tension of his ghostly pursuit.

He stared at the faint smudge clinging to the dead flesh. It sure wasn't ideal, in fact, it was barely there, but, by God, it was a fingerprint—well, almost.

Standing by, patiently waiting for Palmer to finish, was Marilyn Noguchi, a buoyant quipster of a lab tech who would perform the DNA testing on the body. She was a carefree twenty-three to whom human history officially began when her age group was in high school.

After hearing that Marilyn's Japanese-American grandparents had been interned as children during World War II, Jaye had asked Noguchi if she heard internment stories while growing up.

"A lot. But those stories get boring real fast. It was a long time ago. The kids in the family sort of tune them out."

After Palmer removed his equipment, Noguchi stepped in to do her job. As Palmer had been, she was gowned and wore gloves and a mask to avoid contaminating evidence or contracting a disease. Already taken for purposes of elimination were volunteer DNA samples, as well as fingerprints, from the workers who had discovered the dead woman. On permanent file were records of every official on the investigation who might have touched the body.

She first drew blood by which to establish the victim's DNA. She then used a sterile pipette to place one drop of distilled water on each of a succession of swabs, which resembled oversize Q-tips. She ran them gently over the neck area and any other exposed parts of the body that might have made contact with the killer. She followed by scraping the fingernails for DNA evidence, possibly from the victim scratching her assailant.

Noguchi finished and departed. The lab would immediately submit the fingerprints of the corpse to AFIS, the FBI's national database. Also, the corpse's DNA would be submitted to CODIS, the FBI's national DNA database, when lab tests were completed.

Jaye was not eager for her next duty. As lead detective, she was required to observe the autopsy. It was part of the job she hated most, especially the Y incision, where cuts began at the shoulders and merged at the pubis, and then the skin was peeled back. Even worse was the sound of the saw cutting the skull apart, but then the absolute worst was when the organs were removed and weighed, like a morbid butcher shop. Perhaps in ten years, it wouldn't faze her, but not until then.

The four members of Potter's team whiled the time away in the office waiting for their boss. Baker was reading the newspaper and paused to say, "It says here millions of people have Neanderthal genes." He lowered the paper and thought about it. "Can you imagine a homo sapien mating with a Neanderthal?" He shook his head at the image of the Hollywood portrayal of prehistoric people.

Tatum looked up, nodded, and said, "I'd do it. I came close one time, but turned out she was the bartender's girlfriend."

The bland Baker blinked and studied Tatum's face to analyze the humor. Tatum once said Baker was the type of guy who would take notes in traffic school. Almaguer then had said as an aside that Baker would be the unidentified one in the class picture. A raconteur Baker was not, but he could focus on an investigation detail like a cat on a dangling thread.

Jay laughed along with the others as they tossed around the repartee cops called "grab-ass." However, she wasn't tuned-in. Her thoughts were on how she would lay out the case of the murdered homeless woman to the squad.

She and other women on the force would often talk about the minuet they had to dance to bring their two lives into synch. Jaye could spend twenty minutes on makeup on Friday night but also match other cops' grit for grit. She once told Tatum that, for a woman, being both pretty and tough is not mutually exclusive.

She had learned that to be accepted in this man's world, she had to be direct, but not challenging, friendly but not fawning. And most of all—laugh at their jokes. The longer she served, the more assertive and even sassy she became. The guys seemed to like that. Good! Because it was who she was.

Eight years ago, she had been a young wife struggling to put her husband through grad school by hours of ringing up a cash register belonging to someone else. The husband finished with school and with her at about the same time.

With no children or assets involved, the divorce was quick, easy, and painful only to her. She resumed her maiden name, which had the interesting and sometimes irritating, circumstance of sharing its spelling with a well-known Illinois city. She doggedly pointed out to those who misspoke herφ name that it was Italian and was pronounced: "Pe-o-RI-a."

Jaye found the world fascinating, but many of its male occupants tiresome. Unlike her veteran partners, she never complained about the pay or the hours because she remembered the vulnerability of knowing how mean the world could be for a woman with no skills an employer wanted to pay for. Every time she thought of the seventy-five-large that came with her cop job, she got a warm feeling for all the criminals who made it possible.

Jaye knew she was attractive, but not a head-turner: curly, light brunette hair she kept as long as department regs allowed; a round face with a sharp nose an artist would have widened slightly and sloped; mouth a tad too wide, but which smiled well. Beneath was a five-six body that would add pounds if given half a chance, but she was diligent to prevent the chance.

❦

The detectives pushed back their chairs as Potter left his cubicle and grabbed a nearby squeaky swivel chair. Wordlessly, he leafed through papers on his clipboard. "Okay, let's see… Tatum, what you got on the Armand case?"

Tatum glanced down at the blunted fingernails he had clipped that morning. "A blank. The guy just showed up lying on the beach with the inconvenience of neatly placed twenty-two holes behind the ear and through the eye. Clean site; a pro hit. The trigger was a technician. Saludo!"

Tatum didn't have to explain that pros prefer the twenty-two revolver when a hit is controlled and up-close. It's quiet because the bullets are small and sub-sonic; equally important, the casings stay in the chambers instead of flying out for the police to gather.

"No one knows why brother Armand left Tulsa or why he came to San Diego. I've asked Oklahoma cops to interrogate the dirtbags he hung with. He twice served time for dealing; nothing yet."

Potter slammed the clipboard down with a thwack. Team members didn't flinch. Acting out his frustration was nothing more than punctuation to his manner. Tatum once said Potter should have a warning label pinned on his forehead—contents under pressure.

Pressure? Oh, yeah. If there's pressure on the killer to escape, there is almost as much on cops to prevent him from doing so. All of the TV and movie glitz aside, serving in homicide is often a job of brain-numbing routine. However, with it comes the demand to perform, no different than an insurance salesman.

Potter's team had a solved-case record approaching ninety percent. It was a statistic that didn't exactly lie, just puffed-up the truth a little. The fact is, homicide cases are of two kinds: one, those relatively easy to solve where a motive or witnesses point to the guilty like highway markers, and two, those murders that seem to happen without discoverable motive and in view of no one, leaving a trail as difficult to follow as a fox's path.

The first kind of murder—a jealous husband or a drunken bar fight—is by far the majority. The second kind, where someone dies by a stranger's hand, is as hard to grasp as a wet bar of soap. Drug deals are often of that variety and will drive down a detective's batting average like a pitcher with a nasty curve.

Jaye glanced over and saw Potter sitting gingerly on one buttock. A sure sign hemorrhoids were giving him another kick in the butt. Potter's hemorrhoids were a great source of behind-the-back humor for the team. They broke up when it was discovered that he stored his Preparation H in an opaque plastic salad container marked 'personal' inside the lunchroom refrigerator. They often joked about coating one of the suppositories with itching powder, but no one had the nerve to take the leap and do it.

Potter twitched and shifted, vainly seeking comfort. "These goddamn drug killings are ruining our won-loss record. The bastards fly in here, waste some jerk they never met before for no reason anyone knows of, then they hop on a plane back to East Armpit, and then we're supposed to solve it—no motive, no witness, no nothing." Potter continued to frown as he thought of the injustice of it all, not to mention the inconvenience.

Finally, Potter said, "Okay, that's out of my system." He turned to Jaye. "What do we have on the homeless woman in the alley, Peoria?"

She leaned forward and scanned the waiting faces of her squad mates. Her job was to lay out the case and relate what she was doing about it. For a seasoned homicide cop, it was often helpful, but for a rookie, it was scary as hell. She knew her ideas might be swatted down like flies in a kitchen. That was part of the drill, except she hadn't been a player long enough to take the jitters in stride. At least she had become fluent in the "guy" language. She could talk the game.

Jaye had practiced before her bedroom mirror for an hour on what she was about to say, not realizing over-preparation might sound wooden, even professorial, in front of seasoned cops.

She uttered a nervous, dry cough: Well, here goes.

"Let me set the stage with some things we all know.

"Strangulation by itself is an act of anger. It's not robbery; it's not a sex crime, although a sicko might get his rocks off doing it.

"It's also damned difficult. It'd be tough to strangle a cat, let alone an adult. It's almost always man against woman, for obvious reasons.

"It requires some force because it takes four or five minutes to strangle a human to death. The person will fight back and cause a ruckus. So, the act requires strength, isolation, and time." She stopped and looked at blank faces. "I know you know all this," she said, almost pleadingly.

Potter rolled his eyes in the direction of Almaguer, then instantly regretted it.

"She pushed on. Since there was no apparent reason for this woman to be strangled, we have to assume this was a random act—" She paused.

"Assume, not conclude.

"Some creep walked the streets until he found a vulnerable victim in an isolated place." She waited for her words to sink in. "If he gets his jollies by killing a stranger, he probably will do it again. That could suggest a serial killer, either a pro or an amateur wanting to go big-league. Now, we don't know that, but it's a starting point."

Jaye's spirit sank as she picked-up on skepticism vibes from the four men of her audience. "Of course, maybe they knew each other. That's the other possibility," she said lamely, trying to close on the point of consensus.

Almaguer said slowly, "Yeah, well, one murder does not a serial killer make."

"That sounds like Shakespeare," tone-deaf Baker said.

"Don't jump the gun on the serial killer thing, Jaye," Tatum said. "You've got to follow the evidence, not expect it to follow you if that makes any sense."

"Not a whole hell of a lot," Almaguer said jokingly.

"Serial killing is the crime de jure," Baker said. "There's always a temptation to be fashionable."

Almaguer looked knowingly at Tatum. "Don't play hop-scotch with the steps; you might miss a few."

Potter knew it was time to bring this to a merciful end. "What else you got, Peoria?"

Jaye instantly regrouped. "Ignacio maybe found a witness." She looked at Almaguer expectantly.

Almaguer found a sheet he was looking for and reviewed it. "This guy claims to have maybe seen the killing."

Everyone leaned forward. "Who?" Baker said.

"Well, not exactly seen. A guy named Henry Gunnison. He's a late-night clerk at the flophouse across the street called the Bird of Paradise. He's got a direct view of the alley from his desk. The relief clerk said Gunnison told him he saw a disturbance across the street. I got Gunnison's phone number and woke him up. He wasn't too happy. He told me he looked out at 2:40 A.M. and saw two people in that alley. They seemed to be wrestling, and then one went down. The one standing seemed a lot larger than the other. It was quiet the rest of the night. He couldn't make out any faces, but—"

"What the hell," Tatum said. "I checked that motel when we made the first sweep. Why didn't he say anything then?"

Almaguer checked the report he was holding. "He went off duty at 6:00 A.M., before we got there."

"Why didn't he call 911 when he thought it was a fight?" Baker asked.

Tatum laughed and said, "In the East Village? That'd be like reporting kids for playing in a schoolyard."

"Standard time started that morning at 2:00 A.M. Did he turn the clock back, Ignacio?" Jaye said.

"I asked that. He said he did."

"Could he recognize anyone?" Baker said.

Almaguer shook his head. "Too dark."

Potter pursed his lips and said, "Well, at least it gives us a probable time of death; about the time, I figured."

Jaye asked Almaguer, "Can you go back when he's on duty and see if you can coax anything else out of him?"

"I begin my vacation at end of shift today," Almaguer said.

Potter frowned. "Shit. That's right. Every frickin' time we need you, you're going on vacation."

Almaguer shrugged. "I schedule the vacations, not the murders."

Jaye said, "Well, let's make a note to get back to the Gunnison guy. Now, about the autopsy." She reached for the autopsy report. "Just as we thought at the scene, she was strangled—"

"I thought," Potter grumbled.

Jaye glanced at him, then continued. "The victim suffered a fractured hyoid bone." She looked up. "You know, just behind the tongue—"

"Jeeeezus! We know where it is," Potter groused.

Jaye turned to him with an edge. "Sergeant, will you let me run this?"

"Okay, okay," Potter said, a touch contrite. "It's your show."

The others f??? their smiles down.

Jaye cleared her throat again, but louder this time. "There was hemorrhaging at the base of the tongue and the anterior part of the throat. Also, they found petechiae in the whites of the eyes."

"How about toxicology?" Tatum said.

"Nothing. No drugs or alcohol, and nothing unusual in the stomach; in fact, almost nothing at all in the stomach."

"Did they swab for sperm?" Baker said.

She nodded. "The works. Vagina, mouth, and anus. Deep swabs. Nothing. There was no sexual molestation. In fact, we could find no evidence of any kind. I went over that alley like I was cleaning my own kitchen after the CSI did the same, and I found absolutely nothing there, evidence-wise. Same with DNA. They almost mopped the alley with swabs, but the bleach did its job. No DNA on her body or clothes, either." She stopped. "Oh, one thing I found curious: one of her shoes was missing. The right one. We couldn't find it anywhere nearby, and we looked. I don't know what it could mean if anything."

Tatum said, "What'd we get on fingerprints?"

Jaye shook her head and held up two fingers close together. "This much. Palmer tried, but all he could get was a partial on the throat—three points of comparison. That's worthless, untrackable. You need ten points to even submit to the database. Also, the victim's prints aren't on the record. He ran her every which way through the sheriff, the state, and the FBI's AFIS system, with millions of prints. We also will run her DNA through the CODIS crime database when we get lab results, but I don't expect anything. If she had a criminal record, it would have shown up in the fingerprints." She laid down her papers and shrugged. "So far, we have an unidentified body and no leads."

As the briefing came to a close, Potter shifted his eyes to Jaye and studied her.

Jaye returned the gaze, not defiantly or nervously, but with a small, friendly smile and wondering if he was having second thoughts about giving this case to her.

Potter gathered up his clipboard and papers. "Okay, Señor,

have a nice vacation," he said to Almaguer without sarcasm. The others scattered with the scraping of chairs, but Potter signaled for Jaye to stay behind.

"You're new in homicide, Peoria, and I know you want this one real bad. But walk, don't run. You'll see more along the way."

"I'll do my best, Sarge. I still think this might be a serial killing."

"Maybe, but it's way, way too early to tell. Just don't jump to conclusions. It screws up your thinking." He paused. "Also, and this is serious: If word leaks that we think we have a serial killer on our hands, all hell will break loose in the department and the press. We need to watch what we say."

Jaye leafed through her thin manila file as she walked out of the office, not sure where she was headed but feeling the need to be moving to get on with it. She made her way to the cafeteria patio, where a few staffers chatted. She bought coffee, sat on the low stone wall, and let her mind drift as she looked at the Italian cypresses standing in a precise row.

Her thoughts went to the dead woman. She studied the photo taken at the morgue. It looked normal, except there was always something wrong with the eyes—unfocused, half-lidded. Dead.

This woman was not the smiling kid whose parents probably sat proudly as she was given her high school diploma, then the young mother nursing her firstborn. Rather, this was more like her trying heroin the first time or perhaps feeling her mind slipping into dark make-believe.

Jaye imagined the murder victim to be sitting next to her and let her thoughts drift to what she might say if the woman could hear—Lady, I'm not the religious type, so I think you're just dead. Period. That makes what happened to you more the pity. I'm not a romantic, a crusader, or an avenging angel. I'm just a gal trying to make an honest living and maybe do a little bit of good.

When that bastard decided you shouldn't live, I suspect you didn't have family; you didn't have money; you might have been kind of crazy or an addict. If anyone loved you, they couldn't tell you because they maybe had lost track of you. But I saw what he did to you, squeezing the life out of you. It would have taken at least four minutes. An eternity.

Lady, I don't know who you are, but I'll do my best for you. I saw you lying like a thrown-away puppet on dirty concrete next to garbage cans. I was at your autopsy. I saw you lying naked on a steel table. I heard the circular saw cutting through your skull. I smelled burning bone. That was you. I will do my best.

We won't be talking again.

❦

As Jaye walked down the gloomy, green corridor of headquarters, she glanced for the hundredth time at the file, which consisted only of the scene report, autopsy results, and several photos.

She turned into the crime analysis office and approached a thin young uniformed officer who half-dragged a disabled leg to the counter. His mean scowl proclaimed more than his leg was suffering.

"Hi, I'm Jaye Peoria from homicide. I need a little help." Jaye saw resentment in the officer's eyes.

"What?" he asked, but it came out as a demand. The cop-clerk had a reputation for bitterness, but people worked around it out of sympathy.

The hostility hit Jaye like a punch. "Uh, I'm investigating a murder. A woman was strangled. Can I get a printout of everyone arrested in the last year for crimes of violence against women?"

The officer reached down below the counter, grabbed a thick phone book, and dropped it on the counter.

"What's that for?"

He laughed with a snort. "Your list is in here…about half the book."

Jaye closed her eyes and took a deep breath, then glared directly at him. "Look," she said, "I don't give a fuck if you like me or not. But I know goddamned well you're going to help me. Now, how's it going to be?"

(Jaye had, over time, grown comfortable with the colorful, even crass, language of street cops. The language seeps in through your pores. Every woman cop learns to talk the talk or ignore it, maybe just laugh when others do. If not, she goes into administration or gets another job.)

Uncertainty mingled with resentment on the man's face. Jaye let her eyes drift down to his nametag, and she suddenly smiled. "Say, you're Tom Gooden. Didn't I hear about a citation you got a while back?" Actually, Jaye had never heard his name, but any injured officer given clerical work instead of pushed into retirement must have impressed the brass. He was almost certain to have been given a citation. They weren't hard to come by.

Conflicting emotions competed on the man's face; the anger was reluctant to depart, but finally, a weak smile forced itself. "Well, yeah. Not many people remember that."

She put out her hand. "I respect that. Pleased to meet you, Tom. Sorry, I blew my cool a minute ago."

He hesitated, arguing in his mind over how to react. Then, he took her hand. He suddenly noticed she was rather attractive, probably a seven on his scale. "Forget it. I get frustrated myself, shuffling this damned paper."

"Let me tell you what I need, Tom. I'm hoping you can give me a suggestion: a bag lady-type strangled down on Imperial Avenue; no sex angle, no robbery, no real evidence. I need a jump start," she said in her subtle version of a damsel in distress. I'm especially interested if choking is involved."

He thought a moment. "You got a victim ID?"

"I'm working on it."

"That's thin." He tapped his fingers on the counter. "There's obviously a fair chance the killer was someone else on the street. Have you looked at the sheriff's database? It has all criminal records in the county. It even includes field interviews by officers on the street."

"Yeah, I know. I spent some time on it, but for the complicated search I need, I'm better off with an expert like you helping me. That database has nooks and crannies in it like a rabbit burrow."

She gave him a wide, toothy smile. "But it wouldn't lose someone who knows his way around in it."

He reached for a pad and pencil and said, "Strangled, you said?"

"Uh-huh."

"Okay, that's a common M.O. for domestic killings and maybe for stranger attacks. We can check through the computer for all persons arrested for that, misdemeanors and felonies. Let's search for the last two years. We can also check for all major crimes of violence against women within the county."

"Sounds good," she said, nodding. "Can you also narrow it down for violent crimes against women in the early morning? Maybe he works at a job that puts him on the street at that hour."

"I'll see if I can get that. I don't know if we have that. If we do, let's broaden it and go for all late-night arrests for violence during the last year. Maybe our boy is a weirdo on a roll." He was writing rapidly. "You say there was no sex angle?"

"Not conventional. No rape, anyway. But who knows the world of kinkdom."

"Right." Gooden finished writing and put his pen down with satisfaction. "I'll have some printouts for you real soon."

"That's just great. I appreciate it."

He smiled thinly. "Well, that's my job now."

Standing on a corner in East Village among the homeless and wearing a light gray jacket over a blue pants suit, Jaye looked like the guest who didn't know it was a costume party. The fanny pack holding gun and badge was shifted out of sight to the side. She scanned the crowds of homeless people, derelicts, and drunks, wondering who among them might have known the dead bag lady. Street people, she knew, formed their own loose mini-communities, the regulars often being as familiar to each other as Rotarians. These are the people her victim would have moved among.

Coming down here always made Jaye feel uneasy because it was a reminder of her youth of poverty. Even when you leave it, you never quite shake the fear of going back.

She looked around. They were mostly men, often with scruffy, graying beards pushing "liberated" shopping carts or carrying large plastic bags over their shoulders. They didn't appear to speak, even in their clusters gathered in the corners of parking lots. Adrift on a river with no name.

There was no grass; even the weeds seemed stressed. The

midday traffic was light and largely of trucks passing through, watchful black and whites, and tired autos scarred by the dent-wounds of a long life.

The few women tended to be younger and not by accident. Living on the streets was not a place for a woman to grow old. Things happen. The women she saw tended to keep walking en route to a seedy room, or perhaps to see the fellow who sells the meth, or maybe a step behind some guy they should run from like a plague carrier.

There were no children visible, and if there had been, they wouldn't be playing.

There was no reminder of the approaching holiday until… in a small front window of a shabby, tiny house, something was written, facing outward, scrolled free-hand with what looked like soap. It said— "Happy Thanksgiving."

But it said more. It said: "I am here, such as I am, and I haven't given up."

Jaye thought— *Happy Thanksgiving to you, too.* Then, she shook her mind out of its reverie and refocused on why she was down here.

She carried the morgue photo of the woman. Even though it was straight-on of a normal face, something was missing: the spark of life doesn't exist in dead eyes.

She spotted a shabbily dressed man walking toward her with an awkward gait. One leg was bowed and the other unsteady. She figured it was a combination of a bad set of a broken leg and too much cheap wine.

"Pardon me, sir," she said, pulling her badge from her hand-bag. "I'm a police officer. Do you recognize this woman?" She showed him the photo.

He squinted and drew close to the print. "Does she claim to know me?" he asked suspiciously.

"She was murdered near here. We're trying to find out who she is. Can you help?"

"Don't know any women anymore. Don't want to."

"Thank you," Jaye said, concealing her scorn because police never need more enemies, even—especially even—on the street.

She showed the picture to several more. The reaction was invariably the same: ignorance or feigned ignorance, she was often uncertain which. Many of these people had learned that attention was trouble, that safety lay in the shadows, pretending not to exist, knowing nothing and denying everything.

Two persons eventually acknowledged having seen the woman somewhere but had no idea of her identity. Jaye noticed a glimmer of recognition in a few other faces, but even insistent prodding left her empty-handed.

Jaye had walked the streets for almost five hours, and her feet felt like she'd been disco-dancing on a rock pile. The faces she had peered into that day exposed her to so much bad breath and stinking bodies that it seemed the fetid smells had been dropped in the street like a gas grenade. She was beginning to look down the street for more prospects when a Mercedes pulled up to the curb, and an electric window whirred down.

"Hey, honey!" she heard a deep voice call and looked around. "Yeah, you. Come here, baby."

Jaye walked over to the car. "You call me?"

"Yeah, sweetheart, whataya charge?"

"For what?"

"Maybe half and half."

"You got a hard-on, mister?"

The well-dressed man chuckled conspiratorially. "Big enough for you to choke on, little lady."

"Well, I've got something that'll take care of it real fast." Jaye flipped out her badge. "Beat it, buster." She paused and then added in an afterthought that amused her, "Also, get the hell out of here."

The driver screeched the Mercedes away from the curb and into traffic, almost hitting a delivery truck.

Jaye sighed, took out her notebook and read for a moment, then started down the street, which took her past red-eyed hookers in hot-pants back on the job after a morning of drugs, past rent-a-cops guarding pawnshops who watched her curiously, wondering what a clean-looking woman was doing down here; past open-door cheap bars with anthill traffic of grimy drunks stumbling in and out to twangy-voice Willie Nelson; past the Catholic Kitchen with a line of people waiting silently with blank faces for a free hot dog and a plate of beans, looking in their castoff clothes like humble, yet enduring, peasants.

She checked the Downtown Shelter, the Light of God Rescue Mission, and the St. Mary's Women's Center. At each place, a few staffers and volunteers recognized the woman, but no one could give her a name or even identify possible friends. "She just came and went quietly, you know. I guess no one asked her name. I certainly didn't," a sympathetic nun confessed. "So many of them are like that." Her face made a hopeless smile.

Jaye checked off in her notebook again and walked slowly down the street. The woman obviously had a thing about being anonymous. Where might she go where she'd have to reveal her identity? Jaye snapped her fingers. The welfare office. She scolded herself: Of course, stupid! If the woman had ever gone there, as all of them did at one time or another, they'd insist on knowing who she was. With a new spring in her legs, Jaye returned to her car and headed for the county welfare office, driving a little too fast for even a police vehicle.

Mrs. Mathews, the chief caseworker, met her in the waiting room. She was tiny with gray hair cropped short and wire-rimmed glasses perched on the end of her nose, looking as if she had just walked off the cover of a cake mix package. Jaye handed the woman her card. She studied it: "A pleasure to meet you, Detective Peoria."

"Thank you, ma'am. It's Pe-o-RI-a."

The woman looked closely at the photo Jaye held up to her and tsk-tsked with her lips. "Oh, the poor dear. What a shame. I swear, what is this town coming to?"

"Do you recognize her?" Jaye asked anxiously.

She studied the face of the dead woman. "Well, it's hard to tell," she said carefully. "People look different when they're—like this."

"Please try, Mrs. Mathews."

The woman held up the picture. "May I borrow this?"

Jaye nodded. Mrs. Mathews disappeared into an inner office.

After several minutes, she reappeared carrying a manila folder. She led Jaye to a hard vinyl sofa, and they sat facing each other sideways. "I thought I recognized this woman, but I didn't want to get your hopes up, dear," she half-apologized. "I checked with one of the other girls and leafed through our records, and we're certain this is Edna Willows. Yes, it definitely is."

The thrill of success rushed through Jaye like a prairie wind. "Who was she?"

"Poor thing. A volunteer from the homeless civic task force brought her in about a month ago. He said she didn't seem able to fend for herself. He was a nice man. He asked if we could help her."

"And—"

Mrs. Mathews opened the file and read silently for a moment, then turned back to Jaye. "She didn't want to cooperate, but she finally gave us her name and next of kin. She showed us an old driver's license from Minnesota. Of course, it was outdated, but it was her."

"What happened then?"

"Well, since she didn't have a permanent address, there wasn't much we could do—regulations, you know. But we told her to come back the next day, and we'd make some calls." Mrs. Mathews shook her head sadly. "I'm afraid we never saw her again."

"Why, do you suppose?"

Mrs. Mathews leafed through the file. "Our psychologist, Dr. Owens, spent a few minutes with her; that's all the time he had. But he wrote here that she probably had—" Mrs. Mathews adjusted her glasses and read carefully. "An avoidant personality disorder with common schizotypal features."

"I don't know what that means," Jaye said.

Mrs. Mathews looked regretful. "She was afraid of people— and crazy. Pardon me for saying it that way."

"Hello, Mr. Willows? Is this Mr. John Willows of Brainerd, Minnesota? How are you this evening, sir? I'm Jaye Peoria, a detective with the San Diego, California Police Department. Are you the nephew of a woman named Edna Willows? … Mr. Willows, I'm afraid I have bad news for you. Your aunt was murdered last Sunday morning. I'm sorry to have to tell you that… We don't know yet; that's one reason I'm calling you. Was there anyone your aunt was close to? Mr. Willows, everyone has someone, a friend, ex-husband, lover, someone… Really? That's odd. Well, how long since you talked to her?… That long? Hummmm, I see. Mr. Willows, could you come out here for a positive identification? …Well, then, could you send a photo and, most important, some dental X-rays? That would be helpful. I'll email this photo to you. Let me know if there's any doubt… Good, thank you.

"One last thing, sir: the coroner's office will be contacting you about how you would like to arrange for burial or cremation… You mean?… I suppose the county will have to do it in that case. Thank you for your help. May I have your email?… Thank you. If you think of anything, please call me. Goodbye."

Jaye hung up the phone and said aloud, "Up yours, Mr. loving nephew." She cupped her hands over her mouth on a church steeple and stared at the ceiling—I've got a name, but that's all; no motive and no suspects. Where do I go from here? She considered asking Potter's help but decided not yet, not until she could show some progress.

Chapter Three

Driving back to the department, Jaye was lost in thought, trying to fit what she had learned into the puzzle of the Willow's murder. With only half a conscious decision, she turned onto a side street that was out of her way. It was not the first time she had taken the detour.

Jaye drove slowly past a modern office building that had a dignified sign in front with the words "B.L. Spiller & Associates, Civil Engineering." Jaye slowed down and gazed at the sign. That used to be my name, she mused, and remembered herself writing monthly checks for bills and proudly signing them, "M. J. Spiller."

At least she had gotten rid of the name along with him; she had told herself a thousand times. But she knew the reality was Ben got rid of her. She had loved to call herself by Ben's name, but now it was gone, but there were times she missed it. She wasn't going to lie to herself.

Jaye pulled into the headquarters parking lot and sat in the car for several minutes, staring straight ahead as tears seeped from her eyes. She thought of how it had once been when Ben was a student and dependent on the meager salary she earned as a cashier; how they would plan their hamburger leftovers as carefully as the menu at a fancy restaurant; how he would patiently try to explain some complicated engineering principle, which would leave her in a fog; how they would lie awake after lovemaking sharing dreams for the future: several kids, lots of money, big house, Hawaii vacations…

Then, bang! A week before he graduated, the surprise ending—his shame-faced announcement there was someone else. Janet was her name. Yeah. JanetgoddamnedJanet. Not only that, but it had been going on for over a year. All those hours at the cash register, cooking, dreaming, loving, and all those months he had been screwing another woman…sharing *her* dreams, too, no doubt. Jaye laid her head against the steering wheel. Was it her? Did she fail? It was hard. God, it was hard. She knew it was past time to get over it, but she had nothing to replace the memory.

Jaye heard footsteps and quickly reached for her sunglasses. Through her open window, she watched as Slim Hubbell, a detective in burglary she knew from academy days, walked over to the car.

"Hi, Jaye. You okay?"

She grabbed her purse and opened the door. "Hi, Slim. Yeah, I've just got a tough case that's driving me crazy. See ya."

As she rapidly walked away, Hubbell watched her for long seconds. Funny, he thought, work's nothing to cry about, even for a woman.

Mike Palmer looked up from the fingerprint enlargement he was studying to see an attractive brunette standing in his doorway. With a nervous smile, he recognized Detective Peoria from the autopsy.

"Hello, Mike." She strode across the room to shake his hand. "Jaye Peoria from homicide. Remember me?"

Palmer stood up and removed his glasses. "Of course I do. Hi, Jaye. Have a seat." He slipped the prints into a folder. "Nice to see you. What's up?"

"I'm working the Edna Willows case."

A blank look.

"The bag lady murder."

"Oh, yeah."

"Your report said you got a print off her neck, at least part of one. Three points."

"Well, let's see." He sat down at a computer keyboard and typed in some words. While waiting for the machine, he said, "As I recall, it wasn't much of a print." The computer screen suddenly filled, and he said, "Not much at all. Like you said, only three points." He spun his chair around to face Jaye. "Three points is about the equivalent of the earlobe in identifying a face. I won't even testify in court with that." He pulled out a poster-sized enlargement of a sample fingerprint. "Let me show you something. Stop me if I'm being too elementary."

"Don't worry about that. This'll be a refresher of what I might have day-dreamed through in the academy." She knew nothing motivates an expert like a wide-eyed audience, especially if it's female. She knew how to play the game between the lines. She walked over to be closer as he happily launched his spiel. He liked talking to this woman.

"Look at these rows of semi-circular lines; think of them as being like the topographical map of a mountain. See how regular the main lines are? Now, look closer. See the little lines shooting off at right angles into dead ends? Just like gullies off a mountain ridge. Those little gullies are distinctive for every person. We call them points of comparison. They're what we look for when we're trying to match prints."

"What're the most points any person can have?" Jaye asked though she knew the answer.

"Oh, from about fifty to 150."

"And we've only got three," she said, making a face.

Palmer put the display board down. "You see the problem." He went back and looked at the computer screen again. "The only other thing I can tell you is the print I was able to lift was an arch pattern. It must have been in my report."

She knew it wasn't. He probably turned out a half-dozen each day. Occasional omissions were not uncommon. Reports were written by overworked people in a hurry. "Okay," she said. Her patience was starting to pay off.

He leaned back, confident in his knowledge. "There are three types of fingerprint patterns: loop, whorl, and arch. The loop is most common, sixty-five percent of all people have it; the whorl is found in thirty percent. The arch, on the other hand, is common to only five percent."

"Well, that's something, isn't it?" Jaye picked up a pencil and started drumming it against the desktop. "I don't see how we could do a search for just arch patterns."

Palmer thought for a moment. "Unfortunately, no. The AFIS databases we use don't give that breakdown. Besides, you'd have many thousands of them."

"Well, that doesn't mean it's useless," she said. "At least we can use the arch pattern to evaluate suspects. If some guy doesn't have it, it doesn't eliminate him, but it's definitely in his favor."

Palmer nodded. "I checked the prints of everyone who could have touched the body: victim, witnesses, cops; everyone. There were no arches. In my own mind, I can tell you this print belongs to the killer."

Jaye nodded. "Wow. Thanks. Will you help me if I need it?"

A smile spread over his face. "I'd love to."

Jaye yawned and again scrolled the columns of database records Tom Gooden had gathered from ARJIS. After several hours of tedious searches and phone calls, she had converted them into Excel files for three lists. The longest list represented those candidates rejected for a variety of reasons. The discard list had grown since Palmer told her of the arch print evidence.

The second list was of those convicted of violence against women who didn't have alibis for the night Willows was killed or weren't dead or in prison. The third list, and by far the smallest but also by far the most important, was culled from the second one but also included the arch print and choking as a method.

Baker broke the silence by saying, "A gnat under a microscope looks like a monster, but it's still a gnat."

Jaye looked up and stared at him for a long moment, then went back to her list. Baker being Baker.

Tatum walked by and looked over her shoulder. "What's the long list, Jaye, the guys you say no to?"

Jaye looked up, then back to the list, and theatrically ran her finger down the names. "Yeah, here's your name right here, Tatum, in boldface."

Tatum shook his head in dramatic sorrow. "A great loss for both of us."

"I'll try to bear up under the disappointment. It's been a long time since I've gotten turned on by a red sports car. You should have caught me in high school."

He slammed his palm against his forehead in mock chagrin. "God, if you'd told me earlier, I'd have bought a used Focus. Think of the money I've wasted."

Almaguer, sitting nearby, laughed. "Tatum, you'd troll for women in a Christian Science reading room."

Jaye looked down at the lists. "This idea of trying to isolate suspects this way isn't exactly revolutionary, but it's all I've got."

Tatum shrugged. "Fact is, no one cared if that bag lady lived or died, so unless you come up with something concrete or have a witness, you've got a tough job."

Jaye leaned forward and rested her chin on her palm. "Do you think it could have been a sex crime?"

"Well, it sure the hell wasn't robbery. But who understands perverts? When I was in sex crimes, I once arrested a guy for trying to screw a horse."

Baker looked up. "A horse?"

Almaguer laughed. "That's a piece he could have gotten a kick out of."

Tatum was on a roll. "Another case was a guy who started jac—masturbating on the porch when some church kids showed up singing Christmas carols in his neighborhood. After one kid's mother turned him in, I asked him why he did it, and the guy just shrugged and said it got him in the Christmas spirit. I felt like the Grinch when I busted him. Hey, when you're talking sex crimes, you're talking smorgasbord."

Jaye started laughing. "Speaking of self-abuse—"

"Self-what?" Tatum asked teasingly.

"Don't forget, I'm a lady," she said primly. "Anyway, when I was on patrol, we sometimes had to do walk-throughs on the porn shops and theaters."

Almaguer and Baker stopped what they were doing to listen.

Jaye continued. "That's where I saw my first porno flick, in wide-screen and living color. At first, I thought it was open-heart surgery. Then I thought that perhaps it was a Japanese sci-fi film, like maybe the Attack of the Giant Genitalia. Anyway, one time, I was going through this porn shop, checking the booths with the coin movies, you know, to make sure two guys of compatible orientation weren't inside abusing each other. On this one booth, I pulled the door open, and there was this guy fumbling with himself—Tatum, you would describe it more graphically. This guy was exercising Mr. Toad, breathing like he'd just finished a four-minute mile, and he had this wadded-up tissue in his hand." Her laughing increased as the memory came back. "When he saw me in uniform, he took the Kleenex and blew his nose. You know what I did?" Jaye said as she wiped the tears from her eyes. "I asked if he had a cold." Tatum put his head down and convulsed in laughter, pounding his fist on the table.

Baker had left the room when the talk turned raunchy. Being on the edge of the crowd was a familiar place for him. The only time he made waves was when he started keeping a Bible atop his desk. HR objected to it, saying his religious display might offend those who didn't share it. He balked at removing it, which almost led to a union grievance on his behalf. He eventually put the Bible in a drawer, much to the relief of the union, which had not welcomed that fight.

The porn-shop hilarity gradually subsided into chuckles, and then grinned as Almaguer answered his phone. Returning to the original subject, Tatum asked, "How many names you end up with in your likeliest list?"

"Eight. The way this list pared down from when I first got the names, it's like their victims were in a war zone."

"They have," Tatum said, "it's called the streets, and they're cannon fodder."

"With all the other things I have to do, it'll take me time to investigate all these names."

"The woman'll still be dead," Baker said as he resumed his seat.

Tatum said, "This is a trial and error business. Every trial seems to be an error. It takes time."

"Maybe I'll get lucky." Jaye highlighted one on the small list and said, "Here's one. This guy, William Connor, is the president of the big Connor Printing Company. He was arrested for choking and beating his girlfriend in her downtown condo. Did a job, five stitches. The woman lost the desire to prosecute, and his

high-powered lawyers got it pled down to misdemeanor assault."
She paused long enough to frown. "I think I'll have a little talk
with VIP Connor. We'll discuss hurting people—and where he
was on a certain night."

Ordinarily, a detective interviewing a possible suspect would
be accompanied by a partner. But in a business with other workers around, she felt comfortable going alone.

Jaye entered the wide door beneath the huge neon sign flashing "Connor Printing." She came unannounced, hoping total surprise might jar Connor into saying something that would horrify
his lawyer.

Inside were several clerk-types working computers, answering phones, or standing at copy machines watching sheets of paper shoot out. She inquired at reception for William Connor and
was directed to his private secretary.

"I'd like to see Mr. Connor, please," she said to the older
woman wearing an expensive red suit that worked beautifully
and purple eye-liner that didn't. The secretary pulled her glasses
down from atop her head and smiled at Jaye. "May I ask your
name?"

Jaye handed her a card, which the woman studied with interest as her smile faded. Apparently, she lacked confidence in her
boss' moral rectitude. Maybe it wasn't the first such card she'd
been handed. "May I ask the nature of your business with Mr.
Connor?" She glanced at the fanny pack in which Jaye carried
her duty equipment.

Jaye smiled. "No, you may not."

The woman pinned her with an icy stare. "Please have a seat.
I'll check with Mr. Connor." She took Jaye's card and disappeared
into a paneled office. In moments, she was back with an edge of
triumph in her voice, "Mr. Connor is quite busy at the moment.
You'll have to wait."

Jaye spent the next twenty minutes leafing through a three-
month-old issue of *Golf Digest,* a game she'd never played.
Several people walked in and out of Connor's inner office, none

of whom appeared on urgent business. Finally, after hearing loud laughter from within, she approached the secretary again and said pleasantly, "I know Mr. Connor is busy, but I've waited quite a while, and I have a full schedule. Would you please remind him I'm here?"

The secretary's haughty smile fit her gatekeeper role, and she said, "Mr. Connor is quite busy. I'm sure he'll see you just as quickly as possible."

Jaye breathed deeply for control, then said with a forced smile, "Personally, I can wait. I'm totally absorbed in this old *Golf Digest*. It's the police business that's in a hurry. Please tell Mr. Connor if he won't see me *here*, then I'll see him *there*." She didn't have to explain the location of *there*.

The secretary's eyes widened. "Just a minute." She disappeared into Connor's office and returned less than a minute later. "Mr. Connor will see you now."

Jaye stepped into the plush office directly under the malevolent glare of a tall, muscular man with a gray face and a full mustache twitching in anger. He tugged sharply at the French cuffs descending exactly a half-inch below the sleeves of his silk suit. He silently motioned her to a chair opposite the desk as the secretary closed the outer door. Jaye glanced around the office: early decadent country club, exercycle, and golf putter prominent in one corner, walls lined with photos of Connor holding trophies, and grip-and-grins with recognizable politicians. One was with the chief of police. Images of strutting narcissism.

Connor sat in his cushy leather chair and studied her card. "What is it you want, Miss Peoria?"

Jaye forced herself to be unruffled by the condescension of the big shot who was treating her like someone he'd send out for coffee. She'd been there before.

If it's a test of wills he wants, I've got the hammer, she said to herself. Okay, buster, you get it straight.

"It's Pe-o-RI-a. *Detective* Peoria." She let her tone sink in. "Mr. Connor, I'm investigating a crime, and I'd like to ask you if you can account for your whereabouts—"

"What are you talking about?" His back went ramrod. "You

come into my place of business and accuse me…"

"Mr. Connor," she said calmly, "no one is accusing you of anything. I simply asked a courteous question."

"Is that your idea of courtesy? Well, you can talk to my lawyer about this. Of all the outrageous…"

"You're right, sir, you don't have to tell me anything."

He nodded smugly. "I'm glad you at least know that."

Jaye stood up. "Let's go, sir."

"Huh? Go where?"

"To police headquarters. You can call your lawyer from there."

"Are you telling me I'm under arrest?"

"No, since you won't cooperate, I'm taking you in for questioning."

Disbelief covered Connor's face like a thrown cream pie. "No way."

Jaye removed a pair of handcuffs from the fanny pack, where they lay next to her Glock 9-millimeter.

A vein stood out on Connor's forehead. "No way you can put those things on me."

Jaye reached in again and took out a hand radio. "Probably not, but I might embarrass you with the effort. Anyway, you're a businessman—think about the cost-benefit ratio of what you're even thinking about."

Connor shrank in defeat like a scolded puppy. "What is it you'd like to know?"

Jaye resumed her seat and took out a notebook. "Where were you on the night of November fourth and early morning of November fifth?"

He thought for a moment, then with shaking hands, he leafed through the calendar on his desk. "I was in St. Louis. A sales trip to a customer, Gerhard Plastics."

"Can you verify that?"

"I'll call in my sales manager; he was with me." He reached for the phone, then hesitated. "Uh, can we cool this? I mean, can we be discrete?"

"We'll see how it goes."

Connor shook his head and punched in a number. "Sam, can

you come in for a moment?"

Within a minute, the sales manager with an expense-account belly and bright tie peeked around the door and then came all the way in as Connor beckoned. He stood there looking quizzically at Jaye, who had not been introduced.

"Sam," Connor said, busily studying his calendar. "Do you remember the Gerhard proposal in St. Louis?"

"Yeah, sure. I wouldn't forget a big deal like that."

"I'm just going through my schedule," Connor said as he made a show of looking at his calendar. "What day was that, do you remember?"

"Well, sure, it was just Monday, November sixth," Sam said, mystified.

"That's all, Sam. Thanks."

As the sales manager turned, Jaye said to him, "When you say 'we,' do you mean the organization or the two of you?"

Connor's glare promised a slow death at the first opportunity. Sam said, "The boss and me."

"How long were you in St. Louis?" she asked.

Sam thought for a moment and gave his boss a quick glance. "Uh, we left here Saturday morning, got together for dinner with the vice president on Sunday, had the meeting on Monday, and came back on Tuesday." Sam's face was filled with bewilderment.

"I'd like to see your paperwork on the travel."

Sam again looked at Connor, who nodded. "Okay, uh, come with me." Sam walked out the door as Jaye rose and said, "That'll do it for now, Mr. Connor. Sorry to bother you."

"Just a minute, please." He called her back as Sam walked out, and she turned to follow. "Why me?" he asked, almost whining. "I mean, you're *homicide*…why me?"

"Because you were accused of a crime with certain similarities to the one I'm investigating."

"It was just a little spat with my girl—with an acquaintance, a misunderstanding. I was drunk and mad." He sighed deeply. "For all the trouble it caused me…I'm a class-A fool."

Jaye's stare was level. "You might be that, but you're also a woman beater. Convicted."

Outside the office, Jaye leaned against the building, took a deep breath, and let it out slowly. She felt the perspiration in her armpits as the nervousness caught up to her for what she had done. By telling Connor she would take him to the station in handcuffs, she violated department policy and probably the law. She had no evidence or probable cause to place him in custody, so why did she run such a stupid bluff? She asked herself. Probably because he deserved it, the answer came back—the asshole.

Jaye opened her steno notebook and crossed the name Connor off. She scanned the list and found the name of a possible suspect only three blocks away. She closed the notebook and decided to walk to Giardello's Restaurant to interview the owner, Frank Giardello, known to the public for his fine cuisine but known to the police as a man who beat prostitutes for leisure time sport.

Chapter Four

Just before calling it a day, the detectives were decompressing. Almaguer looked over at Baker, grinned, and said, "New jacket there, Art?"

Baker looked down and fingered his polyester mustard-colored sports coat, not more than five years out of date. "You like it? I got it off the clearance rack at Target. Practically stole it."

Tatum looked up. "Really cool, Art. I've got some lime green slacks that'd set it off just right. Can I borrow it for a date sometime?"

"You'd need white bucks, too," Almaguer said.

Keeping a straight face, Tatum said, "Well, of course. Give me some credit, will you?"

Baker figured out he was being ragged on and went back to his magazine. The hell with them, he thought. My wife likes it.

Jaye ignored the teasing as she kicked off her shoes and wiggled her toes in relief. Potter looked across the room and scowled. "Hell, gal, this is a foot-killer job, and you ain't yet got any more miles on you than a showroom Chevy. What you gonna do when you get fifty thousand miles on those legs?"

Jaye looked up and grinned at the overweight sergeant. "Tell you what, Sarge; I'll race you a hundred yards with a side bet. Okay?"

Potter looked up in interest at the challenge, walked over to where she was sitting, and perched one cheek on Tatum's desk.

He puffed out his cheeks and pretended to look indignant. He liked his squad to show moxie, even at his expense—to a point. "Sheeet! I'd blow your doors off. Little lady like you'd fall into the vacuum caused by my body displacing atmosphere. Whoeee," he said, contemplating the speed he'd attain even as he returned to seriousness. "On Willows, how many more names you got on your list?"

Jaye opened the notebook and glanced at the list. "Four. I've talked to printers, restaurant owners, and candle-stick makers. Nothing. Everyone had one reason or another not to be a suspect, though I was willing to beg them to be one. Maybe someone will walk in here and confess. I hope something turns up."

Potter slowly blew out a breath. "I hope so, too, but what the hell, that's showbiz. If it doesn't work, well, we can always beat a confession out of someone."

Tatum chimed in with a falsetto voice. "Don't hit me again, ossifer. I'll talk, I'll talk."

"Spare my school-girl ears such macho-cop talk, you two," Jaye said, slipping her shoes back on and heading for the door. "That's no way to talk around a lady." She flounced her rear just a tiny bit and was out the door.

Potter grinned at Tatum. "That little spitfire kind of grows on you, doesn't she?"

Tatum looked after the departed detective. "Definitely the right word."

Potter locked his cubby-hole office and headed toward the garage to collect his Hyundai and leave the sacred fellowship of cops. If he could, he'd probably put a cot and microwave in his office and make it his home. He was a classic organization man, comfortable mainly in the structure of the Marine Corps or the department.

He was a tough old non-com with a big heart. That's a cliché movie role, but real in him. Potter sometimes reverted to drill instructor. He had been known to handle people's feelings the way Lennie Small handled the puppy in *Of Mice and Men*. Too bad for the puppy. He wasn't a bully, though he sometimes bullied. He was a unique contradiction.

Tatum joked that Potter sat around and watched John Wayne reruns. He had no wife, no family, and no close friends except Jack Daniels, who sometimes visited too long over the weekend. Potter was always sober on duty and almost always solved his cases, which was all the taxpayers of San Diego required of him.

Jaye double-checked the address of the peeled-paint old house in the low sun of late afternoon. She was alert to the dangers of this run-down neighborhood where tinny rap music drifted out of open windows, past torn curtains, and lay above-broken fences and weed-filled yards like an invisible mist.

She was here to see Sylvester Morris, a nasty piece of work who had beaten and choked his girlfriend to the extent of three days in the hospital. She refused to press charges, so he walked.

As Jaye headed up the walk to the unlit house, she noticed a husky black man standing at the corner, watching her with an oddly-disconnected look. She clutched her shoulder bag tighter and kept walking alongside the uniform beside her, a woman cop arbitrarily assigned to accompany her, Alison Pritchard.

She knocked on the broken screen door until a young black woman peeked around the corner. The woman's eyes were red from crying, and her hands shook as she started to unlatch the door, then thought better of it. She stared at Jaye with trepidation, knowing that when cops, even women cops, came all the way down to this neighborhood, they weren't making the trip to drop off the lottery prize.

Jaye thought of showing her badge but decided against it; this woman was upset enough. "Is this the residence of Sylvester Morris?" she asked, remembering the name from her notebook.

The woman nodded in silence.

"Is he home?"

Jaye followed the woman's wide eyes to the man on the corner. "Is that him?" she asked.

The woman nodded.

"Thanks."

The woman's eyes were filled with fear. "Tell him I didn't call you."

Jaye looked at her carefully. "Of course, you didn't. Miss, are you okay?"

The woman shook her head fearfully and disappeared back into the room.

Jaye approached the man warily, put on guard by something strange about him. "Excuse me, are you Sylvester Morris?"

The man turned around with stiff and jerky movements and stared at her. The sweat was pouring off him, though it was a chilly day, and he was wearing a T-shirt. His pupils were pinpoints and wavered in and out of focus.

The signs computed instantly for Jaye: PCP—phencyclidine, also known as angel dust, goon, killer weed, and crystal; developed as anesthesia, first for humans, then animals, and then discarded for both because of the behavior distortions—craziness—it caused.

Jaye quietly shifted the fanny pack holding her pistol from her hip to the front, and unzipped it.

PCP was cheap, quick, and often dangerous, a drug of opportunity in the ghetto. A man on a bad PCP trip is like nitro on a hot day—a cross-eyed look can make him blow. He's an attack awaiting a victim. He feels like he's burning up, and extreme paranoia and irritability can induce uncontrollable rage. The anesthetic properties make him impervious to pain, and though his strength doesn't increase, contrary to myth, the utter abandon of his attack makes it seem so, and his subduing becomes hazardous to the extreme.

Pritchard put a hand on her pistol and started to speak into a collar microphone for back-up. She didn't get two words out.

A hoarse scream ripped from his throat, and he shouted, "You gonna kill my mama!" Without warning, he smashed his fist into the face of the patrol officer, who crumpled to the ground.

Oh, fuck, Jaye thought in a mingling of caution and fright. She backed away as slowly as possible. The man's wild eyes sought her out and finally managed to fix on her. She stood rock still and said nothing, hoping his attention would pass over her. She got her hand on her pistol but no further.

With a herky-jerky movement, he grabbed Jaye's arm in a painful vise and hit her on the side of the head with his fist. The blow exploded in Jaye's brain like cymbals and made her vision flicker and her knees buckle. Before she could react, he shouted, "Leave my mama alone!" and threw Jaye like a discarded match against the trunk of a large oak tree several feet away near the curb. The pistol flew out of the fanny pack.

Jaye hit the tree and felt the rough bark rake her arm like sandpaper. She collapsed at its base and desperately tried to shake the blurriness out of her eyes and somehow defend herself against the next attack, the one she knew could kill her. The man gradually became clear in her vision. He seemed distracted by something else, but she feared it wouldn't last.

As her whipsawed body raged in protest when she moved, Jaye managed to scramble to her feet and limp around to the other side of a car parked next to the tree, hoping for time to locate her dropped piece. The man was attracted by the movement and once again centered his paranoia on Jaye—destroy her, and his mama would be safe, and the unbearable heat would go away.

Jaye watched as he ripped the T-shirt off his chest, and his drooling reminded her of a mad dog. With stiff, Frankenstein steps, he started after her. Jaye knew he had the power to snap her spine. Jaye skittered around the car like a crippled chicken, trying to keep the vehicle between them, playing a deadly kid's game of tag—Where was her damned bag?

As she completed a circle of the car, Jaye spotted the pistol lying on the berm and managed to grab it. Constantly glancing at the man and moving every time he did, she fumbled for her hand radio. She flicked the safety off the 9-mil and turned on the radio. "Cover, Code 3," she shouted into the speaker. "Cover NOW, Code 3."

"Location?" the dispatcher's tense voice instantly replied.

In desperation, Jaye tried to remember where she was, but suddenly the man made another quick move to reach her, and she had to dash around the car to keep her distance. She glanced up at the street sign and spoke breathlessly into the radio. "Seventeenth and Autumn. COVER NOW!"

Jaye knew pepper spray would be worthless. She held the pistol ready and psyched herself up. She realized the sight of it wouldn't deter Morris, but she would do everything possible to avoid killing a man who was out of his head. However, she resolved if he caught her, she would blow his fucking head off.

The cat-and-mouse game went on. He would fake one way, then move the other, and Jaye would push her throbbing body in the opposite direction.

What seemed unending to Jaye were the ninety seconds before the first patrol car, with siren wailing and lights flashing, came to a skidding stop in the intersection. Jaye hadn't even heard the siren, but when she saw the officer, a thick-chested young black man, jump out of the car, she shouted, "PCP."

The officer grabbed the pepper spray canister and nightstick at his belt. He rushed up to Morris and sprayed him full in the face.

Morris shrugged off the pepper spray like a squirt from a water pistol and threw the officer to the ground like a child. Moments later, four more cars arrived, and several more cops jumped on the man, but they were wrestling a raging octopus as obscenities filled the air.

Jaye struggled to her feet, re-engaged the safety, and slipped the pistol back into her bag. She hobbled over to the melee and tried to grab the thrashing foot of the berserk man, but instead of the leg, all she got for her effort was an accidental smash in the face from a cop's elbow.

❦

A terrible odor assaulted Jaye, and she fought to get away from it. She shook the fog out of her eyes to see a paramedic leaning over her with an ammonia capsule. She pushed his arm aside and shook her head but quickly stopped when it started pounding like a Beethoven crescendo.

She looked around to see that what had been a nearly deserted neighborhood only minutes before was transformed into a battlefield. A few feet away lay a struggling Sylvester Morris strapped to a gurney.

The first thing she mumbled was to ask about the cop who had been first attacked. She was told that Alison Pritchard had a broken jaw and probable concussion and had already been taken to the hospital.

Six squad cars were parked in disarray in the street, and cops milled about with nothing to do now that the action was over. Despite her aching body, Jaye felt a rush of warmth for these men, her partners, who had rushed to her aid. Cops truly do take care of cops, she thought. *I'd like to kiss every one of them on the force. Well, a few of them, anyway.*

She felt strong hands steadying her, and she leaned back to see upward. Looking down at her was an upside-down face wearing a big smile. She twisted around to get a better look. She recognized him from somewhere. The man helped prop her against the trunk of an oak and said, "I'm Deputy Chief Will Davis. I happened to be in the neighborhood and picked-up on your call. They tell me this was your show."

"I'm Jaye Peoria, homicide. Pleased to meet you." She glanced over at Sylvester Morris strapped to a gurney. "I was just telling him a joke, and he didn't think it was funny."

"Then you better work on your stand-up routine." Davis' short laugh became a solicitous smile. "How are you feeling, or is that too dumb a question?"

She took quick stock of her body, and about a hundred nerves and muscles provided an angry answer. "Like I've just finished fighting Mike Tyson with a wine hangover."

"Well, Jaye, I want you to go to the hospital to get checked over." He pointed to the strapped-down Morris. "Do you mind riding in the same ambulance with your friend?"

"Of course not. We haven't had a chance to get acquainted yet."

"Let me tell you, officer, what you did was gutsy. A lot of cops would've shot the crazy bastard; then there would have been hell to pay from the ACLU-types. You kept your wits intact and your finger off the trigger. It took a good cop to do that."

An old black man in work clothes who was standing behind Davis began to clear his throat to say something. Both Jaye and Davis looked toward him.

"Ma'am, I live 'round here, and I just want to say thank you from all the decent people in the neighborhood. Sylvester Morris, he be a bad dude, real bad dude. He's been acting like a demon for years, getting on angel dust and scaring folks near to death. He just got out of jail last week after getting sixty days back in Oklahoma for making trouble. We hope he gets ten years this time."

Jaye said, "You're welcome, sir." She smiled broadly at Davis. "I learned about all I need to know about PCP. I don't see the need to do this again."

A paramedic checked her and said to Davis, "Far as I can see, there doesn't look like any serious damage."

Jaye pulled up her pant leg to look down at her scraped leg. "Oh, yes, there is."

They looked at her with sudden concern.

"I ruined these five-dollar knee-highs."

Jaye stood on the emergency room steps and took inventory: she gently touched her temple—a headache reminded her of a shaking tambourine. She put her foot down solidly and winced on a twisted ankle. She touched a tender spot on her cheek and felt a yellowish-purple bruise that no amount of makeup would cover. Raw spots on her body felt like she'd belly-flopped in a gravel pile.

She took out a notebook and scratched the name Sylvester Morris from her narrowing list. She took another step. "Fuck!" she said under her breath as the pain shot up her leg. Being more careful of the ankle, she walked slowly to her car, muttering to herself: "I've got to stop using that word."

Mark Joseph was the next man who had been arrested for abuse of a woman and had arch fingerprints. He was a single thirty-five-year-old accountant at an Indian casino on the edge of San Diego. He had been in town for fifteen months from Las Vegas, where he had been employed at various casinos and at other casinos elsewhere. He apparently was a job-hopper. He came to Jaye's attention because of a misdemeanor arrest in San Diego last September.

He was accused of choking his girlfriend named, Bonnie Fletcher in his automobile at a public parking lot. She subsequently declined to press charges. His fingerprints were on file with the San Diego P.D. and the gaming commissions of three states, but because he wasn't arrested on a felony charge, no DNA sample was taken. He had no prior criminal record in California or Nevada.

Jaye called the detective who handled Bonnie Fletcher's complaint. "What's the real story there, Mike?"

"I think the guy did what she first said he did. The woman was scared with a capital "S" when we saw her."

"Why a misdemeanor instead of a felony?"

"There were no marks on her neck, which was no big surprise. She was adamant at the beginning, but later, she cooled during questioning. Given those circumstances, I wasn't comfortable with a felony. If she was distraught and said he tried to kill her, it would have been a felony straight up. Judgment call. We make them all the time."

"Why do you suppose she refused to press charges?"

"It happens, Jaye—money, fear, remorse, shame, stupidity, misplaced loyalty—and did I say money? Let me say it again."

Bonnie Fletcher had a one-bedroom walk-up in a converted large house in a part of the city once considered stately but had drifted downward to seedy. Bonnie was a cosmetics clerk at a high-end department store. She was early-thirties and of average appearance. Jaye tried to smile her way past Bonnie's initial reaction to a cop coming to the door. She asked if she could come in and visit. Bonnie first stumbled over a couple of words, then stood aside and held the door open.

Jaye tried to put her at ease. "Let me explain. This is not about you. Nothing negative will happen to you from our conversation. I would like to chat in confidence with you about your complaint against Mark Joseph on February 17, last year."

Bonnie shook her head. "I said all I have to say to the DA."

"Okay, Bonnie. Let me be clear: This is not about you but about him. If I can learn something to prevent what happened to you from happening again, it might be because of your cooperation."

Bonnie considered a moment if she trusted this stranger with the gun on her hip. "Are you recording this?"

"I am not. This is strictly between us."

That seemed to relax Bonnie, and she sat down on the couch as Jaye took a chair opposite. "Well, at first, he was nice: flowers, candy, nice dinners, you know the deal. I thought it was a little strange that some days he'd be hyper and other days so sullen he wouldn't talk, but some people are like that, I suppose. Anyway, I wasn't planning to marry him. But then, after he thought I was hooked, he became abusive."

She became subdued with the memory. "It was weird. The night it happened, we were arguing over which movie to see, if you can believe that. And you know how silly arguments tend to go off the rails and get more personal? Well, this one did."

Bonnie scooted to the edge of the couch and put her hands around an imaginary neck. "He started choking me. I was starting to black out, and he suddenly let go. He didn't even apologize.

"The parking lot attendant saw it happening and called the police. They came and took him away in handcuffs. I never saw him again."

Jaye asked, "What do you think would have happened if you were in an isolated place instead of a busy parking lot?"

Bonnie became nervous just at the thought. "I honestly don't know, but I'll tell you, I wouldn't want to find out."

At the door, Jaye asked, "One last question, and this is strictly between us: "Were you paid money to drop your complaint?"

Bonnie studied the floor. "A little."

Jaye learned Joseph worked nights, so she arrived at 5:00 P.M. and asked for Mark Joseph at the casino office. When he appeared, she saw someone a man-hunting woman might call handsome. He was six-feet with a pool-side tan, pretty buff, and pretty angry.

When she showed her badge, he said, "Couldn't this wait until I got home?"

"No," she answered flatly. "This will be as discreet as you choose to cooperate."

They went to a conference room just outside the office suite and sat at opposite ends of an elongated table. He spoke first.

"Look, I apologize for being uptight. I thought all that police stuff was behind me. You can understand." He kept staring at her discolored cheek. "That looks painful."

Jaye ignored the comment. "Mr. Joseph, I'm investigating a violent crime against a woman, and I'm interviewing men who have been arrested for similar crimes."

He winced at the word "crime" but recovered to tell her he was due at a staff meeting and would have to let them know he'd be late. He reached for the phone, punched the numbers, and said to start without him.

Jaye resumed. "First, can you account for your whereabouts in the hours after midnight on this past November fifth?"

He leaned back and thought. "I don't recall. I'd have to think back. Maybe home asleep, like most people. I usually leave work about 1:00 A.M. and go straight home."

"What is your address?"

"117 E. Mariposa Ave."

"House or apartment?"

He squinted. "Why?"

She ignored his question. "Which?"

"A small house, a rental."

"Do you always work until 1:00 A.M.?"

"This is a casino, not a church."

"Can anyone verify you going straight home?"

"Uh, no, not unless they were looking in my window, I suppose."

"Did you stay home?"

"So far as—" He stopped. "Wait… Yeah, okay. That was the weekend… After work, I went home, picked up a bag I already had packed, and started for Las Vegas."

"I'm impressed. You're an organized man."

He smiled at the compliment. "I better be. I'm an accountant. Working in a casino, I know the trouble you can get into by not keeping your ducks in a row."

"You left for Las Vegas after midnight?"

"Yeah. When you work my hours, the clock gets turned upside down. I intended to attend an awards ceremony the next afternoon at a Boys & Girls Club where I used to volunteer. A special kid

I'd worked with was going to be honored."

"Anything else?"

"I was also going to take in a show, maybe see some friends. I have Sunday and Monday nights off."

"That's a long round-trip. You go to your awards event and maybe a show, and then after a day or two, turn around and do a long drive back through that boring desert."

"I enjoy driving. Vegas is still home to me. I was going to take Tuesday off to give me another day."

"Would your day off request be recorded with the casino?"

"I planned to call in sick."

"What show did you want to see?"

He shrugged. "Whatever's playing. I mainly like the ambiance, the atmosphere of the Strip. You can't get that here."

"Can you give me a name at the Boys & Girls Club who can verify your relationship?"

His look became incredulous. "Excuse me? So here you are, a San Diego cop, wanting to call my friends to see if my "alibi" holds up on some serious crime? How would I explain that?" He shook his head as though this couldn't be happening. "I don't think so."

A staff member rapped on the glass door, and Joseph motioned him in.

"Mr. Joseph, I'm sorry to bother you, but I need an okay on this credit chit. The guest is waiting."

Joseph glanced at it and signed. The subordinate scurried out apologetically.

Jaye resumed. "So, you left for Las Vegas. What time was that?"

"Uh, let me think back. Uh, I left work a little early to get a head start. I guess I left work about midnight. I'm not sure. Actually, I didn't go to Vegas after all because I had a minor accident on Rt. 94 near Thirtieth Street. Some late-night drunk."

"What time was that?"

"It was 2:10; close to that. I remember because I heard the officer mention the time, and he was on the scene in just a couple of minutes. It should be on the Highway Patrol report."

Jaye made a show of reviewing her notes to buy a moment

to sort out what he had just told her. "Uh, help me understand something. You were beginning a long drive to Las Vegas for a get-away of only a couple of days. You said you first went to your home located in Del Cerro in the northeast part of the city after coming from your work at the casino located directly east of the city. To begin the trip to Vegas from your house, you only had to drive a few blocks to get on Interstate 15, which takes you directly into Las Vegas. Instead, you had your accident in the southwest part of the city, a good thirty minutes and twenty miles out of your way." She looked at him quizzically. "Why was that, Mr. Joseph?"

He looked at her blankly for a long moment. "I, uh, went to see a lady friend before I left for Vegas. Is that important?"

"May I have her name?"

"I'm sorry. That would be awkward for her."

Jaye looked down at her notes. "The reason I'm talking to you, Mr. Joseph, which you've probably guessed, is the incident of last February 17, when you were arrested for choking Ms. Bonnie Fletcher in a parking lot on Fifth Avenue at 12:30 A.M."

Jaye asked him to recreate in detail the scenario and circumstances of the incident with Bonnie Fletcher. She always remembered what Potter had told her—You want them to lie, to tell lots of lies, because then you've got them. Blowing up a lie is child's play to a good interrogator. A truth teller only has to remember one version; a liar, though, has to remember all his made-up details because getting confused about even one can strip away his deception. That's why you have him repeat it several times. It gets harder and harder to keep the phony details straight.

Joseph avoided the question. He only said, "My version of the event was given to the police. I will just say that some women can take a break-up better than others. But when she had plenty of time to think about it, she refused to press charges. So, you can see, I'm not the woman-beater you came here to find."

"Did you pay money to Bonnie to drop charges?"

His look flashed defiance. "I have no interest in re-opening a closed case."

Jaye locked eyes with him steadily until he surrendered the eye contact and looked away. She said, "By the way, satisfy my curiosity, if you will: When you used the phone, you dialed with your right hand, but when you signed the paper, you used your left. Which are you, right-handed or left-handed?"

He grinned. "You ARE observant." He held up both hands. "I'm ambidextrous. You won't meet many of us."

"Mr. Joseph, would you be willing to take a polygraph?"

He nodded emphatically. "I'd be happy to take a lie test. Why not?"

"Will you give us a DNA sample?"

He uttered a short laugh. "I don't see why not." He paused and appeared to ponder what he had just said. "Uh, this whole thing is making my head spin. We're going a little fast with all this. I think I better talk to a lawyer. You know, I've heard stories… I'll tell you what, Miss Peoria—"

"Detective Peoria, sir."

His voice became contrite. "Sorry. No offense. I'll call my lawyer tomorrow."

Jaye closed her notebook and stood up. "I'll be interested in your decision, Mr. Joseph."

He rose with her. "You know, she did drop the charges."

"Thank you for your time, sir." Jaye left without shaking hands. There was nothing strange about his behavior, but she knew no one tells a cop the truth 100 percent, and she always liked to leave them wondering.

The next afternoon, Jaye called Joseph to schedule his polygraph. Instead, his willingness had turned into refusal. "I'm sorry," he said. "I ran it by my lawyer this morning, and he said no way, absolutely no way. No tests of any kind. He told me that polygraphs, especially, are susceptible to error, and once someone fails the test, even if it's a proven error, the police will never let up on them." He paused, expecting an argument from her, but she said nothing. "I know I said I'd do it, and I feel bad about that, but I've got to go with my lawyer's advice. He's a real hard-liner."

"Thank you," she said in a flat voice.

Jaye's next call was to the CHP to check-out his story of the accident. The clerk pulled up the log, and yes, the accident did happen at the time and location, Joseph said. A perfect alibi.

Chapter Five

Jaye and Tatum normally teamed up on many investigations, as did Baker and Almaguer. So it was normal for them to drive together to a DA's seminar on DNA evidence. The material was familiar to them, so the effort was directed at staying awake. As they drove back to headquarters, Jaye explained some of the information they had been given.

Tatum turned to glance at her. "You're better at this technical crap than me. In college, I only learned two things about science: how to convert Celsius to Fahrenheit, and light travels 186-thousand miles per minute."

"Per second," Jaye said.

"Huh?"

"Light travels 186-thousand miles per *second*," she said.

"Damn. I'm down to one thing."

Tatum parked the unmarked car in the underground garage, and they both walked to their individual cars and drove away in the same direction. After a few blocks, they pulled into a shopping center parking lot, and Jaye parked and got into his car. He drove away silently.

For about the tenth time since morning, Jaye examined the bruised cheek the PCP freak gave her. "Gross." She dabbed another layer of powder over it.

"I think it's sexy," Tatum teased.

As they drove, Jaye gave him her theories about a case he was working on.

When she finished, he said, "That makes some sense. If I catch the perp, I might let you have my body."

Jaye clapped her hands like a delighted teenager. "Oh, will you? Do I have to wait? Huh, huh, do I, do I?"

He pretended to be considering the matter. "I guess I can fit you in tonight."

"No," she said, "I can fit you in."

Tatum and Jaye had been carrying on an affair for three months. It was casual and only when both were in the mood or in the need. Jaye called it "relief sex." Tatum called it "sport fucking."

Their attitude was that both were single and unattached—well, he was separated, no surprise. They were using each other, but each knew it, and each knew the other knew it. They kept their trysts (both would deny it was an affair) secret and distant from their apartments because, though it wasn't against the rules if the department learned of it, they would be split up, and one would have to leave homicide. Neither relished the thought of working patrol on a graveyard shift.

The toilet flushed, and Tatum came out of the bathroom. "Welcome to the Voyager Lodge. Home away from home," he said, waving his arm slowly to encompass the printed sign on the door, the queen-size bed, the old-style TV, the door-less closet, and the wake-up coffee maker.

Jaye sat on the edge of the bed and listened to another couple noisily enter the room next door. One of the interesting things about such motels was the fast turnover of neighbors. Jaye could hear muffled, indistinguishable baritone words, followed by nervous soprano laughter. Shack-up chatter.

Tatum sat down next to her on the lumpy bed, took the wine bottle out of the paper bag, and unscrewed the cap.

They stopped and listened as the couple next door got into bed, and their springs squeaked loudly. Tatum snickered. "Sounds like a quickie is out of the starting gate. This place could use some insulation between rooms. On the other hand, maybe they like it this way. The guests can turn each other on from room to room. They should call it the Voyeur Lodge."

Jaye leaned back on the bed and pulled him down with her. "I don't care where it's at. This works for me." She ran her fingers through his thick brown hair. She stopped abruptly, reached down to her slacks, and took a condom out of the pocket. She wasn't worried about pregnancy, but she knew he was a tomcat, and she wasn't taking any chances. She handed it to him and said, "You know the ground rules."

He grimaced. "Ah, no." She countered, "Ah, yes."

Tatum said, "That's like wearing a raincoat in the bathtub. I knew a fellow who paid for college by going around to gas stations installing empty condom machines in women's restrooms—100 percent profit and no customer complaints."

Jaye laughed. "Even though you undoubtedly just made that up, it's a good story."

He cupped her face in his hands and looked past the deep bruise and into her eyes, including the puffy one. He gently kissed each eyelid. "I do care for you."

She laughed. "Remember, no gushing." She put out her hand. "Let's shake on our joint undertaking in this enterprise."

She flopped back on the bed. "Do you sometimes feel we're being foolish?" she asked.

"No, do you?"

She gazed at a cheap ocean surf print on the wall but looked far beyond it. "I've had my moments. You're technically still married, even though you're not. As I've gotten a little older, I've learned how hard it can be to stop what you start." She looked up with a wan smile. "But I'm here, so be nice to me."

Through the thin wall, they heard bed springs start to squeak rhythmically, and low moans join in counterpoint. They looked at each other and broke out in muffled giggles. Tatum started to hum along with the squeaking. "I know that tune," he said. "Three-quarter time."

Jaye pulled him down. "Come here, you. 'I want you' is just the chorus. We can learn the verses together." She kissed his face in about a dozen places in a flurry of desire.

He stroked her cheek tenderly and said, "Maybe we can make up our own lyrics."

"That's called an extended metaphor," she said.

He looked down at her in exaggerated praise. "I'm impressed."

"I got an A in English."

They kissed deeply, their mouths open and tongues exploring freely.

Sprawled across the bed, they made getting undressed a team

effort, laughing at the clumsiness of undressing each other while kissing and fondling.

They made love with fluidity. For three months, they had been luxuriating in their new-found delight and had made love ardently. She knew his touch, and he knew her feel. They made love like dancing partners, each anticipating practiced moves and both flowing with a rhythm that was silent except in their minds.

Tatum felt his surge beginning somewhere far down, toward the end of his body. It climbed his legs like a slow electrical charge, creeping upward, touching his muscles, his nerve ends, then his center.

"Jaye, I'm—I'm—"

"I know, I know, I can feel it," she answered breathlessly and arched her body against him. Her face flushed deeply as it thrashed from side to side.

They climaxed in quick succession, she first, he close behind, in a chorus of soft groans gradually scaling down to contented sighs. Finally, he spoke for both of them. "Wow!"

They stayed there together without a word, just touching and laying claim. Then, in silence, they became aware of something at the same time and started chuckling together. The chuckles progressed to laughter that left them with tears in their eyes and short of breath.

The squeaking and moaning were still coming from the other side of the wall.

Tatum swiped at his eyes and said, "He's got my respect. My boy next door is dedicated."

Jaye said, "You don't suppose they recorded themselves and are playing back the tape?"

"Maybe it *is* a tape. Piped in. The management is trying to set the mood." Jaye howled.

"I expect you to groan like she does," he said.

Jaye laughed. "Make me."

It was as though they had formed a bond with the anonymous couple in the next room, a bond of seeking the hoped-for, of grabbing the possible.

Jaye used her fingers to comb the hair on his chest and ran her fingertip down the length of the scar on his face. To do so was a familiarity, and it was a sign of comfort with him that she asked, "You never told me how this happened?"

He put his own fingers on the scar. "Uh, a broken bottle."

"On duty?"

"A cop's never off duty. Some guy couldn't hold his liquor. I don't like to talk about it; self-conscious about how it looks, I suppose."

"It makes you look swashbuckling and mysterious," Jaye said as she rolled off the bed and headed for the bathroom.

When she came out, Tatum was nearly dressed, sitting on a plastic-upholstered chair with his feet on the rumpled bed and drinking the remaining wine. He watched quietly as she dressed.

It made her feel good to have his approving eyes on her. It was a lusty sensation but also one of nesting, of feeling possessed and possessing. Watch it, she told herself.

Jaye watched as he attached a pre-knotted necktie. "Why do you wear clip-ons? Rather uncool, don't you think?"

"I got the idea from a backcountry stump-jumper named Billy Roy Edwards."

"Yeah?"

"I once had to arrest the scumbag for child molesting, and he decided to put up a fight. He got hold of my tie—regular type— and pulled me around like a dog on a leash. We waltzed like that for what seemed like a long time, with him doing all the leading. Since then, I've always worn these."

Jaye finished dressing, and they checked the room to make sure nothing had been left. Tatum opened the door to leave, but both stopped short and listened as unease crept up their spines.

The woman in the adjoining room was crying.

He was still riding the high of her Voyager interlude the next morning when her spirits took a glum turn. She had scheduled a follow-up visit with the pathologist that she had seen autopsy, Edna Willows. Those visits were helpful for further questions or perhaps a new twist on previous conclusions.

The most unappealing part of her job was observing autopsies. She would stand around and watch whining saws split skulls down the middle, and smell the acrid burning of bone. The odor of a week-old corpse being opened up made her breathe through her mouth and hope she didn't see it in her dreams.

White-gowned, blood-splattered people with razor scalpels would cut into abdomens like fishermen gutting trout and then hold up the entrails for inspection like prize cuts at a meat market. She couldn't shake those analogies. Even the thought of it made her stomach trying to jump into her throat and left her depressed about the human condition in general.

She studied the process, thinking that knowing the science might make the smell less objectionable. She learned the scientific terms, but words didn't change the naked fact that at the moment of death, an army of microorganisms attack the body in a banzai charge. It was like the bacteria were clustered impatiently behind a wall, and when death opened the gate, they rushed in, trampling each other in their eagerness.

The result in the autopsy room can be like taking week-old fish, rotten eggs, rotting cabbage, and fruit, feces, and garlic, then mixing them all in a plastic bin, covering it for a few days, then jerking off the lid and inhaling deeply. The resulting "Whew!" is the natural process of a life, making space for its replacement.

Jaye hoped, knowing the science would help. It didn't. She abandoned knowledge for two cotton nose plugs. If anyone in the autopsy room thought she was being amateurish…well, have at it.

The subject of the day's dissection was an old man, a presumed suicide by carbon monoxide poisoning. The reason for the autopsy was his widow was suspicious of his grandson from an earlier marriage just released from prison for manslaughter. He stood to benefit from the old man's will. Her suspicion hadn't sounded reasonable, but she had the right to make sure.

Jaye watched because she always learned something, no matter how unpalatable, and she wanted to again see Dr. John Racklin's work.

Ten minutes into the cutting, it was evident the old man had by his own free will filled his car with gas, lowered the garage door, and settled back to wait, and why it might have been a pretty good idea. The cancer had expanded from the colon to the stomach like rot spreading over fruit. Death, the old man must have learned, does not come soon or serenely to those who await it in pain.

Jaye watched as the pathologist finished up, and the other staffers wandered away.

Dr. Racklin had finished washing up when he sensed a presence behind him and turned to see a young woman waiting patiently. He was a stooped, near-sighted man who had spent a long career hunched over unwashed victims of violent San Diego streets, as well as the perfumed remains of high society suicides, and they had become all the same to him. But he never lost the belief that respect for the human they had once been was the last gift they could receive.

He was a man who had learned to see humor in human pre-tension, having minutely studied the end, which equalizes us all. At medical conventions, his peers would joke with him about his specialty, and in rejoinder, he would make the point that, unlike all of them, he had never lost a patient; in fact, all his patients were formerly theirs.

Racklin said, "You waiting for me, miss?"

"Yes, doctor, I'm Jaye Peoria, San Diego P.D. homicide. I'd like to ask if you remember an autopsy on a woman named Edna Willows."

"I remember you, my dear. You observed a couple of my autopsies. I don't recognize the name Willows." He smiled and gestured to the white table with the hastily sewn-up cadaver still on it. "Here, they have no names."

She made a face to acknowledge her stupidity. "I'm sorry. Obviously, you can't remember them all."

"Come into my office. If it's one I did, I'll certainly have notes."

Jaye waited while he leafed through some files, took out a slim one, and studied it for a couple of minutes. "Humm," he said, "strangulation, without a doubt."

"I was just wondering if maybe there was something besides your report you could tell me that might help."

A stern look shot over his glasses. "Young lady, my reports are complete and thorough."

She blushed and stammered. "I—I didn't mean—"

He returned to his notes, "I assume you're referring to both reports."

"Both?"

He seemed mystified. "Yes, the actual report and the addendum."

"We only saw the first."

"What? I filed a supplement to the report two days later. I'd wanted to think about what I added and do a little research."

"You sent a supplement, doctor?" Jaye was suddenly excited—guardedly excited.

"You didn't get it?" he said in exasperation. "That's unpardonable—damned bureaucracy." He reviewed a second sheet of paper. "Well, this is what I think: Based on the angle of damage to the hyoid bone and greater trauma to the tissue on the left side of the throat, I believe the killer's left thumb was considerably stronger, suggesting, of course, he was left-handed."

Jaye started writing in a notebook.

"Understand, young lady," he cautioned, "I didn't include it in the initial report because it's not medically verifiable. The certainty of my supposition is a matter of dispute in the profession. I can't swear to it because it's not provable, that's why I hesitated. But I just decided you're entitled to my thoughts, for whatever they're worth."

"A lot. They're worth a lot. I'll track down the second report." She shook his hand and headed for the door. When she reached a bench in the waiting area, she took out her iPhone, summoned Google, and spent a few minutes reading. When she reached her car, her mind was racing—Let's see: if one person in ten is left-handed, and one in twenty has arch pattern fingerprints, then that cuts down my candidate list a lot. I'm going to get it down to one. The One.

Chapter Six

Brian Fogarty craned his neck to see what the hang-up was. Traffic was hopelessly snarled at the center of the curving, rising hump of the Coronado Bridge, spanning two miles of ocean 200 feet above San Diego Bay, connecting the city with Coronado Island. The bridge seemed to wrap a concrete ribbon around the spectacular ocean-skyline views it connected.

Drivers on the westbound side were leaving their cars and walking quickly toward the middle of the bridge. Gawkers on the opposite side made those lanes equally impassable. Seeing no point in sitting and wondering, Brian left his car in the right-hand lane and started walking toward the crowd. Along the way, he passed a sign, giving a number for suicide prevention, which ended with the words, "We care about you."

As he neared the huddle in the middle of the bridge, murmuring voices carried an ominous message: "Do you think he'll jump? Poor guy; he's got to be crazy. That cop'll talk him down."

"What's going on?" Brian asked a teenager with a punk haircut.

"Dude's out on the edge of the bridge; says he's gonna jump." The boy started to push forward. "This I gotta see."

Brian worked his own way through the crowd made up equally of businessmen, women in suits, and inner-city youths jostling shoulder to shoulder. Each person ignored his neighbor, intent on joining the scene ahead, to which they seemed both entranced and repelled; most concerned that whoever was out there would jump, a few concerned that he wouldn't.

When Brian made it to the front, he saw a young man standing out on the edge of a temporary construction-repair girder extending about five feet into mid-air beyond the waist-high railing.

In the background, he heard a voice say, "Check it out. Cat's goin' for the big splash."

The girder was about two feet wide and black, with bumpy rivets interspersed on its surface. On three sides of it was nothing but air with the choppy waters of the bay far below. The young man was small and thin and appeared to be about twenty-two. The strong breeze whipped his shabby clothes tight against his body so Brian could see the boniness of his arms and legs. His black hair stood straight up in the wind, and he wrapped his arms around his chest as though warding off a chill too deep for others to feel. His face was contorted in despair, and his wild eyes were unable to find a place to rest.

In the distance to the east, the harsh white of sunlight reflected off the splendid new high-rises of downtown San Diego. Below was the green glimmer of the bay. Sailboats, freighters, and dull-gray Navy ships were toys in a bathtub, made tiny by height. They wandered slowly about, ignoring each other like different species of insects. To the north and west, the wooded hills of Point Loma and the flat glitter of the endless Pacific completed a post-card setting that didn't fit the anguish happening on the bridge. Reality playing mood games.

A uniformed officer, only a little older than the man on the girder, leaned over the railing and pleaded, "Come on in, please." Brian could see from the desperation on the officer's face that he had no idea what to do. With anxious eyes, the young cop turned back to the crowd as though seeking a rescuer for the jumper and maybe for himself.

Brian could feel the crowd growing behind him as pressure from new arrivals pushed those in front forward. The excited mumbling was like the drone of bees. He could hear a nervous titter and a couple of people praying aloud. Suddenly, a single, deep gasp rose from the crowd, like watching a game-winning home run. Brian looked up to see the jumper lift a leg into the air so that he was standing on the edge of the beam on one foot.

"God, don't do that," the officer shouted and sounded about ready to cry. Again, he looked back as though seeking reinforcements.

Brian stepped forward. "Excuse me, officer, I don't want to interfere, but I'm a psychologist. Can I help?"

The cop looked relieved at having someone to talk to. "I radioed this in a few minutes ago. My sergeant should be here pretty quick." He gestured toward the jumper. "What can even he do for this guy?"

A second loud "Oooh" from the crowd announced another move by the man toward jumping.

Brian could see that if he kept it up, the man would fall, either deliberately or accidentally. "Mind if I talk to him? I don't mean to inter—"

The cop had the reflexive suspicion of any policeman at civilian help. "You sure you're a psychologist?" When Brian nodded and fished a business card out of his wallet. The cop glanced at it and said, "Okay, but back off if I tell you to, understand?"

Brian nodded and moved slowly to the railing. "Hi. What's your name? Mine's Brian."

The jumper turned his head and stared suspiciously at Brian.

"He's going to jump!" a woman in the crowd screamed.

Brian knew that the man had not jumped already for one of two reasons: either he wanted to be talked down, or he wanted to punish society before going, to make a statement about how life had wronged him.

"It's pretty tough to talk to a guy who won't answer," Brian said with a big smile. "Maybe you're a fellow who has nothing to say."

The jumper seemed to debate with himself for a moment and then hesitantly answered in a soft voice. "That's not true. I have a lot to say, but no one'll ever listen."

Brian smiled. "I'm listening."

"You're nobody."

Brian shook his head. "That's not true. I'm me. That's somebody, just like you're somebody."

The jumper threw his head back and laughed, but the movement knocked him off balance, and for a long moment, he swung his arms, fighting to keep his perch while the crowd screamed. When he had regained his footing, he said, as though nothing had happened, "Do you have a name?"

Brian nodded. "Brian Fogarty."

"Well, I don't. My name was stolen from me."

"Who'd do something like that?"

"Them. The people at the hospital. They were going to take everything from me, but I got away."

Brian guessed the man was paranoid schizophrenic, not a determined suicide in the manner of a deeply depressed person, but still quite capable of taking the plunge to escape his imaginary enemies. "Would you like me to give you back your name?" Brian asked.

The jumper squinted suspiciously at him. "You couldn't."

"Yes, I could. Try me. What did your name use to be?"

"Donnie. Don Mason."

Brian made a giving gesture toward him. "Well, Donnie Mason, I hereby give you back your name. You now have it. I speak it—Donnie Mason."

Several people in the crowd laughed, and Brian turned to the cop and whispered harshly, "Keep those creeps quiet."

As the cop turned to control the crowd, Jaye stepped out of the crowd holding her badge aloft. She had been nearby when the radio call went out. She moved close to the officer. "What can I do?"

"Keep these people back," he said, "and thanks."

Jaye extended her arms, holding up the badge, and moved the crowd back.

Brian ignored the crowd. "See, Donnie Mason, that wasn't tough at all. You've got your name back. There're a lot of things you could do if you'd just come in off that beam. Why, I'll bet you could do anything you wanted to."

"Would you help me?"

"Absolutely." Brian nodded vigorously as though trying to convince himself it could be this easy. Apparently, all the fellow needed was a friendly, reassuring voice. Brian knew that a paranoid schizophrenic could slip out of a persecution delusion as easily as into it, and he wondered what emotion would replace it. "You bet I'll help you, Donnie Mason, and so will a lot of other people. Now, all you have to do, Donnie Mason, is just walk over to me carefully." Behind him, Brian could hear a disturbance and turned around to see three other cops led by an older man who must have been the sergeant. "Who the hell is he?" the sergeant asked, pointing at Brian.

Jaye moved over to him. "He seems to know what he's doing." Brian put his hand behind his back and frantically signaled for quiet while not taking his eyes from Donnie.

"Will you take care of me if I come in?" Donnie asked in a little boy's voice.

"The first thing we'll do, we'll go get some ice cream. How's that sound, Donnie Mason?"

Donnie started to put one foot in front of the other and looked down. Suddenly, as though he had just awoken to find himself on his ledge, a look of panic spread over his face as he stared at the water far below. He gritted his teeth and started to shake.

Brian's heart sank. Panic, not paranoia, was now the enemy. "Take it easy, Donnie Mason. Don't look down. Just one step at a time."

Donnie started to slide one foot forward.

"That's it. Attaboy," Brian encouraged.

Donnie made it halfway through the step and froze again. He couldn't keep his eyes from drifting to the empty air below. His whole body shook, and he started to whine.

Brian knew panic would throw Donnie's coordination off, and he would fall before he could work himself back to the railing. With a desperation that temporarily masked his own fear of heights, Brian turned to the sergeant. "Do you have any rope?"

The sergeant turned around and questioned his subordinates, who shook their heads. Next, he asked the onlookers near the front. One man nodded and ran to his nearby car. In moments, he returned with a length of clothesline and handed it to the sergeant, who in turn passed it on to Brian. Brian looked at the frayed length and said, "Uh-h. This won't do."

"I can radio for some," the sergeant said.

"No time," Brian said and looked around for something. A woman extended a twelve-foot length of clothesline, but it appeared strong. Brian took it and called to Donnie. "I've got a rope here. I'm going to throw one end to you. Tie it around your middle." He gestured for two big men standing nearby to help him hold his end. He flung the rope end to Donnie. It ended at his feet. He didn't react. The second toss hit him in the chest. He ignored it, staring straight ahead.

Brian dropped the rope and turned to the crowd. Just then, a man in work clothes appeared with a long coil of an orange heavy-duty extension cord. Brian knew that the rubber-coated material would be stronger than almost any rope. His first idea was to make a loop and throw it out to Donnie, but the more he thought about it, he realized if Donnie reached out or down to gather it in, he would surely fall. He was frozen in fear.

Brian wrapped the cord through his belt and twice around his waist, so both ends could be held. A cop gave a strong tug to make sure it was secure. He took one end of the clothesline and gave the other to some men standing by. "I'll tie this around him for safety, and then I'll try to guide him in."

"This should be *our* job," the sergeant protested, but none too vehemently.

"I wish it could be," Brian said, "but a policeman going out there might freak him out again." With the cord securely attached and with the clothesline in hand, Brian climbed to the top of the railing and paused. He looked down and saw the water through the girders. Two sailboats bobbed past like bathtub toys. The wind that he hadn't noticed on the bridge floor now seemed to teasingly pluck at him, trying to throw him off balance. He looked behind. Four cops and four burly workmen were holding both ends of the long cord with white-knuckled determination. He turned back to face Donnie standing just a few feet away. The fear came over Brian like a chill, making him shudder at the thought of taking a first step.

He looked out at Donnie standing near the end of the beam, whining like a frightened puppy, and knew he somehow had to force himself to go forward. He looked back at the men bracing themselves against the edge of the railing. "Hold tight," he said unnecessarily, but the words made him feel better. He steadied himself and called, "Be calm, Donnie. I'll be there in just a moment."

Jaye stopped her crowd control for a moment to look back. She prayed briefly, though she greatly doubted her influence.

Brian held his breath and put one foot on the girder. It seemed impossibly narrow. He tried to avoid looking at the water so far below, but he couldn't watch his feet without also seeing the great empty void beyond.

He wondered what would happen if he reached Donnie. Would he be grabbed and pulled off in the other man's panic? He tried to dislodge the thought from his mind. Balancing himself with arms outstretched, he pushed the other foot ahead slowly...slowly. He was within about three feet of the man. "Just relax, Donnie. I'm almost there." He moved the other foot. Then another. One more step, and he could reach out to Donnie and loop the line over him, then guide him to safety. "Hold on, Donnie." Brian concentrated on calming his voice to help put Donnie at ease. "Now, what I want you to do is relax. When I toss the rope loop to you, put it around your waist and let me tie it. I'll lead you back to the railing. Don't look down. Keep your eyes on me." He forced a smile. "Everything's going to be okay." Brian shuffled forward like a man moving through a minefield.

Donnie heard what Brian said, but his muscles were tight with panic; they felt numb, as though he had been outside too long on a freezing day. He jerkily tried to reach out prematurely for the rope.

Brian saw Donnie lean forward too soon. "Hold up a second," he shouted, but Donnie panicked at not being able to grab the rope and leaned forward even more.

Then Donnie was lunging awkwardly. His fingers touched Brian's but then slid off. With a guttural moan, Donnie fought for balance by windmilling his arms.

Brian saw Donnie's face turn from surprise to fear to horror, and he knew from that look alone that the man was gone. Brian heard the high-pitched scream and watched helplessly as Donnie fluttered spread-eagled through the air, getting smaller and smaller and finally hitting the water on his back. Brian watched the tiny splash spread at the impact and then close again as though nothing had happened. Nature yawning at human struggles.

"Just make a careful pivot," the sergeant called out.

Slowly and without a sound, Brian inched 180 degrees and slowly made his way back along the beam, and climbed over the railing as the men reeled in the cord. Stunned people jostled and jabbered in their excitement, but Brian felt nothing and heard nothing. His spirit was on that green water far below.

Police converged on the scene from all directions, giving the impression of being too many, too late.

"Make way for a hero," the sergeant shouted, pointing to Brian pushing his way through the crowd. Jaye gasped as she saw the pain on his face. He ignored the murmurs of praise and the nice-try pats on the back from onlookers as he tried to distance himself from that awful sight. There was something about his grief for a demented stranger's death that deeply touched Jaye.

She walked over and introduced herself. "Come with me," she said with quiet authority and showed her detective's shield. Still stunned, he looked through her and nodded. She gently gripped his forearm and led him through the crowd to the young officer who was starting to fill out his report and needed to talk to Brian.

"Can you get what you need so I can get him out of here?"

The officer nodded understanding and took down Brian's ID information and how he could be contacted. Then, he shifted his notebook and put out his hand to shake Brian's. "You're a hell of a man, is all I've got to say. Thank you."

Brian nodded absently, and Jaye said, "You need a cup of coffee." She looked him in the face closely. "You seem okay to drive. Where's your car?" He pointed it out, and she said, "I'm right over there. Follow me. I'll get us out of this mess."

Jaye gently pushed Brian toward his car. She activated a dashboard red light and drove slowly on the wrong side of the now-closed bridge back into San Diego to a small barrio cafe away from the bridge and the crowd. Inside, she chose a back booth and led him to it. She ordered coffee and watched as he gripped the mug with two shaky hands and sipped. He blinked and took a deep breath. "I'm okay now. I, uh, I've never seen anything like that before."

"No one should."

"It was horrible. He had a life." Tears formed in his eyes and puddled on the Formica tabletop. He made an attempt to brush them away.

"It's okay," she said softly. "You're entitled." She groped for words to describe how wonderful his efforts had been but said nothing.

He gazed at his hands. "I almost had him. His hand reached mine. And then—he was gone. Just gone." He closed his eyes as though that would shutter the memory.

Jaye felt her own eyes moisten. "But, you know something? Before he died, someone who cared reached out and touched him. A lot of people die without that."

She studied Brian as she listened. He was mid-thirties, six foot, medium handsome, reasonably fit, brown hair with just a wisp of premature gray in a widow's peak. Obviously compassionate. A pretty average-seeming guy, except for what he had just done. Nothing average about that.

Brian was still looking at both of his hands, not listening. His thoughts were on a trip of their own. The two of them sat that way for a couple of minutes silently. She watched him stare at his hands. There was no tension, only Jaye waiting for Brian to settle his thoughts.

Finally, he said in a voice of wonderment, "This is weird, but when I was talking with Donnie, I felt power, real power—not over him, but over myself. I was in total control of my life. I approved of myself." He repeated the words, wanting to hear them again. "I approved of myself." He leaned back. "That's a weird thing to say to a stranger, I suppose."

Jaye had no response and wasn't sure what would be appropriate. Finally, she said, "You seemed to know exactly what to do, what to say."

"I deal with people like Donnie every day. I know the language. I'm the director of a halfway house for the mentally challenged. It's called New Hope."

His thoughts returned to the bridge, and he gazed out a window with the top of the bridge in the distance. "My God, do you believe how monstrous life can be?"

Jaye reached out and touched his arm. "Yes."

As they parted, she gave him her business card and hoped he read the intended meaning into it.

Two days later, Jaye answered the phone to hear a voice that was vaguely familiar. "Hi, detective. This is Brian Fogarty."

Yes! He had read the proper meaning— "Uh, what can I do for you, sir?"

"I'm the guy from the bridge that you were nice to."

"Of course. I couldn't forget what you did. How are you? I saw the story on TV last night. You're a hero—Let me change that: You're a *real* hero, not some idiot jock."

He said, "Hey, that's a perfect segue to what I want to ask you. I've got two tickets to the San Diego State-Gonzaga basketball game tomorrow night. Want to share some popcorn with me?"

She hesitated only long enough not to seem too eager. "Well, yes, thank you. Oh, by the way, is it Dr. Fogarty?"

"I just use that when it's advantageous to be a stuffed shirt. But, no, it's just Brian.'"

When Brian picked her up for the game, he walked to her door, and when she answered the bell, he handed her a bag with the name of a framing shop on the cover.

Surprised, she reached in and took out a framed cover from a Nancy Drew mystery. It showed a pretty teenager walking up a dark staircase with a flashlight. The title said *The Hidden Staircase*.

Her eyes widened with delight. Her memory took a quick, pleasant trip back to junior high and checking out this same book from the library. "I love this. You don't know how much. How clever. What's the occasion?"

"You were a friend to a stranger at the bridge. I was lucky to be that stranger."

"Ohhh." She pecked him on the cheek—Too-forward be damned. I'm a big girl—Then she said, "Ladies aren't usually that brazen, but I can always arrest you." She took the framed picture and held it up to the wall experimentally. Then she turned to him. "Here are the ground rules for the evening: Nothing but fun allowed; nothing about murders, suicides, or any kind of violence. We can talk about basketball, but only if you're a State fan. Otherwise, that's off the table, too."

He agreed, and they had a ceremonial handshake.

Seated a few rows behind the visitors' bench, they had a running low-voice conversation. He learned she was divorced, she learned he was separated from his wife. At halftime, she said, "You said you were in the army. What was that about?" She followed that with, "Oops! Don't be nosy, Jaye. You're not on duty tonight." Actually, she didn't mean that. She didn't mind being nosy.

He laughed, then without thinking, said he was in the Rangers in Iraq and immediately regretted it.

"Really?" She arched her eyebrows. "You must have some stories. Give."

He shook his head. "Nah. I was in supply. I passed out towels."

She looked to see if he was joking. "I don't believe you. They got grunts to do that."

"Tell you what," he said, "Remember your ground rules. I think war is covered by the category of violence."

"Touché." However, she said to herself—There's a story here, and I'll learn it, or I'm not a Nancy Drew protégé.

They sat back and watched the game and drank their five-dollar warm beers, but neither was terribly interested. The conversation was muted to escape irritated stares from seat neighbors. Their faces were close together amidst blended scents, aftershave, and perfume. Jaye looked around curiously. "Would you believe I grew up in this city, and this is the first time I've ever been in an actual sports arena?"

"Well, you probably had lots of distractions."

Her voice trilled in an ironic little laugh. "Distractions? I guess you could call being poor that. Yes, 'distraction' is a good word for it. Where I lived, basketball was as far from our thoughts as—well, the price of admission. There wasn't the money, the time, or even the clothes. My dad had trouble keeping a job but no problem drinking up what he did earn, so we kids had to pitch in."

The basketball game was forgotten as she released tucked-away memories. She had to put her lips close to his ear because of the crowd noise. "In high school, I was chosen to be a cheer-leader; I had to refuse because I had to work bussing tables after school at a local café." She gave a single, tight laugh. "To this day, it's the only thing I've been elected to."

Brian faced her and let her talk, ignoring the fans around them, as they were also ignored.

"I wanted to be the first in the family to graduate from college, but the best I could do was two years at community college." She shook her head. "Then, I 'escaped' into marriage."

A tie-breaker-shot cheer broke her reverie. Others around them rose excitedly, but they didn't. Brian saw that her reflective moment had passed, so he asked: "By the way, what was the ruling on the bridge tragedy, Donnie Mason?"

She had been waiting for the question. "Suicide." She looked at him carefully. "How are you with that?"

"I thought that would be it. However, it wasn't technically a suicide. He was trying to get back."

"There is no statistical cubbyhole for 'I changed my mind...'" She stopped and looked at him. "That sounded crass. I apologize."

He rubbed the back of his neck and answered slowly. "Not to worry. I wouldn't think that of you. It is what it is, I guess. I pushed it out of my mind. That's what people do to stay sane. Sublimation can be a gift."

She waited for him to continue. He didn't.

They left in the middle of the fourth quarter to beat the traffic leaving the one-sided game. Walking through the parking lot, Jaye asked, "Did you enjoy the game?"

"To tell you the truth, basketball bores me to tears. Someone gave me these tickets, and I said to myself— 'How can I use these to maximum advantage?'" Then glancing at her slyly, he said. "It was a great excuse to see you again."

"Basketball bores me, too," she said. "Same excuse."

Jaye settled back in Brian's Acura and ran her hand along the upholstery. "You better be careful where you park this around New Hope. Your neighbors could reduce this to an empty tin can in about two minutes." she failed to see Brian wince at her characterization. "That, or have the whole thing in Mexico in an hour."

"Any progress on your murder case?" he asked.

"It's a work in progress, just not enough progress yet."

"God. What's this world coming to?"

Jaye laughed. "Same as it's always been. Nothing's changed, Mr. Psychologist. You should know that."

He sighed. "Sometimes it's a little hard to get used to. I don't see how you do it, dealing with that sort of thing every day."

"It's a living. It's not as grim as a Wal-Mart cash register." Her attention turned to the music coming from the car stereo. "What's that? It's pretty."

Brian listened for a moment. "That's Schubert's *Piano Quintet in A*. It's called "the Trout." What kind of music do you like?"

Jaye hesitated. "Oh, country, pop, but I like that. That music is you."

They drove to a barbecue place that Jaye had heard praised. He parked, and they walked toward the place called "When Pigs Fly BBQ." Brian looked at the sign and said, "Shouldn't that read—'When Pigs Die BBQ'?" Jaye playfully punched him on the arm as they entered.

They had a pleasant dinner, the type both recalled from happier days and which both were pleased to realize could be revisited.

Over dessert, Jaye said, "You're a mysterious guy, and as you know, my job is to solve mysteries."

He chuckled and shook his head. "Nancy Drew would find me boring. Got a marriage that's falling apart—make that fallen—I have a seven-year-old named Traci who's fast approaching perfection, if not already there."

"I'll bet you spoil her right and left," Jaye said.

Brian laughed. "Well, of course. But, you know, someday, I'd like her to have a sister or brother.

"I had four siblings. We grew up middle-class, maybe a bit upper-middle, in Des Moines. Then college. Army. Marriage. Went to work for San Diego Utilities and finished my doctorate on the side. Made good money and helped some folks as a corporate shrink. Got inspired, I guess, and became head of New Hope halfway house. That's about it."

"The truth is in the details," she said.

"That's also where the devil is," he said. "Sometimes I think they don't like each other." For a moment, he lost his smile but quickly regained it.

When it came time to pay the bill, he reached for it. "Do you mind?"

"Nope. My liberation stalled just short of that final step."

It seemed as though they laughed at everything.

Walking out, he reached for her hand, and she gripped his. "Wow! This is like high school," she said happily. "I guess we're now on an official date. Next step is going steady. Then I can take your class ring, make it smaller with yarn, and cover the yarn with fingernail polish. Do you realize I hardly know you, and we're holding hands? Moving pretty fast, buster. Does that make me a wayward woman?"

"No," he said, "it makes more clear what you genuinely are—a quite intriguing woman."

On the street near the parking lot was a touristy wire display that had dozens of padlocks locked onto it, some with notes attached.

"This is called the Wall of Love," Jaye said as they stopped and looked at it. "It used to be an Italian thing, now it's a Chamber of Commerce thing. You're supposed to attach a lock to secure your love."

He frowned. "If you're smart, you won't throw away the key."

"Oh, what a cynic! I'm shocked. I think when I fall in love, I'll attach my handcuffs. That'll tell him he better not screw around."

"That'd be the downside married to you. You'd always have that gun handy."

"And a deadly aim," again, laughter.

Chapter Seven

Jaye was staring at the ceiling, trying to sort out the threads of her case and half-listening to the banter of Tatum and Almaguer.

Almaguer looked up from the magazine he was thumbing. "I've been reading about this white privilege you-all are getting fat off of. How do I get me some of that?"

"It won't be easy," Tatum said.

"My grandfather was a gringo. Do you think that makes me eligible for a quarter privilege?" "You could say you're mainly A-rab trying to cash in on your victim status. Might work."

"Be nice, you redneck," Jaye said, only half listening.

Tatum leaned back thoughtfully but with a grin. "Tell you what: You can have my white privilege if I can have your affirmative action."

Mike Palmer in the crime lab picked up the phone and punched in a number, his anticipation growing like bread yeast.

Jaye answered on the first ring. "Jaye? Hi, this is Mike Palmer over at fingerprints… Right. How are you? Listen, I've got something here you might be interested in. I just saw a request from Central Division to run a print check through the FBI's database, AFIS, on a guy they're holding named Lewis Price. He was arrested for trying to strangle a woman downtown. He's charged with aggravated assault… Yeah, and get this: he's an arch pattern… Right." He laughed. "That sure the hell is the truth. The last one to know anything around here is usually the one who needs to. That's why I called… Hey, you're welcome; my pleasure." He paused and took a deep breath. "Uh, say, Jaye, how about a drink after work someday soon? I've got some theories you might be interested in… Terrific! That sounds great. How about if we meet tomorrow after work at the 10-7?

The 10-7 (police code— "out of service") was a bar that was converted from a large shoe store in a sliding-downhill shopping center on the edge of downtown near headquarters. It was the favorite watering hole for cops, including spouses and dates, deputy DAs, cop groupies, and defense lawyers who were expected to buy more than their share of drinks. What did groupies contribute? Well, that was on a case-by-case basis.

The owner, Frog Thompson, claimed he had been a bookie and brothel operator years before in Chicago. He boasted that he earned the money to open the 10-7 by being a better mouse than Chicago's finest were cats. He was proof that old times can become good times if you ignore all the bad stuff. Frog got his name because another bordello entrepreneur years ago had tried to garrote him with a clothesline, leaving a permanent welt across his neck and a rasping voice from a damaged larynx that impressed with its similarities to the tailless amphibian bearing the same name.

Jaye stood on tiptoes, trying to peer over the bobbing heads crowding the bar of the 10-7. Across the room, she saw Tatum drinking beer with a guy from the sheriff's office and Alice Marko, a uniform from patrol. Alice was a proud lesbian and popular because of her fun nature. Tatum was kidding her about "converting" to hetero. "Give me one night," he said. "Just one night, and I'll turn you around."

She laughed. "Oh, you're so thoughtful, Tatum. What a generous offer, but what do I tell my girlfriend?"

For Tatum, the question was like getting a pony for Christmas. "Bring her along," he said with an expansive wave of his arm. "I'll help both of you."

Frog Thompson spotted Jaye, scanning the room. "Hey, Jaye," he called over in a grating rasp. "You're too late if'n you're looking for work. I just got some fresh girls in from Chicago."

She sought his flaming red face out of the crowd at the bar.

"Frog, as a pimp, you couldn't *give* a movie star away on death row," she shouted. Jaye waited for the she-gotcha-Frog guffaws at the bar to subside, then she asked if anyone had seen Mike Palmer from the crime lab. Seeing the shaking heads, she ordered a beer and leaned against the bar to listen to Frog brag about the old days.

"Shit," Frog said, "in my day, those Chicago cops didn't take no crap off'n nobody. Weren't no Miranda or shit like that. The only warnings you had was when a cop would pull back his arm 'fore he smacked you with the Chicago phone book. I'll tell you, boys and girls, that'd get your attention. You could hear ever one of them phones ringing."

"Did you pay off?" a young detective, whom Jaye recognized as being from burglary, asked.

"Pay off?" Frog repeated incredulously. "Why, in those days, they had ledger books with the word 'graft' printed on the cover. The cops would line up on Fridays, just like a regular factory payday. Some of the boys liked to take theirs out in trade, that's cause my girls'd never give 'em the clap. Well, it happened once, but that were an accident."

"That's terrible," the young detective said.

"I said it was an accident," Frog snapped.

"No, I mean that corruption was so widespread and open."

"Well, it only worked for girls and gambling," Frog said, "and the cops earned enough to support their families. Kept taxes down, too."

"Huh?" someone said.

"Yeah, the City Council knew what was going on, so they just kept cops' salaries low. Let 'em make it on the side, they figured." Frog wiped his hands on checkered polyester pants that hung below his balloon-like belly. "Tell you one thing, though, folks weren't afraid to walk down the street in them days. And if a cop's going to pick my pocket, I want him to protect my ass, too."

Three policemen raised their voices in a good-natured baseball argument as Jaye saw Mike Palmer making his way toward her.

"Sorry I'm late," he said.

"No problem. I was early."

"Can we take a table?" he asked nervously, looking around for anyone he knew.

Jaye picked up her beer. "Follow me, but better grab a drink first. This isn't the Hilton."

Palmer bought a Lite and followed her to a postage-stamp table in a corner. Above them was a revolving red light that Frog had installed as the main decoration. He turned it on when a customer bought a round for the house, usually a lawyer or politician. He claimed that keeping the price of drinks low enough for cheapskate cops didn't allow for any other ornaments, except horns and hats on New Year's Eve, which he collected and reused.

Someone had asked Frog if the red light was meant to honor his police customers. "Shit," he had said. "It reminds me of a whorehouse I used to run in the days when my customers were quality folk, not like here."

When they were settled, Palmer asked, "Did that stuff I gave you on Price help?"

Jaye nodded her thanks. "I've got high hopes we can close this case; really appreciate it."

"I've heard a lot about this place," he said, looking around as a red reflection played across his face.

"You've never been here?" Jaye said, amazed. "It's cheap and safe. If anyone has a snoot full, one of the guys'll make sure he gets home okay."

"Uh, my wife doesn't think much of cop hangouts. Frankly, she doesn't think much of cops. She wants me to get out."

An imitation police siren went off, and Palmer jumped several inches out of his chair. "What the hell was that?"

Jaye laughed. "Frog sets that off whenever he buys a drink for the bar. Wants to make sure everyone knows it. Claims it's a siren taken off an ambulance worn out from picking up all the bodies these cops killed with their throw-downs."

"Quite a place," he said, shaking his head.

"I love it. I can relax here for a few minutes after work without getting hit on. If some guy wandered in and bothered me...well, he'd be happy to be thrown out. It also helps me work on my sick cop humor, which is coming along but occasionally struggling." Jaye raised her glass in a perfunctory toast and took a sip. "You said you had some ideas. I'm all ears."

He fidgeted with his glass. "Yeah, ah, well, I was going to suggest that—" He blushed and grinned self-consciously. "You won't believe this, but I forget what I was going to tell you."

"You're not good at this, you know."

"Huh?"

Jaye smiled wistfully and patted his hand. "Mike, this is not my first waltz. You're a great guy, and I appreciate your help on my case, but the answer is no."

"No? What do you mean?"

"I mean, no. You've got a wife, and—"

"Yeah, I sure the hell do," he said bitterly.

"And regardless of what she's done, I won't do this to her because I've had it done to me."

"I'm sorry."

"What is it? She tired of you, or you of her?"

"We fight a lot. She seems to want me to be someone else, someone she could've married but didn't. She's big on that, all the chances she had, but threw over for me. That's about all I hear anymore."

"People change, Mike. Either that or we never knew them to begin with. In my case, I don't know which, maybe both." She sighed, tired of the familiar thought, one she had lain awake with on too many nights. "I don't know whether they grow tired of the other person or if it's themselves they grow tired of. Either way, the innocent one usually gets hurt. That's a basic law of nature. That's straight from Darwin, probably."

Palmer absent-mindedly tore the label from his beer bottle with a thumb. "She makes fun of my work, calls me a failure because I don't make what all her old school friends do."

"Any kids?"

He shook his head. "Not yet."

"Do you still love her?"

He studied the strips of paper in his fingers. "I don't know. I—I guess I maybe don't. Otherwise, why would I chase you?"

"Don't get carried away, Mike. Don't confuse a handy warm body with the real thing. Either you're a womanizer—cocksman, I believe is the term of art—or you're trying to punish her."

He leaned forward and spoke with intensity. "No, no. I'd never use you. A man'd be a fool not to want you."

She chuckled. "Thanks, that makes me feel good. But, as the saying goes, 'all cats are gray in the dark,' if a cat's all you want." He started to protest, but she said, "No, it's true. Sex is something people have got to do because we're wired for it. But unless there's something emotional between a man and woman, it's also the silliest thing in the world…sweating, groping, moaning, and then—Will he call me tomorrow? That sort of thing is only a temporary fix. It doesn't last."

"That's not what I had in mind."

She patted his hand and smiled. "Of course not."

"You're turned-off, aren't you?"

Her shoulders slumped slightly, and her voice carried a burden. "No, not at all. Men are just people trying to get by best they can, just like women. I'm just extremely tired of people screwing other people over. If God made us this way, I don't like his workmanship, but I sure dig his dry sense of humor."

She looked around. "I'm a lucky woman. I found a home. These cops are my people. I love them, even the ugly, crude, and lecherous ones. Every one of them would risk his life for me."

"And you for them?"

"Yes. And I for them."

He looked penitently at the beer rings on the table. "I'm sorry I lured you here tonight."

She laughed merrily. "Lured? What a lovely, Victorian word. Being lured by you has been fun. I feel like our talk has given me a new friend. You're a nice-looking, good guy, and I'm flattered. Any woman would be. But I'm not your answer. She stood up and kissed him lightly on the forehead. "Go home and get it straightened out, Mike, one way or another."

Potter's bloodshot, baggy eyes indicated he had been on another flight as a test pilot for Jack Daniels. He gestured weakly at Jaye and grunted a hello without smiling. When she was seated in front of his chipped desk, he muttered, "Congratulations."

"Oh-oh, what did I do?"

"Sending Lewis Price's prints and DNA out on the wire was good detective work," he said. "It worked. He's from New Hampshire, Portsmouth. Real name, Lanny Pease. From what I read, upstanding citizen Lewis/Lanny has a long record of abusing women.

Jaye went to her desk and returned with her own notes. "I'm not surprised. In San Diego, he's served time for petty theft but also a conviction of battery on a girl he was dating three years ago; he beat her up bad on some trivial issue, which tells me he did it for the fun of it. Choking was a part of it. I've got a call into the detective who handled it." Of course, his prints don't tie him to the Willows murder because all we have is a partial, and hardly that. Price has an arch pattern, and that's it. But I've got a feeling…"

Potter said, "Sex crimes picked him up. He's in county jail trying to make bond. Burglary also wants to sweat him on some jobs they think he did before he gets out. After they finish, we'll take a shot at him."

Jaye sighed. "If they do, get around to it before he gets released. I've seen those guys drag their heels before."

Potter tapped a pencil on the desk. "We don't want a pissing match with burglary."

He shuffled his papers until he found the right one. "What do you have on the drug hit in Logan Heights last Wednesday night? What was the name, Arrow?"

Jaye said, "Arroyo, Luis. A Mexican cartel drug courier. We're pretty sure he was deep-sixed by his business associate, an upstanding hombre name of Carenza. A snitch told Tatum that Carenza was given the job because the late *Señor* Arroyo was ripping off the cartel. Not a good way to grow old."

"Miguel asshole Carenza. That's a name I know. He manages to stay busy. Too bad it wasn't a murder-suicide," Potter mumbled.

"Sarge?"

"Yeah."

"Do you maybe have a feeling about this Price guy, too?" she asked.

"I try not to think about that until their asses are convicted. It saves making a lot of excuses."

The prisoner was ushered into the interview room by a jailer and handcuffed to a table. He glared at the woman sitting at the plain steel table. The room was otherwise empty except for a digital recorder, which she turned on as soon as he stepped in.

"Lewis Price. I'm Detective Peoria. Welcome."

Price sat uneasily on the edge of the chair. He was in his early thirties, short and muscular, with tousled brown hair and the scars of teenage acne pitting his cheeks. His tattooed arms look like the wall of a subway station toilet. Jailhouse art. His watery eyes conveyed a mocking of most things he looked at, and definitely Jaye Peoria.

"Are you amused by something?" Jaye asked.

"You a real detective?" he said with the trace of an accent that Jaye couldn't identify because, whatever its origins, it was now largely homogenized into middle-American speech.

"Don't worry, I won't threaten your manhood."

He threw his head back in a semi-snarling laugh.

Jaye decided her best chance to break Price would be to lean hard on him. She figured guys like Price abused women because they secretly feared them, and if she were aggressive, he might cave in. Being nice to this guy would just be scorned as a weakness. She knew she was lucky so far that he hadn't demanded to see a lawyer.

She would cut him down to size. "Listen, Price, there's nothing about this you're going to find amusing." She pretended to refer to some papers she had in her hand, following the axiom that criminals are made nervous by official-looking papers, not certain what is being revealed of what they're trying to conceal. "Judging by this history we gathered on you, life doesn't work for you, does it?"

He shrugged. "Bad luck."

Jaye nodded. "Seems that way, especially seeing how you're in for aggravated assault and some other things, our knowledge on which will shortly be revealed to you. On the assault charge, with your 'bad luck,' as you say, it might be upgraded to attempted murder. That hasn't been ruled out."

A worried look flashed across his face. "It seems you attempted to strangle one—" she referred to the paper again— "one Bonnie Jean Lacroix of India Street, San Diego, five nights ago. That right?"

Indignation filled his face. "I didn't try to strangle no one. She cheated me, and I was trying to get my money back."

"She was a prostitute, right? Am I to suppose she swallowed your money, and you were trying to choke it out of her?"

"Yeah? Damn, I thought she was with the Salvation Army." He snorted, preening at his cleverness.

"Let me explain something to you. Whores never take beefs with johns to the cops. If she cheated you and you punched her, she'd just mark it up to the cost of doing business and give back your money. It takes a mighty spooked hooker to turn in a john. You scared the hell out of her, Price. She thought you were trying to kill her."

"Well, she's full of shit."

"Do you like to strangle women, Lewis?"

"I don't strangle no one. That's a stupid way to kill someone."

"According to the record, last year, you were busted for beating another woman. You beat her bad. That woman was fifty-five years old."

"They didn't convict me. Anyway, she was a whore."

"Sorry, tough guy. She was a waitress. You jumped her in a women's room at Balboa Park."

"She was coming on to me."

Jaye looked at him like a pimple in a mirror. "She was peeing, for Christ's sake." She referred back to the papers in her hand. "That's only in San Diego, we don't know yet what you've done elsewhere under a different name. How about it, Price? What other names've you used?"

"I never used another name."

Jaye chuckled and patted the papers in front of her. "You'll understand if I don't regard this information you gave us with the same reverence as the Bible. Let's see now: you guys usually go by similar names… Lewis Price…how about Peter Lewis? Would that be a good guess? How about it?"

"Never."

She paused to change direction and then asked, "Who was it, your mother? Maybe some girl who laughed at you? A wife who took off and left you stuck for car payments?"

"Who was what?"

"The one who turned you against women, made you want to hurt them."

"You're crazy."

"Is that right, hot shot? Listen, buster, nobody settles a beef with a hooker, or anyone else, by strangling them. Maybe a twisted arm or a punch in the face, but strangling? Naw. You strangle someone you want to kill." Her voice became hard. "Where were you the early morning of Sunday, November fifth?"

"Huh?"

"You heard me. November fifth."

He started to fidget. "Ah, let's see… Yeah, I was with this hooker I picked-up on El Cajon Boulevard. We went to her place."

"How long?"

"All night."

"Bullshit. No one stays with a street hooker all night. They're half-hour girls, twenty bucks a trick in a flophouse or the back seat."

"You seem to know a lot about it," he said, leering.

"I'll tell you where you were on the early morning of November fifth—you were killing a homeless woman named Edna Willows."

"Huh?"

She had the hammer, and she used it. "Right now, we've got you for aggravated assault. That can easily be upgraded to attempted murder. That in itself can lead to a long, long stay in the state hotel. I understand the boys in the cell block frown on guys who beat women. The DA's got a lot of interest in you," she lied. "Here's the deal. Right now, the evidence convinces us… we have the right man on the Willows murder—you. And we have a lead on more evidence that points right to you. The Willows murder is a death sentence, for sure. Think about it: a kindly old lady living out in the cold, poverty-stricken, strangled like some animal? Just imagine a jury of decent folks hearing this. You'll be needle-bait, and I don't mean a flu shot.

"If you confess and spare us the trouble of convicting you, the DA might deal on that case and the one you're facing now. You need to think about this. Good offers don't grow on trees."

"Fuck you," he said, glaring.

Her lips tightened, and her voice became hard. "Listen, punk, at this moment, your balls belong to me, and if you give me any shit, I'll cut them off. You're in serious trouble, so you better be looking for all the friends you can get. Got it?"

He stared at her silently, but the smirk was gone.

She raised her voice. "I said, got it?"

He nodded slightly, but Jaye knew the movement was an indication he was scared. She kept the pressure on. "The street hooker, what was her name?"

"Mary Magdalene." His smirk returned but then disappeared again when he saw the look on Jaye's face. "I didn't ask her. You know they don't tell you, anyway."

"Where did she live?"

"It was too dark."

"What did she look like?"

"A spick, maybe. I dunno."

Jaye lowered her voice but kept it tough. "Price, I'll be straight with you. I think you're lying. I think that on November fifth, you strangled a woman named Edna Willows. I think you're a sex murderer, like Richard Speck or Ted Bundy. You must have heard of them; maybe have their pictures on your wall."

"I never killed nobody."

Jaye eased up a bit, giving him an opening. "I'm not saying at this point it was murder. Maybe an accident, who's to say? Maybe you were just trying to scare her. But I'll tell you what, the difference between murder-one and maybe even voluntary manslaughter can be how cooperative you are. The way I see it, the truth's the only way to save your ass. The DA can be reasonable when people don't try to jerk him around."

He shook his head vigorously, saying no, but also trying to make the whole scene go away. "I didn't kill nobody."

"You hang around the Imperial Avenue, don't you?"

"There's no law against that. I don't have no money to live, no place else."

"A nice-looking young guy like you? Come on, Lewis, you could get lots of jobs. Isn't it true you hang out down there because that's where the easy pickings are, women who are alone and weak?"

"I didn't kill nobody, I swear, ma'am. What kind of a monster you think I am?"

"I want to find that out—and I will… Where else you wanted?"

"Nowhere."

"Don't bullshit me, Price. Guys like you collect warrants like parking tickets. Come on, what's your real name?"

"Lewis Price."

"What's the matter? Didn't you like Lanny Pease, or was that name getting too hot?"

He looked at her open-mouthed. "How?—

"Because we're smarter than you, Lewis-Lanny. Now tell me, why Edna Willows?"

"Who?"

"You know who, the woman you killed. Why'd you pick her?"

"I didn't kill nobody."

"We got fingerprints, did you know that? Off her neck."

"Not mine."

"Would I be talking to you if you were in the clear?"

"I didn't kill nobody."

"This is your chance to confess. If we have to charge you, the DA's going to be pissed, and you won't like that—you definitely won't like that."

"I'm not going to say one more word."

"Will you take a polygraph?"

"Fuck you."

Jaye asked several more questions, but he only stared straight ahead in silence. Jaye's heart sank. The moment of vulnerability had passed. Finally, she gestured to the guard. "Take him away. He's too dumb to know what's good for him."

As Price started to walk out the door, Jaye said, "If you change your mind, just ask for me." Then, just before the door closed, "Price, are you right-handed or left?"

"Left. Is that a crime too?"

Potter's face resembled an hour in a steam bath. "You what?"

She tried to look innocent. "I questioned Price. I didn't want to bother you."

Potter's hemorrhoid suddenly flared up, and he leaned onto one buttock for relief. "You can be a real pain in the ass, you know that? Damnit, Peoria, we try to get along in this department." He caught his breath as a sharp pain reminded him what an actual pain in the ass was and that a head-strong female was only the second worst type.

"Please, Sarge, no sermons until I spend about eight hours at the 10-7."

Potter sputtered and slammed his fist on the desk. "God damn it. Without talking to anybody, you just defy instructions and waltz up to the jail to do whatever the hell you want to do. Price is not your prisoner. The guys in burglary are all pissed off, and I don't blame them. Now I got to go over there and grovel and listen to them whine for an hour. "

"Murder trumps burglary, Sarge. What was the harm? That son of a bitch Price is guilty, I just know it. The arch pattern prints his history, left-handed, the M.O., the same part of town… The whole thing points right at him," Jaye said as she pounded her fist in her palm and paced the squad room.

"I'll tell you what the harm is: The burglary guys wanted to talk to him about some other stuff before he got his guard up. Now, after stewing in his cell, he won't talk at all. In a day or two, he'll be released and fly away like a big-ass bird." That's called harm, capital H.

Chapter Eight

What a friend we have in Jesus, all our sins and grief to bear.
What a privilege to carry everything to God in prayer.
Lila Brown sang the old hymn as she rhythmically shuffled behind her cart along the Ocean Beach pier, letting the beat and lyrics of the hymn dictate when to sway and when to dip. Though the old wooden structure, which extended several hundred feet into the ocean, was usually lined by fishermen and strollers, at 3:00 A.M., it was deserted. Lila's song competed only with the soft splash of the surf against the pilings. She sang it in the way of her Mississippi upbringing, swooping down with a rich alto in one place, then ascending with trills and falsetto and lingering where another singer might plow right through.

Lila knew she was a feeling woman. She had loved a dozen men and raised almost as many kids. Although the fat now jiggled on her arms and made her barrel thighs wearisome to push along, she liked to fancy herself as she used to be, a sleek and sloe-eyed, man-damning, lovin' gal with nostrils flared in passion and moonlight glinting off shining chestnut skin.

Men's eyes had once followed her with open delight as she paraded down the street. Their lustful pleas still drifted in her mind like the songs of ghosts: "Hey, mama, you shore is fine." She had stored the words and lived off the memories, and my, oh my, what memories they were.

At age sixty-eight, the men had disappeared, and the children were dead or traveled on. She spent her time collecting aluminum cans to sell for thirty cents a pound at day's end. On a good day, a Monday following a sunny weekend when the harbor and beaches were filled with can-dropping tourists, and if she started early, she could make about fifteen dollars. That supplemented what she could get from welfare. Adding charity services, she could get by just fine. It allowed her to say she didn't depend on "no worthless, fool man." She was, after all, that deep well of resourcefulness, chippy attitude, and rock of tireless servitude, the American black woman, and she could survive.

In front of her was the brisk breeze of salt air; behind were the soft lights of a city asleep. Lila smiled because she had beaten the other collectors to the streets.

Eager to take advantage, she pushed her wire grocery cart toward a dark corner of a bait shop at the end of the pier where a coke machine was located and where she knew a recycling container of cans would be found.

Like a north woods trapper, her instincts led her straight to the cache. Happily, she hummed another gospel tune as the cans clinked into the bottom of her basket.

Suddenly, something caught her attention. She stopped, and the whites of her eyes turned toward the shadows of the low building.

"Who there?" she called out crossly. "Why you want to scare an old lady?"

A foot scraped, but nothing else.

Lila returned to collecting cans, but her song became low as she warily kept glancing at the shadows. When she was almost finished, a man quietly stepped toward her. He said nothing, and as he emerged into the dim light, Lila could read nothing on his face.

"These be my cans; now you go on and get out of here."

He kept moving closer, deliberately, in no hurry.

Lila's nostrils quivered as though the wind had carried something to her. She moved around the cart, keeping it between them. "What you want, mister? Now, you just go 'fore I start hollering."

The man said something, almost in a whisper.

"What's that? What you sayin'? Home? I ain't going home with you. What's the matter with you? I'm an old lady."

He was next to her now, and for a moment, they were face to face. Her eyes were round and white with fear, searching for something or someone that might tell her this wasn't happening.

In an instant, his hands were around her throat, squeezing. The seconds followed each other like the slow beat of a gong. The pressure mounted until her eyes started to water, and only a thin, guttural squawk could be forced past her lips. She wanted to tell him that whatever he wanted, she would give. He could have the cans; he could have her body… anything to breathe again.

Because she was a big woman, her bulk made her difficult to handle, but the man's strength overpowered her, although his grunts could be heard as a counterpoint to the formless sounds that came ever more weakly from her throat. In a last-moment lurch, Lila pushed against him and half-fell, her great weight tearing her from his grasp. She fell against a wooden post, causing blood to gush from her head and her body to land at the edge of the pier.

He reached down and gave her body a push under the bottom board of the railing, and she disappeared into the black night. A heavy splash was followed by the sound of heavy steps retreating quickly on the planks.

The detectives watched patiently as Potter leafed through the sheets in front of him.

Tatum turned to the others, and said, "I always wondered what he'd say if you could get the pope drunk…'We take over the Sistine Chapel Saturday nights. It rocks, man.'"

Potter was ready. "Okay, what do we have on the black woman found in the water? Mike Peters' squad responded and covered the autopsy, but they're up to their asses in alligators, so they passed it on to us," he said, using his all-purpose alligator analogy.

"I've given you all copies of the autopsy report. Her head was bashed against a post on the Ocean Beach pier, or she fell against it, which is not likely. She either rolled off the pier or was pushed; pushed seems more likely. No drugs or alcohol in her system. She had a small amount of water in her lungs, which probably meant her breathing was extremely shallow. But she was alive when she hit the water. The body was wedged between two pilings. The medical examiner estimates she was in the water for three days. The crabs went right to work. The M.E. didn't see signs of sexual molestation, but, you know, being in the water that long…" Potter looked again at the report. "Cause of death: drowning, preceded by blunt trauma to the head. There was no DNA or fingerprints; no surprise there."

Tatum asked, "Could she have been killed elsewhere, and the body floated to where it was discovered?

Potter shook his head. "No. Her cart was on the pier. Probably pilfered a dozen times. However, her daughter examined Brown's possessions and said the only thing she knew was missing, because the family wanted it, was a gold-plated bracelet with the names Catty and J.R. inscribed on it with two valentine-type hearts." He nodded wisely. "That might be something a bum would take."

Almaguer said, "I already checked with her family and some people on the streets who knew her. She was all alone, not even a boyfriend and certainly no enemies. Lived in a tenement room. I went over the room—nothing of any use. Sounds like a robbery or a drunken fight. Those people down there can fight about anything."

Potter looked at him. "*Señor*, you just talked yourself into a case. It's all yours."

Almaguer sighed. "Why do I get all the sure things?"

"Say, Sarge," Jaye said, "why don't I take this one?"

"A volunteer?" Tatum asked in wonder.

"I'm suspicious already," Potter mumbled. "Why do you want this one, Peoria?"

"It seems similar to the Willows case."

"Which?" Baker asked.

"Edna Willows, three months ago."

Potter nodded. "Yeah, the bag lady. Why?"

"Well, they were both killed in the downtown area, one strangled and one bludgeoned, if that's what happened to Brown. Both were down-and-out; both were older; neither was sexually assaulted."

Potter said, "They don't know that about the black woman—which raises another point: She was black."

"So what?" Jaye countered. "We have to regard her race as meaningless at this point."

Potter held up his hand. "I appreciate your enthusiasm, Peoria, but you've got enough on your plate. I just don't see the similarity. It could have been a robbery—her cart was overturned and riffled through."

"Who would rob a grocery cart filled with rags?" she asked.

Tatum said, "Plenty. To some of those derelicts, those carts are like banks, filled with deposits ready to be robbed." He smiled, pleased with his metaphor.

"I just got a gut feeling on this one," Jaye said. "Like, could we have a serial killer here?"

Potter said, "Whoa, Peoria. You've got to dismount that horse. We're not even close to that. Gut feelings don't put handcuffs on bad guys, and they ain't admissible in court," Potter said.

"A gut feeling can give you heartburn," Baker said, then grinned and looked around for cleverness cred.

Potter shook his head slowly. "On this case, we got nothing, folks, a big round zero."

Jaye sensed the argument was over but tried one more time. "Every serial killing investigation starts this way, right? First, one victim, then two. But even if it's not a serial, it makes sense to investigate them together, at least as similar cases."

Potter sighed deeply, almost exasperated. "Peoria, you're like the energizer bunny. I hope that battery is running down."

"She makes some sense," Tatum said.

"I vote for Jaye to get this case," Almaguer said, laughing.

Irritation flashed on Potter's face. "We've already talked about this. It's like you've got serial-killeritis. Let's back off."

Potter softened his tone. "I appreciate your gung-ho attitude, Peoria, I do. But you already have an opinion on the case, and that tells me you're not the one to handle it. Isn't that what the scumbag lawyers call a rush to judgment? No, this goes to Almaguer."

Potter stood up. "That about wraps it up, folks. Go forth and earn the largess the gullible and overly generous taxpayers bestow on you." As the detectives stood and began to scatter, Potter said, "Peoria, stay a second." She looked at him expectantly. Potter said, "We heard from New Hampshire this morning."

"Something tells me there's more to come," Jaye said.

"Yeah. You just lost a suspect."

"How so?"

"They want Lanny Pease, alias Lewis Price, real bad—suspicion of rape. Fella, I talked to said model citizen Lewis/Lanny has a long record of abusing women. Thinks theirs is a solid case. Our problem is, their investigation places him back there the night Edna Willows was sent to her reward."

"Hell," Jaye muttered. "Why didn't that damned Price just tell us that?"

Potter said, "Truth is not an obligation he feels toward you. The bastard was caught by the short hairs. What does he do, admit he's wanted and get extradited for rape, or take his chances on us clearing him here and then shaking the dust? Tough option for the nasty bugger."

Jaye put Price out of her mind and went to her desk, where she stared at the ceiling and tapped a pencil, deep in thought. Finally, she walked over to Almaguer and said, "Hey, Ignacio. A couple of questions about Lila Brown still bother me. Mind if I inquire of Dr. Racklin? I'll share with you what I get."

"Be my guest," he said. "Any and all help appreciated. Just add it to my bill."

Jaye called Dr. Racklin at the coroner's office. "Hi, doctor, this is Detective Jaye Peoria. Remember me?"

The old man thought for a moment. "No, I'm afraid I don't."

"I'm from homicide. We talked about the Willows case.

There was silence for a moment, then, "Ah, yes. There was a time I wouldn't have forgotten such a pretty lady."

She chuckled. "Well, thank you, doctor. I have a question, if you don't mind. You did the Lila Brown autopsy day before yesterday. The cause of death was drowning. I'm just wondering: Is there a chance she might have been strangled before she had the head trauma and entered the water?"

"I have my notes right here, Miss Peoria, just a moment." The line was silent for a long pause before he again spoke: "I found no evidence of that, one way or the other. The hyoid bone was not broken, but that doesn't always happen in strangulations. Her neck had a great deal of fatty tissue. All I can definitively say is that she died of drowning. What happened to her before she entered the water or how she suffered the head injury, I cannot say. Water, more than time, is the great eraser of evidence."

"I understand, doctor. Thank you." Jaye put the phone down in disappointment. Time to move on from Lila Brown, she told herself.

Jaye walked out in the hall to a vending machine to get a cup of coffee, then returned to her desk and kicked off her shoes. Even with holes poked in it, her theory was like a humming mosquito that can't be swatted away.

Perhaps the killer came from elsewhere, and if she could place his M.O. in another city, that could be a jump start. She reached for the nationwide police telephone directory. She started with the most likely, Los Angeles, and then San Francisco, tracking down lieutenants or sergeants of homicide in those departments to inquire about cases similar to Willows.

It was mid-morning when she started by phoning Dave Browning, a homicide sergeant on the L.A.P.D. whom she had met at a regional workshop when they were both on patrol and with whom she had shared an Italian dinner.

"Hi, Jaye," his husky voice said with delight. "Good to hear from you. Ready for more chicken parmesan?"

"Ummm," she said, "with wine sauce. Especially since the taxpayers picked up the tab."

"Drop what you're doing and come up to L.A.," he said, teasing.

"Sorry, Dave," there's a man here who says I can't."

He sighed theatrically. "Ah, dammit, a rival."

"Hardly. My boss. He has an irritating idea that I should work."

"Did they finally put you in charge of the meter maids?"

"Don't get smart, pig. No, worse than even that. I think we might have a serial killer here. It has earmarks."

"Congratulations. Sounds like San Diego's going big-time."

"We've had only one killing so far, maybe two, at least I think so. I'm winging this on a prayer. If you think voodoo might help, tell me. Anyway, I want to pursue that idea, at least for a little way. I'm looking for some tracks like maybe the guy learned his business somewhere else."

"Well, you called the right number. If L.A.'s anything, it's the home of freaky murders; regular flea market. What's the M.O.?"

"This guy strangled an older street woman, a bag lady; no robbery, no sexual abuse. My hunch is that he's not committed to homeless women; he just finds them convenient and easy targets, plus he probably figures no one much cares."

Browning said, "He doesn't display his victims, right?"

"That's right. He leaves them where they fall."

"Then that tells you he's not boastful, that he's pretty calculating, and that translates to crafty. Probably harder to catch. The thing about killers is they all look like your mailman," he said.

"Yeah, I'm afraid of that. All we have is an arch-type print on one of the bodies and a probability of him being left-handed. He apparently likes to use bleach on the body to obscure evidence. Like I say, I'm flying in fog on this one."

He chuckled lightly. "Well, one victim is not exactly an epidemic."

"There might be two, but not for sure."

Browning said, "Sometimes you have to trust instinct, up to a point, and you have to decide what that point is. Intuition has solved more crimes than DNA."

"Speaking of DNA, let me give you a tip: fingernails. These killers, especially stranglers, are fearful of fingernails. A victim is sure to scratch, and they often get DNA skin cells beneath their nails. A few of these animals are aware that some of their fellow monsters have ridden old sparky because of that."

Browning went silent for a few thinking moments. "I heard about something a while back—let me knock some cobwebs down and check with a couple of people. I'll get back to you later. No promises, but we'll see."

Bingo! Jaye thought. If I could hit it first call, it'd make up for a lot of frustration. Humming to herself, she started calling: San Francisco, nothing; Seattle, no similar cases; Las Vegas, nothing like that; Oakland, every kind but that. The calls and no's piled up equally as the hours passed, and the list of cities slimmed down to mid-size in-state cities like Fresno and Anaheim. At 5:00 P.M., she had just hung up on Bakersfield when her phone jangled. She tensed with expectation when she heard Dave Browning's voice.

"Glad I reached you, Jaye. I did some checking, and afraid I've got bad news. We don't have anything like you described. When we talked, I thought of one in Van Nuys, but they told me they caught the guy. Sorry."

"Damn!"

He chuckled. "I understand. Listen, I'll pass the word. Stay out of trouble."

Jaye hung-up, sighed wearily, and patted her freshly-styled hairdo.

Almaguer called across the room, "Don't worry, it's beautiful."

Jaye looked at him. "Huh?"

"Your hair," he said.

"Huh? Oh, thanks." Hair was the furthest thing from her mind.

Jaye realized how tired she was. She stared at the telephone and decided she would rather put a finger in a thumbscrew than use it to pick up that damned thing again. In weary disappointment, she put away her directories, collected her purse, and headed home.

Finally able to kick her shoes off, Jaye browsed through some CDs. She settled on Neil Diamond's *Hot August Night* album. She hadn't listened to him for years, but his voice was upbeat and romantic. She turned up the volume and ran a tub full of hot water, to which she added a double portion of bubble bath. She found a few lavender-scented candles that she didn't realize she had and lit and placed them around the tub. Finally, she went to the kitchen and opened an eight-dollar bottle of Beringer Reisling, taking it and her sole crystal wine glass back to her bath.

Jaye tied up her hair and eased down into the hot water, savoring the lavender scent and sighing as the heat massaged her tired body. She looked at the full-length mirror on the door and saw herself in the flickering light with the water barely covering the swell of her breasts, one smooth knee emerging from the water, and the curls of her hair dangling like a Greek statue she had seen somewhere.

She toasted the image and sipped the fruity wine. "If I were a man, I wouldn't kick you out of bed," she said softly to the mirror. She leaned back and closed her eyes while Neil Diamond sang to her of happy love. She drank the bottle halfway down as her thoughts drifted languidly, and the images that appeared were of strong arms and tender caresses from a man whose face was dimly beyond recognition. She caressed her own body and cried out softly in her desire to be loved.

Why not me? she asked herself.

As the water turned first tepid, then cold, she toweled herself and put on her best negligee, a light blue silk as soft and filmy as a butterfly's wings.

She whirled before the mirror and then snuffed the candles. She switched to classical music from a Schubert CD she had bought because that was the beautiful music Brian had played. She slipped into bed, where she lay against fluffy pillows, and finished a final glass as moonlight flowed through the window. The floating melody of Schubert's *Ave Maria* coaxed her to believe in dreams.

She let her mind wander as the faces of men she considered worthy of a daydream flitted through her thoughts like pages of a slowly perused magazine.

The music clicked off as she finished the wine, and a cloud passed over the moon. Suddenly, the room was dark and silent, and the bed empty and cold.

Staring at the ceiling, there was nothing to protect Jaye from old memories, bad memories, heart-breaking memories of the terrible wrong done to her by a man she trusted:

Why couldn't he just have gone away without changing my life forever?

Jaye pulled the covers up and closed her eyes. Just as sleep dropped its curtain, her dreams came to rest on that intriguing psychologist. He was a man completely unlike the crusty cops she spent her days with and the sordid people she couldn't avoid. The moonlight found its way back through the window, and its golden beams were her lullaby.

✣

Baker looked up from what he was reading. "Hey, maybe Jaye's name got mixed up. Maybe the town should be Pe-o-RI-a, Illinois. Ya think?"

Jaye looked up from her reading and grimaced. She returned to her notes and let out a long breath, then looked at her colleagues unhappily. "I need some help, guys. There's just damned little to go on."

Baker asked about the FBI database umbrella under which serial killings and their characteristics are tracked, and information between cops and experts is shared. "What about ViCAP? Does it have anything?"

Almaguer, overhearing, said, "You still hot on that serial killer angle? That's sure to piss Potter off."

"It's my case," she said a bit defensively. "I'm just poking around quietly, covering all the bases."

Jaye returned to the ViCAP question and shook her head. "I jumped through all their hoops, found no matches, and just a couple of slim leads, which I checked out. There are all kinds of stranglers, but nothing that waves a red flag.

One killing in Missouri sounded similar, but that guy had a distinct signature; he took pains to position the body in a suggestive pose. Our killer didn't do anything like that.

She spread her fingers to tick off her points as she scanned her written summary of her investigation:

One, a partial arch-type fingerprint with just three points; two, a strong opinion by the M.E. that he's left-handed; three, our killer doesn't seem to have a signature. Willows' right shoe was missing, and that could have been a souvenir, but maybe not; four, I've called a lot of metro cop shops about a similar M.O., and nothing; five, I've checked-out local men guilty of extreme violence against women who are not family members, especially choking, and who have arch prints, and zip on that, but I'll go back to them later to see if their stories change; six, no one on the street seems to know anything, at least that they're saying; seven, I've checked Willows' background, as much as there is, and she had no enemies, not even a jealous high school boyfriend; eight, there is no perpetrator DNA; nine, we've had one medium-warm suspect, a dirtbag named Lanny Pease, aka, Lewis Price, but it seems he was back east when Willows was killed. Even so, I'm going to follow up on him."

She let her hands fall to her lap. "That's where we stand."

Baker rubbed his nose. "You still need a motive."

Tatum said, "Those guys don't need motives, Art, at least ones that a normal human could understand. The fact that a motive is not apparent strengthens the idea that we might have a serial killer on our hands, it seems to me. Maybe Jaye's on to something."

Almaguer laughed. "Oh-oh. I think Jaye might have a convert."

Potter was listening from his office but chose to ignore the serial-killer talk. He walked over and plopped down heavily in a chair, and studied Jaye's face. "You just have to keep working the streets, Peoria. That, and review the evidence over and over and over again, just like you're doing. Is it frustrating? Hell, yes. That's why we have near-geniuses like you four to lead us to victory." He ignored Almaguer rolling his eyes.

"And speaking of geniuses, I would remind Detective Tatum that just because you don't know a killer's motive doesn't mean he doesn't have one. Go discover it." Potter thought for a moment. "Look, maybe we do have a serial killer, but maybe not. But if he is not a serial killer, he'll be happy for us to think he is. That's my worry about thinking we know what we don't." He stood up to leave. "This'll play itself out, one way or another. They always do."

"But how many women will die before that happens, Sarge?" she said.

Potter shrugged. "Well, then, go catch him. He's sure as hell not going to have a fit of remorse and surrender. Keep plugging away. It helps keep you sane. Determination is your partner."

Tatum acted shocked. "Sarge, I didn't know you were a philosopher."

"I'm an even better disciplinarian, Tatum, so get your ass back to work."

Jaye tried not to stare, but no one had told her: The old man was so different from what she expected that she had to force her eyes away.

He read her thoughts. "Don't be embarrassed. A man in a wheelchair is rare enough to get a second look. That's a good thing when you think about it."

"I'm sorry, it's rude to stare."

"Nah. If it doesn't bother me, don't let it bother you."

Frank Archibald, Ph.D., professor of clinical psychology at San Diego State University, laughed, and the heavy wrinkles on his face crinkled like creased leather. He extended a powerful hand for her to shake.

Jaye leaned forward and took his hand. "I'm grateful for your time, professor."

He looked at her with a fake frown. "Do you plan on asking the questions that are on your mind at this moment?"

Jaye was perplexed. "What?"

Archibald patted the arms of the wheelchair. "For one, how I got tied to this contraption. Two, do I know anything about practical police work."

"I don't think the wheelchair is any of my business. Besides, the FBI says you are an expert on serial killers, big time."

He grimaced. "Twenty percent of what the FBI says is bullshit, just a slightly higher percentage than the rest of us. I assume you're working on such a case, and you came here to pick my brain. Let's talk. You have to find out if there's anything there."

He wheeled to a point directly in front of her and patted the arm of his chair.

"Since you haven't satisfied your curiosity, I'll tell you. Years ago, I was a vice detective in New York City. A crazy pimp I busted got me in the back with a twenty-two. A lousy little twenty-two. But I got him with a thirty-eight. The arithmetic was on my side. However, he left me with C-6 paralysis, which would have pleased him no end if he were alive to enjoy it.

"I was retired with honors and full pay. The full pay was more useful. When I got tired of feeling sorry for myself, I went back to school, and here I am."

He motioned for Jaye to sit down. "Now, what exactly can I do for you? From what you told me on the phone, you think there's a serial killer loose in San Diego, the man who killed the homeless woman a while back."

"Yes, professor. I have a detailed summary of the case right here." She opened her briefcase and removed a thick sheath of papers. "This is as complete as I can make it. Sorry about the grammar. I'm not used to having college professors read what I write."

"You're making a huge assumption about a serial killer, aren't you?" he said.

"You sound like everyone else. However, if I don't have any answers and darned little evidence, then every assumption is huge." She handed him the papers. "Serial killer or not, anything I learn from you will make this a good day."

He glanced at her papers, then said, "Pretty slick talker, aren't you? He chuckled. "We'll talk. I've picked up a few things along the way. And don't be taken in by that 'professor' crap. Some of the dumbest people I know are college professors. Also, please stop that doctor bullshit; you're not a freshman. This is just cop-to-cop. Frank and Jaye."

He looked at his watch. "Tell you what, it's almost one o'clock, and I have to see a grad student. Why don't you wander around the campus, get a sandwich, and then come back here at, say, two-thirty so we can discuss this?"

Jaye wandered like a pilgrim in a holy place among the campus oaks, emerald expanses of lawn, and stately buildings. She soaked in the ambiance of the happy chatter along the sidewalks and scanned the shelves of texts in the bookstore. She looked at the frowning concentration of the young scholars reading at library tables, hanging around the student center playing rock music and acting happy at being twenty and on the verge of conquering the world, or at least correcting it.

"Why didn't I have this?" she said aloud and drew a glance from people standing nearby. Oblivious to their curiosity, she vowed to read better books and listen to more classical music.

When she returned to Archibald's office, she found the old man just finishing her notes. "Hi, there," he said. "Enjoy the campus?"

"It's absolutely lovely," she said. "I've lived here all my life and never took the time to notice it."

"Well, there's nothing lovely about this case I've been reading."

"I need your opinion," Jaye said, sitting down and removing a pen and notebook from her shoulder bag and sitting poised as she thought one of his students might. The heavy clunk of her handgun drew a knowing smile from him. She said, "Granted, it's only one case, but from what I've learned, it seems to have some of the earmarks of a typical serial killer."

He said, "I wish I had something more solid, but what behavioral science has on serial murder is pretty thin. Trying to figure out why a man kills repeatedly is like trying to understand why one person gambles, another drives drunk, and another might shoplift what she could easily afford. All the academic BS aside, the fact is, the puzzle of human behavior has far too many pieces for us to fit them all in."

Jaye uncrossed her legs and leaned forward. "Then give me some educated guesses."

"Well, for one, serial killing is, in part, at least, a pseudosexual act."

Jaye said, "My killer didn't have sex with his victim or molest her."

"My dear, there is sex, and then there is sex. Nothing is darker in the human psyche. Normal men have sex with women. These killers do sex to them or against them. Sex becomes a vengeance-punitive weapon." Archibald reached for a book on his desk with a slip of paper marking a page. "There's a case study in here I want to read to you." He found the right page and said, "Listen to this paragraph. Here's a serial killer talking about his experiences:

"Something would just happen inside of me. I'd feel this uncontrollable rage. I would have nothing against the woman personally, but I couldn't keep myself from acting. During the attack I would feel a thrill, but afterward, I'd feel disgusted with myself. But even so, the pressure would be gone. I could be normal again."

Archibald put the book down. "The motivation that gets these men to act on their compunctions is not pleasure but relief of stress."

"What kind of stress?"

"The stress that's unique to them put there by a myriad of possible reasons. By committing the act, the killer satisfies a driving urge deep within himself."

"It makes sense that the guy probably had a problem with his mother," she said.

"That's possible, but it's also a cliché." He wheeled his power chair around in a slow circle, thinking as he talked the way someone else might pace the floor. "Look, you're in homicide, so let me ask you, Why do people murder?"

"For lots of reasons, obviously. I know *how* people murder, but I'm always trying to figure out *why*. Understanding someone who might kill for kicks is like voodoo."

"You just answered my question. People murder for lots of reasons: experiential, environmental, physical, or even genetic—maybe especially genetic."

"Physical?"

"Right. For example, a man might have rage against women because of an inordinately small penis that makes normal intercourse difficult or the inability to sustain an erection under normal stimulus. Maybe some woman laughed at him. Even the smell of a certain perfume or hearing a song with a negative memory could conceivably trigger the act."

"Aren't we getting pretty far out?"

Archibald shook both index fingers to emphasize his point. "When we're talking about what makes the human animal turn rogue, nothing is too far out. Men and women are susceptible to unlimited stimuli that can compel aberrant behavior." She squinted at his language, and he added, "You know something else? The more I see of people, the more I think a few are created just plain evil."

"Amen to that."

"The best old-fashioned word to describe your guy is evil, and that makes everyone nervous. When we can say that someone is crazy, we put space between him and the rest of us. But just plain evil? Uh-uh. We don't like to think 'normal' folks just like us could do evil things. However, if a psychopath is clinically mentally ill, or 'sick,' as we like to say, we haven't proved it yet."

"Anything recognizable about my guy?"

"Not much. He might be dumb as a board in normal life, or maybe he's a genius. There's a good chance he might be a failure in life or see himself as such, even though he might have a good job. He often thinks the world does not appreciate him." Archibald leaned forward. "Don't you see, that's part of why he kills. He's become good at it, which shows *them*, and it satisfies his revenge against *them*, at least temporarily.

"On the other hand, he can be gregarious, manipulative, articulate, and successful. He makes a game of ingratiating himself to people. Take Ted Bundy.

He saw people as something to toy with, to manipulate, even the women he killed. He was one icy bastard."

Jaye asked, "Then why? Why does he need to kill instead of just beating his victims, or humiliating them, or even just walking away, or working his frustrations out on a stamp collection?"

"You might as well ask why birds chirp or snakes slither. A lot of people make handsome livings convincing people they're smarter than they are about all this."

"So, Frank, give me something concrete to take away."

"I would say don't get hung up on what motivates him. You can get lost in those woods. Concentrate on what he does. I'm talking about his pattern, his area of operations. If it's a small area, then he works or lives nearby—if that's his 'work place,' he's a commuter. If the killings are over a great distance, then he's a wanderer or maybe a seasonal worker."

She said, "He seems to have just popped up in San Diego. Maybe he'll move."

Archibald hesitated, then spoke. "Maybe I shouldn't say this. It's going to sound macabre, even heartless. I'll say it to you because you're a pro. The cold fact is, if he relocates, some department somewhere else will have to start all over, and it likely won't be as professional as yours or have a cop as dedicated as you. It's better he stays in one place. Right here. Big picture—if he kills, say, two people in San Diego, it's no different than if he kills two in Des Moines. We just want to keep him from killing a dozen more."

"I hear what you're saying. However, it's not the most welcome compliment I've ever gotten," she said.

"If he's systematic or creative in how he goes about his killing, then try to get a sense of his education or occupation. Almost every one of these guys has a signature, something they repeat over and over. It may be symbolic, or it might be a technique of killing. But it's purposeful, so discover the purpose."

Archibald closed the book in his lap to signal that the interview was about to end.

She shook his hand, and he said, "After all is said and done, you'll probably catch him on a fluke—a traffic ticket, a computer he used that can be traced, a lucky victim who escapes, or even a flat tire leaving one of his scenes."

"Life can sure suck, can't it?" she said.

He smiled. "I wouldn't know. I've got a *power* wheelchair. I can still make love. I'm a lucky man."

Chapter Nine

andy Martin was desperate for a fix. She wiped her runny nose on the sleeve of her blouse and mentally rejoiced at the ten-dollar bill in her handbag. Only ten dollars more, and she'd have enough. With renewed desperation, she again looked up and down the street. She saw a group of sailors huddled in the shadows outside a tattoo parlor and headed for them. Along the way, she happened to glance in the grimy window of a pawn shop. She stopped for a moment to study her reflection: Ratty shoulder-length brown hair, red velvet hot pants hanging on skinny hips like wash on a line, gaudy jewelry dangling from neck and scabby arms, eyes sunk in a bony face like a Third World famine victim. She was twenty, looked fifteen, and felt fifty.

For a moment, Mandy wanted to be a little girl again. However, a wave of nausea that raked her body reminded her of the drugs she was being deprived of, and she turned away from the window. The past is irrelevant when the present is hell.

She saw a sailor, about eighteen or nineteen, standing off to himself, ogling pictures of strippers in the window of a topless bar. The young ones were easiest, especially coming out of the strip joints with their juices boiling. Even Mandy's hard, unkempt appearance didn't mute their raging hormones. He turned just as she sauntered up, eyes wide with the newly-discovered wonders of wickedness.

"What's your name, big guy?"

"Uh, Billy. Billy Samuels."

She ran her fingers lightly over his face. "Feel like a good time, Billy Samuels?"

The sailor almost said, "Gosh, yes," but stopped himself and said, in a voice straining to be deep, "That depends on what you got in mind, baby."

Mandy was about to make her pitch when the sailor's eyes shifted to over her shoulder, and then a loud voice boomed out behind her. "All right, you two, move on. Don't you know this is a whore? Move along."

"Who the hell are you?" challenged one of the sailors standing a few feet away.

Mandy turned around, and the big voice materialized as a man in his thirties, of medium size, with sandy hair and a worn corduroy jacket. He pulled out a badge in response and said, "Vice. Now move on, or I'll call Shore Patrol."

The sailors grumbled and started down the street. The vice cop turned to Mandy and said, without sarcasm, "Sorry, sweetheart. I know it's tough to be a working girl. Now, move along, or we'll take a ride." The cop knew if he booked her, she'd be back on the street in a couple of hours, but by then, the best business of the night would have been missed.

Mandy gave the most insolent look she dared and walked down the street with a bravado swinging of hips. She put two corners between herself and the cop and reached a dark side street before starting to scout again. She saw a delivery man carrying a box of liquor into the rear of a bar and waited for him to come out. When he did, she was leaning against his van. "Hi, baby, 'bout time for a break?"

The delivery man walked up to her and said, "A break for what?"

Mandy smiled seductively. "Maybe coffee with sugar in it; maybe just the sugar."

"Shit, you gotta be kidding," he said, and roughly grabbed her arm and turned it to look at the forearm. "Look at them tracks. Girl. You're a walking case of AIDS. Man'd be a fool to get near you. My dick starts to itch just thinking about it."

Mandy wrenched her arm free and said, "Fuck you, Jack. I'm clean."

He sneered. "Down the road, junkie."

She swallowed her pride. The need was getting worse. "Quick head for twenty bucks?"

He ignored her.

"We can do it right in your van. Just a few minutes. There's nothing to worry about with head."

"Beat it."

"You beat it, asshole," she screamed after the van as it pulled away. Mandy felt weak and leaned against a wall. It felt like her skin had been stripped off, and someone was running a vegetable scraper over her raw flesh. Cramps attacked, and then she bent over with the dry heaves.

She found a Kleenex in her purse and blew her nose, then used it to wipe her eyes as she started to cry. The tears were not because of the condition of her life, nothing as long-range as that.

The prayer she wept was for just one little sanity-saving fix. She leaned back and tried to pretend that the sweet, sustaining narcotic was flowing warmly into her veins right then, hoping to reconstruct the exhilaration from memory, but her body couldn't be fooled and replied with a savage muscle cramp that made her whine and silently beg for mercy. "Shit," she swore and beat her fist against the wall, then turned around and was startled to see a man watching her intently from a few yards away. She quickly dabbed at her eyes with the Kleenex and blew her nose again. She smiled and tried to walk seductively toward him, but it came out as sort of a mechanical totter. She had never seen him before and knew he might be a vice cop, but she didn't care. He also had a look about him that made her uneasy, but it was not the time to be picky. He also was wearing latex gloves. Weird, but who the hell cares? Half of her customers were named kinky.

"Hi, fella," she said. "I've been waiting for you." She put her hand on his arm and looked into his face. She tried to make the muscles in her face go soft and seductive and panted words at him: "I need to fuck. I need it bad. I want to feel your cock in me. Oh, please, baby."

He didn't respond, so she altered the approach and rubbed against his groin with her pelvis. "You like that, big fella? There's more I can do, a lot more." He stared at her without expression. "Ten dollars, just ten dollars for the most wonderful blow job of your life. Like that?" she nodded encouragingly. He just looked at her silently, so she tugged at his arm. "I know where we can go." He followed, so she led him about a half-block away to a closed-up restaurant that she had discovered could be entered through a fire exit that had a broken lock.

Inside, there was only the dark ruin of a dining room with broken chairs and refuse scattered about. There was no sound except the creaks that come when a building feels pain. It was a building awaiting the wrecker's ball and was atmospheric for the despairing event within its walls.

Mandy wondered that he had not said a word, but she was used to all kinds. She saw all johns as sick freaks. She reached down and teased the zipper on his fly. "You like that, baby? Well, let's see the ten bucks, and then I'll take you for a ride to heaven." She looked up at him expectantly, but he just stared into her eyes and put his arms on her shoulders. She took a close look at his face for the first time, and a foreboding came over her that crowded the nagging of addiction from her mind. "I—I think we should just forget it. Let's go." She tried to turn toward the exit, but his hands on her shoulders tightened. She twisted in an attempt to get free, but she was a toy in his grasp.

"Let me go, or I'll call a cop."

He switched his grip to her neck.

"I'm warning you, mister, I'll—" Mandy tried to say more, but he squeezed her throat shut. The pressure made her head swim, and tears poured from her eyes. Frantically, she dug her fingers into his arms and tried to shove him away, but he didn't budge.

He talked to her in a low monotone, but Mandy didn't hear the words. She managed to force her knee into his groin with just enough pressure that he groaned and loosened his grip. She gave a desperate push, and he fell backward as his feet slipped on shards of glass. Waving his arms, he tumbled over a broken table and into a heap of debris.

Mandy turned in search of the fire exit, but panic caused her to lose all perspective, and she ran blindly in the most plausible direction—away from the man. She turned a couple of corners and ended up in a large room with dimly-seen countertops and sinks identified as the kitchen. She looked around for a way out but, with heart-tearing dismay, realized there was none. Like a trapped rodent, she searched for a place to burrow and quickly found a cabinet underneath a sink. It was so small that one wouldn't look for a child in it, but because Mandy was naturally supple and thin, she managed to squeeze herself into it and pull the door shut.

She heard the footsteps from afar at first, but gradually they came closer until they seemed to be coming at her. She knew he was in the kitchen, looking for her hiding place. Luckily, it had been a large restaurant, and the direction she had run was only one of several wings of the building. Even so, the man took his time and searched the kitchen from one end to the other. Three times he stopped within inches of Mandy's hiding place, but each time, as she held her breath, he moved on. Gradually, the steps faded, and her lips moved silently as she thanked God fervently for her deliverance.

After deciding he was no longer near, Mandy allowed her breath to expel and inhaled another carefully, as though he still might be able to hear the air entering her lungs. She decided to wait an hour before moving, and she remembered that one could count time by slowly saying each second by thousandths. She calculated that an hour would mean counting to three thousand, six hundred. She began: One thousand one, one thousand two…

Hearing no further footsteps and mesmerized by the rhythmic pattern of her counting, Mandy relaxed and let her thoughts run. Strangely, the need for heroin seemed to have left her, and for the first time since she was sixteen, she felt free of its grip. She was exhilarated at still being alive and decided that her close call was a sign from God that her life could be renewed. She made plans to phone her mother and then get started on a drug program. Maybe she could go back and finish school; maybe have a nice family and a little house. Thank you, God, for opening my eyes while there's still time, she prayed and smiled with happiness.

Mandy counted the last few numbers impatiently, then carefully crept out of the cupboard, stood in the kitchen, and listened to the silence while she rubbed the circulation back into her thin arms and legs. She gave a start as a rat scampered across the floor but then relaxed when she realized what it was. Warily but with growing confidence, she moved quietly in the direction of the fire exit. Step after step, her anticipation of safety grew, and when she saw the door, she almost sang out in joy. It was so close. She hurried her pace, but just as she reached for the handle, he stepped out of the shadows.

She screamed, but as their eyes met, she was surprised at the absence of violence in his. She wanted to understand how that could be, but there was no time.

His fingers closed around her throat. The last words she gasped were, "Don't! Please, don't." Then, there was no more air.

The killer stood over her body and poured the liquid over her neck to erase fingerprints, reached down, and splashed on one hand when he was distracted by a banging in the front of the closed restaurant as some junkies tried to force the door to have a place to shoot up.

In his haste, he dropped the plastic bottle, and the contents spilled onto the floor as he hurried for the fire exit.

All attempts to identify the dead woman failed. She carried no identification or address in her handbag. It was as though she had never existed. The few street people who had contact with her only knew her variously as Mandy Martin, Melissa Miller, Misty Mills, or Mary Masters. They even tried to find a pimp but were not surprised that none stepped forward. Her fingerprints and photo were sent out nationwide and got no hits. The same result for her DNA, which was expedited by the lab.

No one knew the young woman's true identity. People who say no one can make themselves disappear in America don't know what they're talking about. She was the second unidentified female of the year. She was given a new name, Jane Doe 18-2, aka Martin, Mandy, followed by the other aliases police learned about.

From the moment he heard about the killing, Potter decided it was Jaye's case, given the similarities to the Willows murder.

He called a squad meeting on a day he was wallowing in a downer state of mind. His face was red on the edge of purple. His eyes resembled a road map. There were three possible causes for his mood: a bad hangover, heat from the brass above, or just whatever…

Art Baker, unfortunately for him, stepped into the maelstrom. He had covered the autopsy and lab work for Jaye, who had been at a conference in Denver. Baker opened the thin file with the catalog-type name the medical examiner had given her. He slipped easily back into the unwanted role of Potter's whipping boy.

Potter grumbled, "Okay, Flanders, let's hear it."

Baker stiffened to hear the disliked nickname. He cleared his voice. "Well, we don't have the actual reports yet. They're still working on it. With all the junkie traffic, the scene might as well have been an airport waiting room. But from what information I've picked up so far, she was strangled, probably by a left-handed perpetrator. Lividity showed the body hadn't been moved. Rigor mortis had disappeared. Given the temperature of the room, the M.E. estimated ten hours for the development of rigor, about eighteen hours while it was in force, and about eight hours for it to disappear. That means 18-2 was dead at least two days before being found. That's all we got so far."

Jaye interrupted. "Don't call her 18-2. That's so Philistine."

Almaguer said, "Philistine? Isn't that from the Bible? What's it mean?"

"Boorish or crass," Baker said.

"It means asshole-ish," Tatum added.

Potter frowned. "Let's get back to it. Go ahead, Flanders. How about body temperature?"

Baker returned to the report. "That supports the time estimate. She was at room temperature. Her rectal temperature was sixty-nine, slightly above ambient room temperature due to bacteria activity. If you subtract that from normal temperature and multiply by one-point-five, that gives you forty-five, the estimated number of hours since death. Two days."

"Why the hell don't you have the full lab report yet? Don't you know this is a murder investigation? I swear, sometimes..."

Baker's lips compressed. "We'll get it tomorrow. It takes a little time. You've got to remember the scene was an old restaurant being used as a crash pad. There might be evidence from 100 people. The place is filled with junk. There wasn't a thing on or near the body that would point to an assailant. Syringes and empty opioid packaging were all over the place."

"Not even a single print?"

Baker shook his head. "There were hundreds of prints of junkies dating back to the restaurant closing, I suppose. The print tech checked the body and her possessions, but just like in the Willows case, nothing except hers. Her neck had bleach-burn marks, and there was an empty bottle of bleach by her body. The label said Oxyclean. That's a type of bleach that has oxygen in it. It obscures DNA and fingerprints better than ordinary bleach. It was clean. He must have been wearing gloves."

Potter picked up a yellow pencil and tossed it down in disgust. "That's all you got? Christ, Flanders." He rolled his eyes.

Baker stared at Potter and saw everyone in his whole life that had dumped on him as the wimp object of his quiet self-loathing. With frustration built up over a lifetime—a slow drip, drip like a stalactite in a cave—he crunched up the papers in his hand. He stood up with fists clenched and veins pounding in his neck and forehead. His bird-like nose flared, and his eyes glistened. "Fuck you, Potter. Stick Flanders up your ass." He pointed a long, accusing finger in the face of his sergeant. "Treat me with respect!"

Potter leaned way back in his chair and looked at his subordinate with shock.

Jaye, Tatum, and Almaguer, sitting around the table, looked at each other with— progressively—astonishment, amusement, and then admiration.

Tatum said, "Did I hear correctly, or did Art use the "F" word?"

The room was silent, but it was a strained silence. Potter looked around, then grinned weakly. "Yes, sir," he said, and there was no sarcasm in it. "Now, Detective Baker, would you please continue."

Baker looked around and saw new-found respect on all their faces. He grinned sheepishly. "I forgot where I was."

Tatum tried to lighten the mood. "Did they check the used condoms for fingerprints?" He looked around to see if his joke was appreciated.

"They might get mixed in with yours," Potter said, welcoming the humor.

Almaguer laughed and said, "Tatum won't be happy until all his competition has ED."

Jaye looked down at her notes, just wanting the subject of Tatum's sex life to pass. "What was in her pockets and her purse?"

Baker was relieved to get back to business. "She wore a dress with no pockets. Next to her was a bag with some cosmetics and a ten-dollar bill."

Jaye said, "There is no way a homeless person or anyone else hanging out in that area would let ten dollars escape. That says to me it was not robbery. The murderer didn't care about a small amount of money right there for the taking. Personally, to me, I think that says something."

"Maybe you can find a pissed-off pimp on this one," Tatum said.

"Pimps kick their asses, they don't strangle the merchandise," Almaguer said.

"True," Tatum conceded.

Jaye said, "I've checked out 18-2's"—she checked herself—"the victim's known activities, such as they were: no known enemies in the area she apparently frequented. Just like Willows, she seems to have been a random target."

Potter wasn't listening. He went over and gave Baker a friendly chuck on the shoulder. "You bastard, I wondered when you'd do that. The Marine way always works." He nodded emphatically as though a great truth had emerged.

Watching that, Jaye thought: Bullshit, Sarge. You're just trying to save face. But there's nothing wrong with that.

Potter cleared his throat to indicate a change of subject and faced the group. "Thank you, Fl—Art. Now, boys and girls, as you know, this is Peoria's case. It's possible, even likely, I suppose, that the same guy killed Willows; no copycat would know about the bleach. We've got to amp up our work on this. Who's going to work with Peoria?" He looked at Tatum.

"Hey, Sarge, I'm up to my ass in alligators with that drive-by killing two nights ago."

"Hey, Tatum, those are the Sarge's alligators," Jaye said with a smirk that earned a dirty look from Potter.

Almaguer, when he saw Potter's eyes shift to him, said, "I'm going on vacation."

Potter threw up his hands. "*Señor*, you just got back from vacation."

Almaguer shrugged. "Can I help it if the department forces me to take five weeks? Next year, Sarge, I'll put in a grievance when they say, 'Use it or lose it.' I'll demand the right to stay here and work."

Potter turned to Baker. "Art, you did a good job on that report. I guess you're the man."

"You da man," Tatum said.

Everyone watched to see how Baker would react to Potter. He didn't. Jaye broke the silence. "I sound like a broken record, but this is the work of a serial killer. I'll bet on it."

Tatum joined in. "I agree with Jaye." He flashed a smile toward her.

Jaye returned his smile and said, "The strangulation sort of makes it obvious. So, why? Who knows. A serial killer's motivation will be as screwy as Alice in Wonderland." She looked around and nodded to affirm her own thoughts.

"He's also a physically strong man. He doesn't even use a ligature. To garrote with, say, a rope, would be easier and faster, but you would have to stand behind the person. He wants to face his victims to make his killings up close and personal. For some reason, it's worth it to him, and he isn't likely to change.

"He kills in a single geographic location, for which there are two probable reasons: It's where the homeless congregate— homeless means helpless. Also, it might be the general area where he lives or works. Serial killers, with some notable exceptions, tend to like familiarity. Finally, for all the reasons I said earlier, he almost certainly is not one of the homeless men in East Village."

"Methinks, the lady, has done some homework, Sarge," Tatum said, and Almaguer nodded his support.

Baker was also impressed. "She sounds like a textbook."

Jaye said, "After we catch this guy, maybe I'll write one."

Potter stood. "Okay, that's it." The detectives started to disperse, but he said, "Peoria, Fl--Baker, I want to see you."

When they were seated in his small office, he said, "Art, you're good at working records, you know all the databases. Also, I want you to concentrate on examining all the field interviews that come in from patrol and coordinate the public outreach. You know what to do. Also, you can help Peoria by keeping in touch with ViCAP."

He looked at Jaye. "You in agreement with that, Peoria?"

"Whatever you want, Sarge," she said sardonically. She wanted to remind him it was her case, but she held her tongue.

Potter looked at Jaye thoughtfully. "We have to keep open the possibility—possibility, I say—that these two killings are unrelated crimes or copycat killings done in a violent part of town. However, it's now pretty obvious to me there's a serial killer out there until I'm shown otherwise. But because it's all the rage now in those stupid TV crime shows, let's low-key it. The public could go crazy. Because we don't have any forensic evidence to tie these two killings together, I want to proceed quietly. I don't want to be pushed to premature conclusions. Zip. Nada. We can't get sucked into ignoring other possibilities. Not long ago, San Diego County had over fifty murders in one year. It's not exactly a rare event around here."

Jaye said, "I've had several talks with the FBI." She nodded toward Baker. "Art will have more. They have no active serial cases that resemble this guy's work. Two similar murders in half a year are beyond a coincidence to me. Usually, these guys are in no great hurry to kill again. They seem to savor their last one for a while until the urge gets powerful again. Anyway, ViCAP doesn't offer any hot candidates. He's either a slick operator or new to the business or new to the area."

Jaye was on a roll. "There hasn't been an unsolved strangulation of a woman in this county for thirteen years before Willows. Now, there are two in five months. And, as you both know, I believe Lila Brown might be a third victim."

"Okay, Peoria," Potter said, "but please, just no surprises, okay?"

She smiled mischievously.

Needing to acquaint herself with the murder scene, Jaye looked over the large room with the sadness of one viewing a crumbling monument. The La Brava Restaurant had been where she had come with her date for midnight supper after a high school prom. The walls had been papered in a rich red and ivory velvet with a fleur-de-lis pattern. The chairs had been soft black leather, and the carpeting burgundy and plush. That night she had her first and only taste of cherries jubilee.

Now, it was a barren wreck, serving as a community trash dump for hookers, junkies, and derelicts. Keeping them out would be like trying to keep flies off the pudding. Just another sad relic of urban decay.

The chalk outline showing the location of 18-2's body was smudged but still visible in the dim light. Jaye wondered what the girl had felt and thought with his hands around her throat in the gloom of her final night. Had she the time to know her life was over, that she would never breathe again, and that her body would rot like a dead animal alongside a road?

Jaye pushed the morbidity out of her mind and, using her flashlight in the dimness, began a close inspection of the trash on the floor, starting in widening circles from the chalk marks. She pushed away the used condoms with her foot and, wearing rubber gloves, gingerly opened smelly old paper sacks. She carefully inspected everything in sight, from discarded hamburger wrappings to moldy blankets, and saw nothing suspicious. "Ick!" she thought more than once.

Looking even closer at the dirty floor, she saw hypodermic syringes with needles still attached and carefully dropped the two next to the chalk outline into clear plastic evidence envelopes for fingerprint checks; a futile exercise probably, but the improbables had to be checked out. Lying next to the chalk outline were three round, mustard-colored tablets with "WW 22" inscribed on them. These she collected with tweezers.

She also noticed a wide splatter area close to the outline that looked freshly scrubbed with no dust showing. She studied it and said one confirming word: "bleach." There would be no other reason to clean a small area of this floor.

She gave the dreary room a final backward glance and closed the door to what had once been La Brava. She walked away, feeling the haunting ache that comes from glimpsing the empty locust shell of one's own youth.

Chapter Ten

If the regular police reporter had not gone on vacation and had been there to do his normal lazy, inattentive job, it wouldn't have become a big deal. If prying, pushy Rick Wasserman's girlfriend hadn't dumped him, he'd have been in Hawaii. Instead, here he was, snooping around police headquarters as a sub on the cop shop beat.

Wasserman had already purchased the tickets. However, his girl chose the Wednesday before departure to tell him she had hooked up with someone else, a stockbroker, someone with a brighter future. He had simply said, "Thank you a lot, and I hope you'll be happy, you conniving, greedy bitch."

He didn't utter the last part, but he thought it. He had just smiled gamely, backed out of the apartment, hurried down to cash in the tickets, and started looking for another girl or two. When he needed consoling, he reminded himself that she could have told him after they got back and all his money had been spent.

When Wasserman thought about it, he shook his head in disgust. Stock fucking brokers. Assholes. Plastic pimps with pinky rings. Jeans from L.L. Bean and French from Berlitz bullshit. When he saw the money they threw around to hit on the same girls he was trying to connect with, Wasserman sometimes wished he had become someone affluently vacuous, too. But then he thought about it and decided no girl, no apartment, no sports car was worth what he would see in the mirror. He had to be himself. He was a reporter and damned proud of it.

Standing at the counter in the public affairs office, Wasserman was still grumbling to himself. He should be getting laid in Maui. At least the clerk was cooperative and showed him where the records were kept. One of the first he examined was the file on the murder of Jane Doe 18-2, aka Martin, Mandy, and some other names. He took a few notes that he knew would wind up in a kiss-off story at the bottom of a back page as just another murder of a nobody. As he started to return the file to the clerk, he said, "I don't cover this regularly, but this Jane Doe entry is intriguing; anything you can tell me about it?"

The clerk looked at it. "Yeah, another strangling. This makes two in the last few months."

"Isn't that pretty unusual?" Wasserman asked.

"Not especially for murder, per se, but stranglings? Yeah, pretty unusual crime. But who knows? Probably some nut can't get it up any other way."

"Who would I see to get more details on this?"

The clerk looked at a sheet in the file and scribbled a name—Detective Peoria, homicide.

Wasserman took the elevator down to the homicide floor and caught Jaye just as she was returning from her inspection of the restaurant. "Hi, Detective Peoria," he said.

"Pe-o-RI-a," she said.

"Sorry. Have you got a minute?" He introduced himself and told her he wanted to talk about the two strangulation murders. It was the first time in her life that Jaye had ever been approached by a reporter, and the thought gave her a tingling of self-impor-tance. He was unfamiliar with police procedures, so she patiently spelled out details of the murders that hadn't been kept back from the public. After a half hour, he thanked her and left, giving no hint of what he had planned.

Jaye let the interview drift from her mind as she picked up the phone and arranged to have the crime lab run a test on the pills found on the restaurant floor. Had she the knowledge of the next day's headlines, her composure would have vanished like ice in August.

The next morning, thousands of San Diegans picked up their morning newspaper to the shock of a page one headline:

SERIAL KILLER POSSIBLE IN S.D., DETECTIVE SAYS
By Rick Wasserman
Sun Staff Writer

"The second strangulation in recent months of a woman in San Diego has led police to believe in the possibility of a dark-street assassin preying on vulnerable women.

"The murder last Tuesday of an anonymous street prostitute, who went by the possibly false name of Mandy Martin and other aliases, follows the murder of Edna Willows last November. Both died of strangulation, and both women were known to live in the downtrodden part of the East Village.

"A serial killer is one who commits multiple murders over a period of time, usually in a repeat pattern of victims and methods. In the San Diego homicides, the similarities are the method of death and the fact that both victims belonged to the loosely defined group known as homeless or street people.

"Homicide Detective Jaye Peoria, who is heading up the investigation, said that no strong clues have yet been uncovered.

"'We are exploring many different angles, including the obvious one that these killings may be entirely unrelated. At this point, we can't afford to close the door on any possibility,' she said.

"Peoria urged women in the area to be cautious about strangers and report any suspicious behavior to police.

"'We're working hard on this case, and if it is a serial killer, we want to solve it before another murder happens. But I remind people we're not sure of that. Also, I want to remind people, especially women, that caution is not the same as panic,' she said."

The story went on to give known details of both killings and trace the history of serial killers, beginning with Jack the Ripper, who eviscerated prostitutes in London's East End slums more than a century ago. Wasserman also interviewed a psychologist who gave a possible profile of such a criminal and also feminist activists who saw the crimes as an outgrowth of male suppression. It concluded with tips on how women might spot a potential attacker.

When Jaye went to work after the story ran, she found a half-dozen phone messages from television, radio, and newspaper reporters. Within an hour, she found herself on the steps outside the police station with the department PR woman standing by uneasily. Several cameras were pointed at her, and reporters took turns interviewing her on what had become the biggest story in the city. It was no longer the "possibility" of a serial killer; journalistic enthusiasm had blurred that distinction.

It was now commonly accepted that a serial killer was loose, ready to visit terror on vulnerable females, which, of course, included thousands of women who had never even driven through East Village.

Wasserman's casual phrase, dark-street assassin, caught the public imagination. The name was heard on the streets, in homes, on talk shows, and in print. It lost its hyphen and became capitalized. Like its predecessors, Son of Sam and the Boston Strangler, the Dark Street Assassin became the verbal epitome of fear.

Journalists, used to suspicious, middle-aged male cops, took to Jaye like a frog to a wet April. Here was the ultimate good-gal, bad-guy scenario: a lurking, maniacal killer pitted against the valiant lady detective, pretty and purposeful, buxom and righteous. Before the day was out, Jaye had been interviewed by talk shows for a newspaper lifestyle spread and had even hung up on a long-distance query about posing nude for a girlie magazine.

The San Diego Sun was determined to keep its lead on the Wasserman story. Story after story followed every conceivable angle. Teams of reporters swept into the East Village to ask profound questions of street people who didn't even know the day of the week. A nasty implication could be fairly deduced that as long as the killer stayed in that part of town, it was a good sport for all. But the nagging question persisted: What if he didn't?

The editors of the Sun also used the incident as a focal point for a long-standing crusade against the presence of homeless people in an area of considerable commercial promise. Stories on lost retail revenue, dwindling building activity, rising welfare costs, and tarnished city image pointed accusingly at the homeless. It was as though street people had invited the killer into town just to make more trouble for downtown business interests.

Letters to the editor and radio call-in shows quickly reflected the public's willingness to find an easy scapegoat. Shrill dowagers and rumbling retired navy chiefs expounded on the evils of the welfare system and how the country was going to hell because it coddled sex-crazed perverts and bums too lazy to work. The homeless quickly became pariahs responsible for many of the ills of society.

The stories about the serial killer also roiled fears and spooked imaginations. Jaye's office phone rang incessantly with tips from neurotic shut-ins who had peered out between curtains and seen suspicious-looking characters walking by; from embittered women reporting that ex-sons-in-law or kicked-out husbands were woman beaters and should be checked out; from religious fanatics and psychics who assured her of their ability to learn the killer's identity, either with or without God's help.

Some of the calls were more serious and had to be listened to and checked out. One man said he heard a drunk in a bar bragging about the women he had "wasted." A volunteer at the Salvation Army called to report a man in the middle of a soup line mumbling threats against all the bitches who had ruined his life.

It got deadly serious on a morning Jaye arrived at her desk and saw a letter addressed to her marked "personal." She opened it to a single sheet of typing paper with a blunt warning— "I'm coming for you, bitch."

Tatum noticed the shocked look on her face and walked over. "What's up?" he said and reached for the letter.

"Don't touch it," she said. While Tatum and the others of the squad milled about studying the letter, Jaye called the crime lab to come pick it up.

The next day, the lab reported that both envelope and letter carried the DNA and prints of Jaye and two mailroom clerks. No surprise there. The only other evidence found was a smudged print and one unidentified DNA sample on the letter. It was run through the department database and also CODIS, and nothing matched. That deepened suspicions that the letter came from the killer.

Toward the end of the day, Potter called her in, and as she sat across the desk, he told her, "How you doin', kid? You okay?"

"Never been better," she lied. "Actually, this is great. If it's from him, the letter is a break from his M.O. pattern. He's trying to be cute—Keep it up, slick! Come to Mama."

Potter nodded. "I agree… Well, I've been in a conference with the chief himself and some other brass about this." He gave a "how-about-that?" gesture. "That's a first for me."

"Congratulations, Sarge. Glad to help make it happen."

They both laughed, then he got serious. "Look, we're concerned for you. Everybody is. We obviously can't assign a bodyguard to you. How would that look? The cops guarding a cop, especially a woman."

"Of course."

"What we're going to do is put an alarm system in your apartment and have patrol make frequent runs by your place. Don't go into suspicious places alone at night. And keep your off-duty piece handy."

"Check, Sarge. Thanks."

He nodded solemnly. "We protect our own."

Jaye said, "I just wish he had given a return address. I'd have a message for him."

"What's that?"

Jaye stood up to leave. "I would have said, 'You're coming after me? What a coincidence because I'm coming after you.'"

That night, Jaye sat on her couch sipping Grand Marnier on the rocks with a lamp on low and the muted TV showing a Seinfeld rerun. She wasn't in the mood to laugh. Her bravado since the letter arrived was a mask. Of course, it worried her. No one would enjoy becoming the target of a madman, cop, or no cop.

She had known from the first day the stories about her appeared that the killer would read the newspaper or watch TV. He would see her face and know she was the one working every day to achieve his capture and maybe his death. Wouldn't hers be a scalp he could hang proudly? Yeah, it worried Jaye, maybe even scared her.

Jaye's angst over her vulnerability intensified as she finished her third liqueur and turned the bedroom lights out. She stared into nothing long after her head hit the pillow.

The worst part of a nightmare can be when the sleeper wakes the instant the demon is about to strike.

Jarred awake, Jaye felt the damp sweat of her fear. She pushed the fog out of her mind and blinked her eyes open in the darkened room. Slowly, she pieced together the terrifying images that had flicked through her dream. She had been trapped in a dark closet with a man slamming against the door. She remembered putting her hand on the door and feeling the thin boards vibrate as they weakened under the pounding.

As she sat up in bed, the terror she had felt was still real as she remembered groping around the closet for her gun, which she had somewhere laid down. She scrambled on hands and knees and finally found the pistol when the door shattered, and the silhouette of a man stood looming in the doorway. She picked up the pistol and pointed it but couldn't find the release lever on the safety. Desperately, she felt where it should be on the automatic, but it wasn't there. Then, the man took a step forward…

Jaye shook her head, trying to dislodge the ugly residue of her fear. Then, she heard it. Soft footsteps moving slowly somewhere in her building, somewhere close. She scrambled out of bed and grabbed her duty pistol, which she always kept on a nightstand.

Slowly, she crept her way in the dark toward her back door. She froze as the footsteps stopped, started, stopped, then started again, then faded. She edged toward the blind and lifted it far enough to see out. Nothing. Jaye listened for a long minute. Still nothing.

She went to the kitchen and turned on the overhead, then checked the clock. It read 4:45. She had assumed it was the middle of the night. Then she remembered the Barra fellow in the unit above working a pre-dawn shift at the airport.

She scolded herself: Idiot! You gotta get a grip, girl. This will not be a coffee-break story at the office. She went back to bed, hoping for another hour's sleep.

Two days later, she happened to see a friendly neighbor at the mailbox and made an idle mention that it was thoughtful of Mr. Barra not to disturb people when he leaves so early.

The woman chuckled and said, "The reason he's so quiet is that he moved out last month."

"Oh, I didn't know that," she said to the woman, but to herself, she said—What the hell?

At lunchtime that day, she went to a gun shop and bought a tiny .22-magnum derringer as a purse gun and as a backup to her .380 back-up. Granted, a .22 is small, but she remembered what Potter had once said: "A .22 is underrated. It can give you a hell of a headache, but only briefly."

Jaye found comfort in her tiny arsenal. "I'll meet you at the OK Corral, you bastard," she muttered.

She also phoned Professor Archibald to ask his opinion about the letter. He said, "It's your life at stake, so weigh my advice as purely academic. I'm just a has-been-cop teacher who spends his days telling kids things he himself is not sure of.

"From what you tell me, Jaye, I'd be cautious and stay out of dark alleys. However, I wouldn't be deeply worried."

"Why?' she asked, eager to get any reassurance that might come her way.

"This guy has shown three things: He's cautious, he's clever, and he's cowardly. Those are the reasons he chooses weak, homeless women as his victims and how he's evaded press attention and capture. Given that, do you think he's eager to take on an alert, armed, strong woman? I don't think you'd make a promising subject for strangulation. You probably worry the hell out of him, and he's trying to scare you off his track. All of that assumes he's the one who wrote the letter instead of some nut job. Frankly, I doubt it."

"That makes me feel better."

"Not too much better, I hope. If he ever had a clean shot at wasting you, he'd do it," he said. "I don't want to stand up at your funeral and say, 'Sorry, but I was wrong.'"

Captain John Burton supervised the police department PR function, which meant keeping everything out of the press except attaboy/attagirl awards, promotions, and the Christmas toy party for poor children. He was what they called an admin cop, which meant he rose through the ranks by shuffling paper, going to conferences, and serving on committees.

He was often at the side of the chief, looking for an opportunity to agree on something. He was what one cop called a "leg humper." Almaguer once said, "He's so disliked he doesn't even get spam." Burton had one significant ability: a skill at making those of higher rank comfortable with him. He was not a threat and not a challenge, and only a minor nuisance.

Burton threw the newspaper down on Potter's desk. "A dark-street assassin, for Christ's sake," he snarled. "What does that stupid Peoria think she's doing?"

"Gee, captain, she didn't say that," Potter said weakly.

"She talked to the fucking reporter who did say it, didn't she? Now, we've got half the dames of the whole stinking town clamoring for us to arrest every man they don't like for this silly shit. All of a sudden, a couple of murders of some street women turn into the great manhunt." Burton glared at Potter. "The mayor is running for reelection this fall, and this makes him look like he has a lousy police department that can't protect women on the street."

"We can't be concerned with politics," Potter said.

Burton sneered. "Oh, really? Who do you think approves our budget? Who do you think appoints our chief, the man who holds your balls in his hand?"

The sergeant fumbled with his hands on the desk as though they were foreign objects. When he spoke, it was in the imploring voice of an underling who knows he's done wrong and hopes a whipped-dog manner will make up for it. Twenty years in the corps had taught him that forelock tugging was the way to handle blowhard desk warriors like Burton. "I know, captain, but what could I do? You know, affirmative action and all that. We gotta be careful. And just like you said, I put her on cases where there wasn't much public interest. How was I to know this would happen?"

"Well, I'll tell you one thing, this is not going to continue."

"What do you mean, captain?"

Burton thought about the question. "I don't know yet, but until I decide, you tell her to watch her damned mouth around nosey, goddamned reporters."

"Do you want me to keep her away from reporters?"

Burton considered the matter, then said, "Nothing would

please me more, but we can't afford to get in a pissing match with the press over who they can and can't interview. Just tell her to clear what she says in advance. Let me think on it. We're going to have to live with the situation—for the time being."

The way Burton said the last phrase chilled Potter.

"Roger that, captain."

❧

Potter's bluster was gone, and he was solemn as a politician at a funeral. He summoned his most serious game face and looked at Jaye. "Jesus, Peoria, what did I tell you about low-keying this 'dark-street assassin' thing?" He shook his head forlornly. "All I can tell you is that the brass is pissed off. I mean, big-time pissed."

Jaye spread her arms in appeal. "But what did I do? The guy just asked some questions, and I answered them. I didn't say anything about a serial killer. Those were Wasserman's words."

"Maybe you shouldn't have said anything."

"But, Sarge, you always said to cooperate with the press."

"I meant on little things."

"How am I supposed to know what that reporter considered little or big? A guy I'd never laid eyes on before." She shook her head in dismay. "Sometimes I feel like I'm in a deep hole with smooth sides."

"Look, I'm not going to argue about this. The fact is, when you talk to these jokers, you have to watch every word. Now we've got to deal with some righteously pissed-off brass. This thing has all of a sudden become a monster, and we're no closer than when we started to solve it. If things don't improve, some changes are maybe going to have to be made, and we both have to face that."

Jaye's expression switched from frustration to suspicion. "What changes?"

Potter's face became vague. "I can't answer that."

"Whatdya mean, you can't answer that?" She paused and studied her boss for a moment. "What's going on, Sarge? Are you going to back me on this—whatever the hell it is?"

"I'll do what's best for you and the department, like

always—Go back to work, Peoria."

The phone call from Burton was the one Potter had dreaded hearing. It completed the back-stabbing to which he was forced to be an accomplice.

An hour later, after he had screwed up his nerve, Potter picked up the phone to summon Jaye to his office, he was as subdued as a preacher discussing the devil.

It was with relief that she excused herself from the jangling media calls and a wide-eyed student reporter from a college newspaper who wanted to know if she considered herself a target of the killer, which she laughed off.

"Wow! Thanks for getting me out of that," she said as she casually plopped down on a chair in front of Potter's desk. "I wish these reporters would finally get what they need and leave me alone. All the kooks are climbing out of the cracks, too. That phone is driving me crazy. Some guy called and said if I'd meet him for a drink tonight, he'd confess. Such a deal."

Those words were the ones he definitely didn't want to hear. "That a new outfit?" he asked lamely.

Jaye looked down and smoothed the green fabric, which represented her clothing budget for two months. "Yes. Like it?"

"I'd like it better if you dressed less like a TV personality and more like a working cop; in fact, if you were a working cop."

Jaye reacted like she had been slapped. She stood up. "That's unfair. I've been putting in twelve- and fourteen-hour days on these cases, and you know it. There's nothing wrong with wanting to look nice. Would the department prefer me to look dikey, to better fit the image of women cops in the minds of some people, like a certain captain we both know who shall go nameless?"

"Sit down," Potter said.

Something in his voice told her she needed to be sitting for what he next had to say.

"Jaye, this case you're on has grown into the biggest thing in the department. Because of all the publicity you invited—"

"I never invited anything. You know that."

"Maybe you didn't ask, but you sure didn't discourage them, either."

She exhaled heavily in resignation. "Go on."

"Anyway, because this case has gotten so big, the brass is taking the situation real seriously."

"That's terrific. I can use help on the phones, and we can blanket the East Village with a repeat check of all the regulars down there. Maybe that—"

"You're not hearing me," Potter said. He stared at her until the enthusiasm vanished from her face and then said, "Running a major investigation like this requires a lot of experience. There's a lot involved in heading up a—"

Jaye's voice turned cold. "What are you using a lot of extra words to say? Are you telling me I won't lead the investigation?"

"Not only will you not lead it, you're leaving the unit."

Her mouth dropped open. "Taken off my case? Leaving the Unit? You can't mean that. Why, that's an insult. That's like saying I'm incompetent. That would finish me in this police department. You know that."

His voice was barely more than a whisper. "No, it won't."

"Say what you've got to say." Her voice was ice.

"You're promoted to Juvenile. You'll be the key liaison with school safety officers throughout the city. It's an increase in responsibility with a merit pay increase. Effective next week. It will be announced as a deserved promotion that has been in the works for some time. Art Baker will take over as lead for the time being."

"Promotion? My ass. That'll fool exactly no one." She laughed but without humor. "Juvenile? That's the dead end of the department, and you know it. Juvenile! My ass! Women's work, eh? Chasing candy store shoplifters and lecturing truants." Her voice raised, and she almost sputtered. "Well, I won't do it. I'll go to the union. I'll fight you, Dave, you and that-that—reptilian asshole Burton who I just know is behind all this, right?"

He shook his head. "No, you won't."

"Won't what?"

"You won't fight it because that would wash you up around here and any other department you might want to apply to. Let me give you some advice. Take your transfer, swallow your pride, and enjoy your life."

His words hit Jaye like hot grease. Her voice quivered, and she prayed the tears wouldn't flow, but they did. "What would you know about fighting? Did you fight for me? Is this how you 'protect your own'?— Your exact words." He started to reply, but she waved him silent. "Thanks, Potter. Thanks a lot. Big, tough fucking Marine. Semper Fi. Hit those beaches, gyrenes, and all that bullshit.

"Just like all your phony macho business and your ragging on Art Baker. It's just hot air. If I ever hit any beaches with you, Sarge, I don't want you behind me." She glared for a moment, then said, "I recall reading an old word that I remember because I thought it was funny. But it's not a funny word. The word is toady."

She stood up and started to leave, then stopped. "You know, a part of you is a pretty nice guy. The problem is, it's not a big enough part."

"Go back to work, detective."

She slammed out of the office. Potter watched her go and didn't feel good about himself, but he knew that when he got home, Jack Daniels would understand.

Jaye needed something to feel good about, so she decided to drown her disappointment in sweat. Maybe a hard workout would lift her spirits.

She looked at her nude body in the bedroom mirror and reflected on life. She tightened her buttock muscles. Hmm, not as tight as last time. She ran her hand down the outside of her thigh and pinched some flesh. Jesus, is that cellulite? She moaned in protest—my job turns to crap, I get screwed by the system, I don't save any money, I've got old, I'm still sleeping alone, and on top of everything else, my body is going to pot.

The fact that most women her age would have sacrificed their workout videos for her shape was no consolation. She was the one whose body was falling apart. Morosely, she slipped on her jogging outfit, stretched, and headed for the high school quarter-mile track a couple of blocks away. She stepped onto the running surface and started a warm-up jog.

It was a warm evening, and she was sweating hard and out of breath after only an easy lap. That was good. Maybe she could punish herself out of the dumps, like self-flagellation in the Middle Ages. She felt as uptight as a 7-Eleven clerk at 3:00 A.M. with a biker coming in the door.

She was sweating and breathless as her thoughts raced down a dark path—damn the police suits for using me like an old mop. Damn, Ben Spiller, for coming home one day and telling me he loved someone else.

She took the curve near the football scoreboard and passed a man about her own age. That made her feel better.

She slowed to a walk and scolded herself aloud, sounding like a heavy breather in a porno flick. "Okay, stop the whining, bitch. I'm getting tired of hearing it." She resumed her silent argument—Remember, you can be useful in juvenile crimes. That's better than a transfer where you totally disappear, like the records department. While you're at it, think something nice about dear old Ben Spiller... Fuck him.

Jaye stood near the start line and let her breath even out. Maybe her anger could translate into a sensational run. She clenched her jaw and readied herself for the big push, for the break-neck, mad dash to set the all-time record, to smash through that magical barrier—the eight-minute mile! She set her watch at zero and accelerated as she passed the starting point. Her breathing started to labor. Careful, girl. Remember, pace will get you to the place... I wonder if I could become the first woman chief. Hey, that'd be something: A salary I could hardly carry home, a new Chrysler, and a driver giving speeches to Rotarians. Oh, yeah!

One lap done. She looked at her watch: 2:06. Too slow. Haul ass. ... God, that Brian Fogarty's sexy.

Second lap: 4:04. Better, but I've got to gut it out the last half. Pick it up, pick it up.... You know you're being used, don't you? Going from homicide to juvenile is like moving from Beverly Hills to the Mohave Desert.

Third lap: 6:02. Sensational: Another like that, and I'll finally do it before I get too old.

Jaye gritted her teeth and told herself—preached, scolded, pleaded—that in only two minutes, it would be over, and she could rest. Damn, it hurts. Keep going. Gotta stop cussing so much. I know it's the cop environment, but no one likes a dirty-mouthed broad. Oh, it hurts. Just one minute more, sixty ticks. Don't think about it… I just know the department is sending me over there just to get me out of homicide, just to give that bastard Benton a chance to put his flunky in there, as everyone says. They don't have a real reason—do they? What reason could they have?... Just a hundred yards more. Kick, damn you. Now, pour it on! Oh, oh.

She finished the fourth lap and stopped her watch, then fell on the football field grass where she lay stretched out, gasping for air and asking the pain in her lungs to hurry and go away. Finally, she sat up on one elbow and looked down at the watch. It read 8:01.

Damn. Nothing's going right.

Chapter Eleven

"Uh, margarita, I guess."

"Mister, this is a bar, not a beauty parlor. One guy came in here and ordered something like that, then went to the can and tried to grab a vice cop's pecker. We had to go in and rescue him. Now, you don't want to be led away in handcuffs, do you?"

Brian looked at the homely old man to see if he were laughing, but Frog Thompson gazed back stolidly.

"How about a Bud Lite?"

Frog nodded. "Welcome to the 10-7, fellow American."

Brian looked around. This was the place Jaye had told him about, where she occasionally stopped. The 10-7 was boisterous and filled with coarse jokes, friendly insults, and catcalls, which volleyed around the room like pinballs. Country-western on the jukebox backgrounded the crowd with laments about loves lost and folks done wrong. Brian, though, was content to stare at the glass in front of him and watch a large table of laughing men and women. There was a common drinks pot in the center with a pile of bills and change. He didn't see Jaye, who was out of sight behind a beefy detective who had the floor.

The cop was ragging on a popular detective named Hornbeck, who was targeted because this was his birthday. Sort of an ad-hoc roast.

The cop said, "Horny's going to sex crimes from the burglary was a noble experiment. Only the burglars objected." He flashed a smile of familiarity across at his buddy. "What the hell, why should burglars get all the breaks?"

A cop named Tatum said, "One time, a bunch of us went fishing up in the mountains."

Hornbeck interjected by rolling his eyes and saying, "Oh, here we go again." He turned imploringly to the table. "Don't believe this bullshit. It's not true, some of it."

"We want to hear the evidence, then we'll render a verdict," one of the wives said, laughing.

Tatum continued. "A few years ago, Horny and some of us decided to go fishing up by Mammoth. Well, after a few hours, we throw all the gear into the trunk and go to town for some medium-to-heavy hoisting. We're bending elbows with the sheriff, a good ole boy I'd met at a conference somewhere. All of a sudden, Horny starts acting—you guessed it—horny. He's freshly divorced, so he says to the sheriff, 'Is there any place around here where a fella can lay some pipe.'

"Well, the sheriff, being a reasonable gentleman wanting to be collegial with visiting lawmen and all that, and having a flexible attitude toward victimless crime, directs him to a small whorehouse on the outskirts of town." Tatum starts laughing at the memory. "Horny here goes out the door like a goosed gopher, and he doesn't return for about two hours.

"When he comes back, I ask what took so long, and he says, with a wink, 'You know, those girls'll do things your wife won't.' Hearing that, the sheriff, who is pretty ripped by then, says, 'Maybe your wife needs a better teacher.'"

The others broke into loud laughter, and Scarborough, from patrol, said, "Horny's ex-wife thought fellatio was some kind of pasta sauce."

"You jerks, don't you know there are ladies present," Jaye said.

Hornbeck lifted up from his chair and swiveled his head around the room. "Where?" he said, and the group exploded in laughter.

Frog brought a round of beer and took money from the pot.

"Search him," someone yelled as Frog turned to leave.

L.T. Turner, one of the first blacks on the force and now a sergeant near retirement, reached for the bottle Frog put in front of him and said: "Heard ol' Joe Martin got busted up this morning by some PCP freak. Guess the freak threw his ass into a bed of prickly pear. They maced and tasered the mother, but that didn't work, so it took about ten of our city's finest to get cuffs on him. Probably took more than that to pick the needles out of Joe's ass. Man, that PCP sure is the Wheaties of drugs. It'll turn a ninety-pound wimp into Dick Butkus."

"Tell me about it," Jaye muttered.

Instead of sympathizing, the others at the table concurrently imagined their old friend Martin landing on cacti and started to chuckle.

"Hope he didn't tear those green polyester pants he wears," Scarborough said.

"He only wears them every other day, so there's a fifty-fifty chance he didn't. Besides, he needs a purple pair to complete his wardrobe," Turner said, draining his glass. "I'll buy a round," and threw a twenty into the pot.

Brian was sort of listening to the cops and held his empty glass up to order another Bud. After an hour and three beers, he was still moping on his stool when he felt a hand on his shoulder.

"Hey, Brian, what are you doing here?"

He swung around, and his eyes took a moment to focus like a rusty camera. "Oh, hey. Hi, Jaye."

Jaye was holding her own third beer and spoke with the slightly-too-loud liquid happiness of someone trying to chase away unhappiness. "I didn't expect to find you slumming in a cop bar."

He looked around again. "Is that what this is?"

"If you're looking for psychological case studies, then this is the Klondike, and you just struck gold. I mean, Fucked-upville USA—oh, excuse my language." She motioned toward the laughing group at the table she had just left. "Come on down and join us. At that table, we got a regular lazy susan for a shrink: broken marriages, job burn-out, misdirected anger, alcoholism. Take your pick."

He shook his head in a wide arc and patted the adjoining stool. "Naw, you stay here. I'll buy you one."

Jaye was too oiled to realize he was only in the 10-7 because he hoped she would also be. She made an exaggerated gesture and sat down. "You're quite persuasive. Down there, I have to buy my own. They aren't gentlemen. I hope you have something to celebrate because I sure don't."

A sad expression covered his face. "Celebrate? No. This is a wake."

"Oh, who died?"

"My marriage. Kaput. Murder most foul. This is my anniversary—Hah! Congratulations to me."

"You don't say? Listen, I'm a homicide cop, so why don't you tell me what the clues are? Maybe we can find the murderer, the per-" she stopped to burp politely. "The perpetrator."

Brian shook his head again. "Naw, she'd just claim self-defense, and she's too pretty for a jury to convict."

Jaye looked sorrowful. "Just as well, 'cause I'm not in homicide anymore, anyway."

Brian wrinkled his eyebrows in deep concern. "No!"

"Yeah, they schent," she said as 'sent' and 'shifted' collided on her tongue, "me to juvenile. The kiddie corps. Woman's work." She stared at Brian. "Tell me—no bullshit—did you think I was good in homicide?" She didn't wait for an answer.

"When I first came to homicide, they gave me all the shit details just to see how I'd do. We do that to all fresh meat. One time, we went out on a scene where this fat old guy had been locked up dead in a house trailer for over a week.

"It was the middle of an August heat wave, and Tatum said—Tatum's my sidekick—anyway, he said—" Jaye made her voice deeper—"'Peoria, why don't you check out the scene?' The bastards stood around while I went in that flipping trailer, not having any idea what to expect." She made a gagging pantomime. "God, I'd never smelled anything like that in my life. It was like—like rotten cheese left in a closet. Like a dead mouse in a drawer. Like a thousand mouses—mice. No, it was worse. That body looked like a moldy, overstuffed sausage, all purple, brown, and bloated. I almost threw up, but I never did. I put on rubber gloves like you're supposed to, but when I moved the body just a little, it started to fall apart. I could hear those bastards outside laughing." Her face wrinkled in the first stages of weeping. "I miss those bastards."

"All you did was get transferred. I lost my wife."

"I've been that route, too, and do you know which hurts worse?"

"Tell me."

"The one at the time."

Brian ordered two more drinks, and Jaye said, "We got this, Captain Burton, a real asshole—pardon me. When he's around the top brass, his best move is the kowtow. One of the secretaries made these cute little marshmallow ducks for Easter and put them on everyone's desk." She outlined the shape of a little duck with her hands. "Bunch of us took some and put them under the glass on Burton's desk; squashed them flater'n shit—sorry; marshmallow spread all over. Then we put on a sign that said, 'Pressed duck under glass.'" She laughed at the memory. "He almost wet his pants, he was so pissed. Do you know what that jerk did? He had the sign dusted for prints. Know whose he got? His own. We used gloves and his stationery."

"Sounds paranoid," Brian said.

"Paranoid? Fucked-up, you mean. 'Scuse me, I'm trying to quit saying that word." Her thoughts drifted, and she started laughing and rested her hand on his shoulder to keep from swaying. "Another time—this'll kill you—we were just sitting around, and all of a sudden, Tatum says, 'Captain Burton has an undescended testicle.' I asked him how he knew. He just shrugged and said, 'I'm a detective.'"

Brian said, "Sounds like a colonel I had in the army. He doubled-down on versatility: he could be a jerk and a fool at the same time."

She said, "I never asked you about the army."

He drank from his glass. "Don't... You ever use your gun?"

Jaye cocked her head and said, "Why is it everyone always asks cops if they ever shot anyone?"

"Well, did you?"

"Just once; shot the ear off a mugger."

"The ear?"

"Yeah, he was running away, and I called for him to stop, and he didn't." Jaye pretended to sight down her finger. "Soooo, plink! The perp thanked me later for only shooting his ear."

"What'd you say to him?"

"I told him he was lucky. I was aiming for his head."

Brian blinked a couple of times, then they started laughing together at the old cop story. He almost fell off the stool and grabbed her for support. Jaye poured them both some more beer and said, "Speaking of Tatum, it was my first week, and I'd just arrived at this suicide scene, and ol' Tatum came out of a bedroom and said, 'Jaye, there's a guy in there you need to question.' So like a dumb broad, I just walked right in, and right in front of me was this guy—ugh! You know how when you shoot a big gun like a thirty-eight in your mouth, the gas has nowhere to go?"

"I never thought about that."

"Well, this guy had done that, and the gas had blown his eyes out, just like a cod you pull up too fast from the bottom of the ocean. Boy! I screamed and ran out of there like—"

Brian shook his head. "That's pretty mean."

"No, no. They were just baptizing me into the job. That's stuff I had to get used to."

"Itch—it is— nice to be able to get your laughs on the job," Brian said.

Jaye thought about that for a moment. "Aw, I'm sorry. That was tacky of me. I forgot you're not a cop. …You know," she continued, "at a party, there are two jobs that you should never tell people you do: doctor and cop. People always want to know if a doctor has saved a life and if a cop has taken one."

Brian drew patterns with his finger on the wet bar. "Why the hell didn't I just stay at my regular job? Had everything: money and a wife. I was a big shot at the utilities company. Do you know what it's like being a big shot?"

"No, but I think I'm about to learn," Jaye said with disinterest.

Brian thought for a long moment, then said, "It's like shit."

They both laughed as if some hilarious joke had been told. Then, Jaye wailed, "I miss those guys."

"I got a question," Brian said. "What'd you think of a guy dumb enough to love a woman who screwed around on him?"

Jaye stared at him. "Cut his balls off. He's too wimpy to deserve 'em. Plenty of women who won't do that crap would kill for a loyal man."

Brian winced. "Is that so bad? I mean—"

"Who we talking about?"

He made a cavalier gesture. "Guy I know."

She shrugged. "Okay, Mr. guy, tell me about it."

Brian looked at her with awe. "You are smart. Wow! You are smart. You're one of the smartest people I've ever met."

"I'm a detective. That was easy."

Brian proceeded to talk for a half-hour to spill all the disappointments of his marriage to Maureen. Some of it was beer talk, but the pain of his failed marriage could never hide behind alcohol." He stopped abruptly with a sudden idea. "Do you carry an off-duty gun?"

"Of course. What did you think I have in this bra? Pistol on one side, ammo on the other."

"Maybe I could borrow it; put myself out of my misery."

Jaye thought about that. "Maybe a good idea. I would loan mine to you, except there'd be a lot of paperwork, I'd probably be suspended, and I need the paycheck."

Jaye put her hand on his shoulder, both to commiserate, and to steady herself, and said, sympathetically, "You're better off. Screw her—oops."

That did not make him feel better.

Jaye's friends sent reinforcements over for the beers that already lined the bar like advancing infantry.

Time passed, and the clock neared 1:00 A.M. Brian weaved his way back to the bar from the men's room. Positioning himself carefully on the stool, he said, "Let me tell you something I've never told anyone else in the entire world."

"What's that?" she leaned over close to him.

He looked around, then whispered. "She's fucking someone else."

"No!" Jaye said with mixed shock and sympathy.

He nodded mournfully. "Does that make me half-a-man, as they say in the movies?" He looked at Jaye expectantly.

She returned the look for a long moment. "Yes."

They burst out laughing, clapping each other on the back. Suddenly, Jaye backed off and said, "What's wrong with me?"

Brian studied her closely. "You mean besides being ugly?"

She waited for his laughter to die down, then said, "Let me tell you something. You kind of scare me."

"Nooo," he protested, as though she had just called him a child molester.

"Yeah, it's true. You're too smart for me. I can't use the big words you do. I don't know all that classical music and stuff. I cuss way, way too much. I only finished community college." Tears started to run down her cheeks. "No one could ever want me."

Brian awkwardly patted her on the back. "Don't cry. Maybe someone might, someday."

Brian put his elbow on the bar and leaned on his fist, Rodin fashion. He tried to concentrate. "I guess it's like a great philosopher once said—" He paused to let a heavy thought form. "Life is shit, and then you die." They didn't laugh at that.

"Okay, you two, time to hit it," a jovial, sober voice said from behind them. They turned and could barely make out the blurred face of one of Jaye's friends. "I got the taxi detail tonight. Let's go."

Jaye and Brian were helped into the back seat, and the cop, whose name was Julian, said, "I know where Jaye lives, but how about you, pal?"

"I can't go home like this. I live in a half-way house."

"He runs it. He's not a half-way," Jaye explained hastily.

"I'm staying with her," Brian managed to slur.

"That right, Jaye?" Julian asked.

"Yeah," she mumbled from semi-sleep, "but he better keep his ass on the couch."

Julian laughed. "Okay." He had been in the academy with Jaye. He knew of the raw deal she had been given and understood why she was in his backseat drunk. This would not become a story.

The car pulled up close to the door, and the two of them stumbled up the steps, and then Jaye dropped her keys. After about five minutes of fumbling around in the flower bed next to the step, whispering too loudly and shushing even more loudly, they managed to get the door open. Almost tripping over each other, they banged into the kitchen, where Jaye opened a beer for each of them. Sitting at the table, she put her head in her arms and started to cry.

"I'm getting old. I'm all alone, and nothing ever goes right."

Brian patted her on the head. "D'ya have any chili? I'd like some chili."

She waved vaguely toward a cupboard, and Brian rummaged around and muttered a pained curse when a can of green beans dropped on his foot. He eventually found some Nalley's and a can opener, which proved as easy for him to manage as Rubik's Cube. He finally discarded the whole operation and returned to the table and his beer. "I think we got to get it on," he pronounced solemnly. "That'll show 'em. Whatya say?"

He awaited her response, but she ignored the question.

Jaye got up and made her way to her bedroom, and closed the door.

He wandered into the living room and plopped down on the sofa. He tried to concentrate on something that seemed terribly important but which he couldn't get a fix on. He closed his eyes and waited for the room to stop spinning, then the dark slipped up and closed around him.

The next thing Brian knew, he was being shaken, and he forced his eyes open despite the gravel under the lids. An angry colony of ants wearing football cleats was trapped inside his skull. Maggots had died in his mouth. An image swam into place, and it was Jaye, standing over him in a housecoat, handing him a cup of coffee and looking, with stringy hair and red eyes, like a dismounted horsewoman of the apocalypse.

"Get up, time to go."

"Wha—what time is it?"

"Six o'clock. I'll call a cab, and you can wait down at the corner. Neighbors. They think I'm a good girl. Sorry."

He swung his legs over, and they found the floor. "I'll pay you a thousand dollars for a swig of mouthwash."

"It's on the house. Whew! In fact, I'll pay you."

Brian stood on the street corner and concentrated on his misery, symptom by symptom. His pounding head made every step as cautious as walking on coals.

His mouth had again become day-old bile. His socks were sticky from having slept in his shoes. Nausea in his stomach percolated like hot lava. Standing at the same corner was an elderly woman waiting for a bus. She kept glancing haughtily at Brian and sniffing the air. Finally, he said, "Lady, that's one of the problems working in AIDS research, some of it gets on you." She skittered across the street with an alarmed glare.

When the cab arrived, he got in and collapsed against the back seat. The driver took a look in his mirror and chuckled. "Been there myself, pal. Hope it was worth it."

Brian squinted out the window at the sunrise, then closed his eyes. "Just drive," he mumbled. On the trip back to his car and then on his drive to New Hope, Brian thought of that fateful drive with Maureen, the one that shot a merciful bullet into a dying marriage. It was after a company party, and they were in the car she just had to have, that damned BMW. Now, with a bad hangover, alone in his own car and urged on by raging hangover remorse, he relived it. He couldn't not relive it…

On the way home—where she continued to live, and he no longer did—Maureen drove, and Brian stared out the window. The social temperature became January in Juneau.

"Something on your mind?" Brian asked after a few moments of corrosive quiet.

"I'm thinking."

"Uh-huh," he mumbled, not knowing what else to say.

"Okay, let's talk now," she said a little too firmly.

He hesitated and stumbled slightly in his response. "Uh, sure."

"Brian," she began, "are you happy?"

"No. Sleeping on a friend's couch is not my idea of homesteading." It was a sarcastic comment that he instantly regretted.

"You know that's not what I meant. I mean in the big picture."

His voice softened. "I want to be, but I guess your question is a roundabout way of saying you're not happy—in the big picture."

"No, I'm not. I'm sorry, but I guess there's no soft way to say it. I haven't been for a long time." She twisted the wheel sharply to avoid a careless driver. "Bastard!" she shouted through the closed window, venting her tension at a stranger. She returned her attention to Brian without looking at him. "Damn," she muttered,

"I practiced these words all afternoon. I wanted to be unemotional and rational about this."

He said nothing.

"We have nothing in common, Brian. We're just…just too different."

"What's wrong with that, Mo? Are you saying we have to be clones of each other? We're individuals, different people, honey. I respect you when you disagree with me. I don't see that as a problem."

"Differences I could handle; different people is something else."

Brian lifted his shoulders and let them drop in resignation. She continued, "The differences I'm talking about go right to the core of the kind of people we are. And, in that way, we don't even live on the same planet."

"Maureen, ever since we got married, I've tried to please you. You wanted this house— you got it; you wanted me to go to work for a big corporation—you got it; you wanted a BMW—well, you got it. Seems to me, when the givings and the gots were passed out, you did pretty well on the got side."

"I paid my dues," she said defensively. "When we met, you were fresh out of the army. You were a basket case. I've spent years watching you eat at yourself over what happened in the army."

"I wouldn't say that. I had some issues to work out."

"Did you?" she said. "I think your 'issues' left you with a great sense of obligation, I guess you could call it. I could never figure out to whom." She turned more fully to look at him. "I wish I was as good at giving as you, but I'm not. However, that doesn't solve our problem."

"We've said all this before, Maureen."

She took a deep breath. "I want a divorce."

They traveled several blocks without speaking. As they rode down streets that Brian knew so well and realized how close they were to journey's end, he said, "I know it won't do any good, but I just want it on the record: I still love you."

"I'm sorry. You'll learn not to."

They traveled the rest of the distance in silence until Maureen turned into the driveway and switched off the engine. She turned to face him fully. "And Brian…"

"What?"

"I want the BMW."

Chapter Twelve

Standing alone at a bus stop at 10:00 P.M., undercover officer Dorothy Mullin resisted the urge to scratch where the wig she wore made her scalp itch. In her twelve years on the force, she had done more than her share of "shit detail" work: scraping motorist remains off of pavements, trying to comfort molested children, getting slugged in bar brawls, and standing between furious husbands and berating wives. However, the duty she hated most was that of decoy, where she was hung out like a trussed-up goose waiting for some pervert or sadist to come on to her. But here she was again, dressed to look like an old hag with a gray wig, a padded dress to make her appear hunched and shapeless, and make-up that made her face resemble the product of a tanning factory.

If I have to do much more of this crap, I won't need the make-up. This'd turn anyone into an old woman, the forty-year-old thought crossly.

Mullin was decoying herself on a mainly deserted East Village street because a rash of purse-snatchings had hit the area in previous weeks. A gang of black teenagers had been preying on the defenseless old ladies living in halfway houses and shelters, especially during the nights immediately following the mailing of Social Security and disability checks. Several of the women had struggled to hold on to the tattered handbags that often represented all they owned, and more than one broken hip or arm had been the result of brittle bones cracked on concrete.

She was also aware, acutely so, of the serial killer prowling these same streets late at night. Like here and now.

At least Mullin knew she wasn't alone. Two uniformed policemen were hanging back a long block away. They were distant enough to lull any tempted snatchers but close enough to swoop down in seconds and have them in cuffs before they could say "motherfucker." The two waited in an unmarked car and tried to relax in a limbo of anticipation, like fishermen watching the big one circle the bait, knowing the calm waters could begin foaming at any moment. Steve Jablonski, a rookie, and Joe Hansen, a paunchy veteran of twenty years, were connected to Mullin by a cigarette-pack-size transmitter taped to her upper chest, which carried every word she whispered back to them.

Mullin told them she was heading toward a dark area in the middle of the next block, and Jablonski jerkily let the clutch out to move the manual shift Corvette forward. It was a car that had been confiscated in a drug deal and turned over to the San Diego PD by the DEA for undercover work.

"Shit, kid, you've been jumping this crate along like a toad on speed. Just ease it down the road," Hansen said, drawing 'ease' out slowly to make the point.

"Sorry. I haven't driven a stick in a long while. I'll get used to it pretty soon."

"You shoulda said something when we checked it out," Hansen grumbled, miffed at the possibility of having to drive himself.

In the long pauses when the transmitter was silent, the two would talk casually about food, the neighborhood, women, or baseball. But when Mullin's whisper came over, they would stop in mid-sentence and tensely lean forward to catch the words, ready to race to her aid.

Mullin hobbled down the dark side street using the rheumatic-looking stiff gait she had practiced back at the station. Directly in front of her, outlined by the weak light of a store window, she noticed an alcoholic sprawled across the curb and into the gutter. A rolled-up sleeping bag lay next to him, and a bottle was clutched loosely in his hand. Vomit shimmered in a stagnant puddle next to his face. A fellow derelict walked by and stopped to study the situation. He reached down, pulled the man out of the gutter, and stretched him out on the sidewalk. He propped the sleeping bag under the man's head and straightened up as though to move on. Then, almost as an after-thought, he reached down, pulled the bottle from the limp fingers, and drank deeply until it was empty. Finally, he tossed the empty onto the man's chest and moved on down the street.

"I'll bet that guy's an ex-cop," Mullin whispered with a chuckle as she described the scene. "Of course, maybe he's not an ex, maybe it's his night off." She couldn't hear the responding laughter as she resumed her shuffle down the street.

Mullin's voice grew tense as she said, "Here come three black males, approximately sixteen or seventeen. Headed south, toward me, about half a block."

In the car, Jablonski unconsciously revved the engine, and both men stared out the windshield toward a threat they couldn't see.

Mullin let the bulky purse dangle from her left arm. "About a hundred feet now," Mullin whispered. "They're looking at me." Her voice developed a slight tremor. "Be ready."

Hansen reached down to unsnap his pistol. Jablonski gripped the steering wheel and inclined his head toward the transmitter speaker on the seat between them. Long seconds passed with no sound.

"What the fuck's happening?" Jablonski said, angry at the silence.

"Quiet," Hansen said, holding up his hand.

"It's all right," Mullin's voice finally said. "One even said 'Good evening, ma'am' to me."

"Well, whatdya know," Hansen said, "a miracle."

Jablonski wasn't amused by the racial barb, but he laughed anyway to release his tension and then slipped the gear-shift into neutral to flex the leg unaccustomed to working a clutch. "I thought sure as hell that was it," he said.

"Probably the only three Boy Scouts in this end of town," Hansen said with a deep laugh that set off a hacking smoker's cough.

"You know what's black and tan and looks good on a mugger?" Jablonski asked.

"What?" Hansen bit.

"A Doberman."

Relieved but also disappointed, they turned their attention back to Mullin's voice as her whisper resumed. "Wow! I can swallow now. Street's empty now. Just a couple of cars… Chicano lowriders, and—wait a minute, here comes someone." She was silent for a moment, then said, "It's okay, just a white male. He's standing under the street light. Can't tell much. About six feet. Now, he's headed this way. Probably looking for the bus stop."

Hansen and Jablonski relaxed when they heard the description. White males were not on the menu. Suddenly, Mullin's voice returned, but with a serrated edge of tension. "What do you want?… Stop that!… Leave me—" Her voice disintegrated into frantic squawks, and the two officers could hear the sounds of struggling through the speaker.

"What the fuck!" Hansen shouted. "GO! God damn it."

Jablonski tried to slam the car into first, but a loud grinding was all that happened. Frantically, he looked down and tried to figure it out.

"MOVE THIS FUCKING THING!" Hansen roared.

Jablonski finally got the car into gear but released the clutch too fast, and the car jumped to a halt.

"GOD DAMN IT. LET'S GO!"

Jablonski gritted his teeth and ground the starter for long seconds that seemed interminable. Turning to Hansen in a voice filled with panic, he said, "It's flooded."

"SHIT! MOVE!" Hansen was out the door and running down the street before Jablonski could respond.

Jablonski caught the lumbering Hansen within a few yards, but both men slowed to a hesitant walk when they came to the dark place where Mullin had said she was standing. The night was silent and empty. Not a person could be seen.

"Where is she?" Jablonski frantically called.

"I don't know. Look, for Christ's sake."

Both men turned in bewildered circles, not knowing what else to do. Hansen turned his flashlight onto a small alley that seemed even darker than the street. "Check in there," he ordered, and Jablonski disappeared through the narrow entrance. Hansen kept muttering to himself, "Be okay, be okay, be okay."

The shout from the alley startled Hansen, and in an instant, he was in the alley and beside Jablonski.

The two cops gazed in astonishment, then burst out laughing.

Standing and grinning at them was Dorothy Mullin with her badge in one hand and a small automatic pointed at the head of a young man standing three feet away in utter shock.

"Hey, what kind of fish did you catch?" Hansen said.

"Cuff him, will you? I got my hands full."

"What did you have that this fine young man wanted?" Hansen said.

"He was after my purse—he says."

Jablonski read Miranda to the man, then Hansen questioned him. His name was Eduardo Martinez. He was a nineteen-year-old Navy sailor from Chula Vista, close to the border, who had just returned from a long cruise to Japan. He said he had spent all his pay in a strip club, and he needed money to buy his parents a present.

"I've never done anything wrong before," he pleaded in a quivering voice.

As a squad car rolled up to take the kid into custody, Hansen had something smart to say to the sailor, but he kept quiet. There was nothing funny about a young guy maybe ruining his life.

"Peoria!"

Jaye's head snapped up from the report on juvenile violence she had been trying to study.

"Some guy out front to see you," the gruff older female sergeant named Ardath shouted across the room at her.

"Who?" she asked automatically.

"How should I know."

Another woman, Trudy, also assigned to what was called the KKK—the kiddie karnage korps looked up and said with a laugh, "Maybe you'll hit it lucky, and it won't be a cop. That means there's a remote chance he's a gentleman."

"What do you know about men, cops or otherwise?" Ardath demanded of Trudy.

Trudy sighed. "Nothing anymore. I've forgotten everything since I came to this department."

"What?" Ardath demanded.

"Never mind," Trudy said and looked back down at the mug shots she had been studying of known juvenile thieves, none of whom looked older than twelve. "I'd just be happy for a chance to gaze at a male with pubic hair."

Jaye walked into the next room and was surprised to see Brian standing a bit nervously near the door.

Extending her hand and smiling, she said, "Nice to see you."

He took her hand briefly. "I'm just glad you're not throwing things at me."

"Why?"

"After the way I acted the other night, you know, at the 10-7."

"Oh, that." She laughed. "That was just a little R and R. You needed to blow off some steam. And so did I, by the way."

"I'm glad no one got scalded."

"Amen to that. I hope you don't think I do that every night," she said.

Brian relaxed a little. "If you did, you wouldn't be one-tenth as pretty as you are."

Jaye blushed. "You know it's a crime to flatter a cop on duty, don't you?"

He glanced around and shuffled his feet slightly. "Uh, if you have work to do, I—"

Jaye touched his arm. "Come with me. I know where I can buy you the worst cup of coffee in town," and led the way to the department cafeteria.

When they entered the large room filled with the chatter of cops, they started for an empty table when she heard, "Hey, Jaye!"

She turned to the sound and saw Tatum beckoning. "You grab the table. I'll be right there with the coffee—regular, okay?" On her way to the coffee line, she stopped by the table of Tatum and Almaguer.

Tatum beckoned her over. "Hey, Jaye. I just wanted to alert you about a tip I got that a gang of six-year-old terrorists is going to attack a daycare center. Thought you'd like to know."

She leaned on the table. "Tatum, stick it where the sun don't shine. You're just jealous I got juvenile 'stead of you. You probably dream about all the mothers you could have met."

Almaguer laughed, said, "Ouch," and punched Tatum lightly on the shoulder.

"How's it going, babe?" Tatum asked.

"Aw, as good as I can expect, I suppose."

He said, "It's an open secret the reason Burton got rid of you is he wants your spot in homicide for his flunky. Everyone thinks you got a raw deal."

Almaguer agreed. "Burton's as popular as a prostate exam." Then, he said, "You got screwed, Jaye. But you'll make it back."

"See ya." She smiled and gave a little wave.

"See ya."

Jaye picked up two cups of coffee and joined Brian. "Friends of yours?" he asked as he stirred in a packet of Equal.

"Buddies from homicide. Yeah, good friends."

He glanced sideways at her. "I hope I didn't say anything out of line the other night."

She chuckled. "I'm sure you did, but how would I know?" Their laughter burst and died, and they sat for a moment nervously in search of a transition.

Finally, Brian said, "You probably date a lot of your colleagues. They certainly seem to like you."

"Once in a rare while," she said, "but it's usually not a good idea."

He smiled whimsically. "The idea of dating makes me feel like a high school kid. It's been so long…"

Jaye waved dismissively. "It's just like riding a bicycle again; one block and you're pedaling full speed."

"Did you find it that way after your, uh—"

"My divorce?" She paused. "No, but it sounded like what you needed to hear."

"I like your sense of humor," he said. "It's therapeutic."

"So now the therapist himself is being—what would the verb be, therapeuterized?"

"Yeah, I think grammatically that's called verbification."

"Oh, shut up," she said, laughing.

"This therapist volunteers for an extended session, doctor."

She said, "I have a brazen-hussy request."

"That sounds inviting."

"How about dinner Saturday night? My place at eight."

"Thanks. I'll be there. In the meantime, I better start practicing."

"What?"

"Riding a bicycle."

The dinner had gone well. Brian dutifully praised Jaye's cooking, and she was delighted with the wine he brought. There was a feeling in the room—not exactly of tension, but an air of uncertainty on the part of each: Where is this going, and do I want to make the trip?

Excusing herself, Jaye stared into the bathroom mirror. She said to herself— I've accustomed myself to live without a man's presence, a man's voice, a man's touch. What would he demand of me, and even if I chose him, could I—would I— give it?

Inside her brain, the spurned-wife chemistry boiled: the memory of the pain, the scars of loss and disappointment, and the hurt of rejection. Those misgivings were counterbalanced by the need to be wanted, intensified by the arousal of desire. She stood rooted in indecision.

Decide, damn it, she demanded of herself. She closed her eyes and listened to her doubts. She weighed them against the hunger that surged through her and made her shiver.

Jaye slowly walked back toward the living room. In the few feet to the couch where Brian waited, she would have to decide.

Silently she took his hand and led the way to her bedroom. She lit candles and stood before him, and began to undress. Without taking his eyes off her, he began to fumble with his own clothes. She seemed shy but also mature, as though to say, I don't do this lightly, but I'm not afraid of it.

Brian watched her full breasts swing as she leaned over to turn down the bed and felt himself grow hard.

In bed, they kissed tenderly, then passionately, as they felt the stirrings in each other. Jaye guided him atop her and close to the moment they both wanted.

Then it happened. Brian felt his erection fade like a dream from his memory. At first, his limp penis surprised him, then that feeling turned to shock and embarrassment as he felt Jaye grasp him and also react with surprise.

"I—this has never happened before."

Jaye smiled gently and pushed him back against the pillow. Her head disappeared, and he felt her massaging him, trying to restore what she had a right to expect.

Nothing she did helped. No matter how he fantasized, concentrated, and tried to respond to her urgings, it was dead, dead, dead.

"Jaye, please believe me, it's not you." He looked at her body and sighed, "My God, it could never be you." He rolled over, raised himself on his elbows, and stared sadly at the headboard. "This has never happened to me before. I feel like—like… God, how embarrassing!"

She rubbed his back softly. "I understand. I hope you believe that I do understand. The truth is, I respect you more because it wasn't easy for you. I wouldn't want a man who could waltz away from a marriage with no emotional turmoil. I think you're terrific."

He turned to face her. "I want you to know that I do desire you. A lot. I, well…damn."

She kissed him on the cheek, and he said, "I can still do something for you."

She shook her head. "That would be admitting we have to settle for less. Our time will come. In the meantime, come over here."

They lay together languidly, sipping wine, cuddling, and nuzzling, and listening to Mozart's Piano Concerto Number twenty-one, a CD that she had recently bought. All of a sudden, Jaye gave a play shriek and rustled under the sheet. "Do you have a gun, or are you glad to see me?"

Brian threw back the sheet to reveal a proud erection, an almost arrogant erection. "Anything to please a lady."

She playfully clasped her hands together. "Is that for meeee?"

"As much as you want."

"I'll take it all."

They made love, not sex-starved, but languidly, as friends, mutual admirers, and grateful for the pleasure of each other's company.

At the end, Brian cupped her face in his hands and said, "You have quickly become my dear friend, and I welcome you into my heart."

She hugged him. "And I welcome you into mine."

Chapter Thirteen

Potter felt miserable, like a kid who had accidentally killed a robin with a rock. The way he had let Burton force him into mistreating Jaye Peoria had seemed unavoidable at the time, but as he sat and thought about it, shame chewed at him like a July chigger.

For an old Marine like Potter, the code of obedience and loyalty was everything. It was his justification for having to do a lot of nasty things. Potter didn't emerge from the Corps after three enlistments without having that stamped on his brain like a shore-leave tattoo.

He poured another Jack Daniels and looked at the hockey game on TV without seeing it. True, the idea of women cops once roiled in his gut like a spoiled sausage, but, to be fair, Peoria had worked hard, and she was smart and gutsy. She kept her end of the deal. What it came down to was that Burton didn't like her because he wanted to move his own favorite into homicide, and Potter was his subordinate. Orders were orders. But—and he had to think about this, too—the department had told him to turn her into a homicide detective, and he didn't fail. So what should be his guide? The brass' orders or the squad assigned to him?

He looked around at his cluttered one-bedroom bachelor pad and then studied the brown liquid in his glass. Was this what life came down to, getting a snoot-full alone in a walk-up apartment and quibbling with his conscience? If he had to live in a twelve-hundred-per-month stucco rabbit warren with a pool and game room, he could at least ask himself what was the purpose of it all.

Potter's family consisted of a woman on the floor above who liked to party and occasionally invited him up and some nice-enough fellows who would sit at the bar with him and watch whatever sport was showing, like kids at a cartoon festival. As an antidote for loneliness, the whole bunch of them were no more than a Band-Aid for a snakebite.

He wasn't bitter because he didn't know many people who were better off. He was just mystified because it seemed as though there should have been more to it this life.

Despite his bluster, Potter was by nature a go-along, get-along guy; a little insecure, okay? He could think of only three or four times in his life when he had taken a stand against the code and had done something because he thought it was right, despite regs. He remembered the feeling he got from doing it was almost giddiness, like a child who had done something well that an adult believed he couldn't. He asked himself, why so few times?

He took a long sip and said to himself— You're not an eighteen-year-old recruit anymore. Are you going to knuckle under to that conniving jerk Burton just because he's got some rank, or are you going to do what the mother-lovin' people of San Diego pay you for?

Potter put down the glass and turned off the TV. He picked up the phone and dialed a number he knew well. "Deputy Chief Will Davis, please," he said to the switchboard operator. After a moment's wait, he said, "This is Sergeant Dave Potter, homicide. I'd like to see Chief Davis as soon as possible."

Will Davis leaned back in his chair and smiled at the man he had known for more than twenty years. "You're looking well, John," he said to Captain Burton. "Thanks for coming by."

"Good to see you, too, Will. Been a long time," Burton said and dropped comfortably into a nearby chair.

The two veteran cops exchanged whatever-happened-to's and a few stories about the early days, then Davis said, "John, I've got some good news for you. We figure you've spent enough time on the front lines." He gave his most concerned smile. "John, we need your help, a job we think you'd be bang-up in." Davis paused and took a breath. "Cerrullo in records is retiring, so we're transferring you over to take his place."

Burton's face went ashen. "Cerrullo? Records? Why, that's nothing but a bone yard. Cerrullo was sent there after he screwed up that big arson case. You've got to be joking."

Davis smiled easily. "You're being silly, John. It's an import-ant job. Every branch of this department depends in one way or another on records."

"Don't bullshit me. That's a kiss-off job, and you know it. I don't know a damned thing about records. … What'd I do wrong?"

Davis ignored the question. His attitude became cooler, more businesslike. "Records runs itself. There're plenty of people over there who know what to do."

"If I refuse to go?"

"You mean resign? That'd be foolish with just two years left for your pension, but it's up to you."

His lack of leverage was sinking in, and Burton nervously ran his fingers around the arm of the chair. "I'm not a man to plead, Will, but I'm asking you, I'm saying, please let me finish in operations, not in a job that everyone knows is for fuck-ups. I'm asking that of you for the old days."

"The old days are over, John. The department is changing, and smart guys learn to go with the flow. Modernize, and update the old ideas. You bend, or you break." He shook his head, solemnly but firmly. "See it as a challenge, John."

"What did I do to make you do this to me?" Burton asked bitterly.

"You're not accused of anything. If you were, you'd know it by now."

"I get it. You're dumping me, but you don't have the guts to say why."

Davis' face reddened. "Don't push."

"Why shouldn't I? You're pushing me. If I'm going to be stabbed, I don't want it in the back."

"Okay, here it is, right to your face. If you insist, we're pre-pared to bring charges of sex discrimination for your treatment of a woman homicide detective, Jaye Peoria. You ran her off her assignment and out of homicide."

"Ran her off? Discrimination? She was promoted to juvenile, for God's sake."

Davis made a face. "Bullshit."

"She was incompetent. You have to trust me on that."

"Under other circumstances, I might. But her record says otherwise. She's a good cop."

"I stand by my actions," Burton said stubbornly.

"If that's what you want, you'll have your chance. I'll prepare charges and have the papers delivered to you. It'll be the department's first sex discrimination case in eight years, so there'll be a lot of interest." He leaned forward and studied Burton impassively. "Seems a funny way to end a career, but the choice is yours."

"So one broad complains, and this is what happens to me."

"She didn't say a word."

"Then who was the Judas?"

"If you need a villain, try the mirror."

Burton knew he was beaten. "I'll take your damned transfer, Davis, but never call me friend again."

"I'm sorry for that, John because you have been a friend."

Burton spun on his heel and walked out without another word and with his back stiffly arched.

Davis stared sadly at the door for a long moment, allowing himself to remember when the two were young together. He picked up the phone and said, "Please ask Jaye Peoria in juvenile to come see me this afternoon."

She sat tensely before the big desk, wondering—Now what?

Davis finished his phone call. "I apologize. I had to take that. Uh, detective, let me get right to the point. I hope you don't mind going back to homicide. We think we need you there more than in juvenile. Of course, you'll keep your merit increase." Davis said it coaxingly, as though she had to be persuaded.

"Mind? No way." Jaye savored it like a bon-bon. "Do I get my old caseload back?"

Davis smiled. "That's up to Sergeant Potter, but since he asked for you back, I'm sure you can come to a meeting of the minds."

Jaye was surprised. "Huh?"

"It was his request."

"How will this look, sir? Out of homicide, then, presto! Right back in."

"It'll look like what it is. No one is fooled by what happened to you. They'll be happy to see the department righting a wrong. We'll just tell the press, if they ask, which I doubt, that staffing pressures delayed your promotion, then it'll be forgotten. A little white lie."

Jaye sensed by Davis' glances at the door that the interview was over. "Well, I guess I better get started. Is that all, sir?"

When Jaye reported back to homicide the next morning, people throughout the unit rose one after another and clapped softly as she walked by. She blushed, blew kisses, and hoped her tears weren't noticed. Out of the corner of her eye, she saw Potter at his desk looking at papers, but she knew he was pretending. She walked to his office door and stood there until he looked up. She simply said, "Thank you, Sarge. I'd kiss you if you were better looking."

He smiled and said, "You've got your caseload to tend to." He went back to his reading. She went to her desk, picked up where she left off and asked for a meeting to discuss evidence.

Later, as the meeting broke up, Potter and Almaguer huddled in Potter's cubicle, and Baker left for a meeting at the DA's. Tatum and Jaye walked to their desks on the far side of the squad area. Tatum looked around, and, seeing no one, asked in a low voice: "Tonight? The Voyager?"

She also looked around, then turned to him and said, "Afraid not, lover. It's over. I met a guy. I want to give it a chance. You and I are back to being just pals."

He pursed his lips and looked down at her. "Not one for the road, huh?"

She smiled. "You wouldn't want me fantasizing about him while you performed, would you?"

He grinned. "My ego—and something else—wouldn't stand for that."

"You just better not say 'easy come, easy go.' Remember, I'm armed." She took his hand and slipped something into it. "Here's a parting gift." He opened his hand to see a packaged condom. "That's one left over," she said, "don't waste it."

They both laughed. "Smart ass. That's cold," he said.

Two days later, Potter came up to Jaye and said, "Deputy Chief Davis wants to see us. Right now."

After motioning them to chairs in front of his desk, Davis said, "Yesterday, the chief of police and I met with the mayor. As you know, he's prone to nervousness. He's fidgety about the fuss kicked by these Dark Street Assassin stories I think you've heard of." He glanced at Jaye and smiled. "Thank God those stories have quieted down. At least they're off the front page, and TV has moved on."

Davis continued, "We talked about putting together a task force on this. We decided not to for the time being. Here's our reasoning: For one thing, there have been only two murders." He paused. "Pardon me for saying 'only,' but the two murders might possibly—repeat, possibly—not be the action of one man. We don't know. Also, the accepted definition of a serial killer is three murders. We're one short, thank God. On top of that, task forces have a mixed record. In some cases, it's been investigators falling all over each other and quibbling over power trips. Anyway, we're going to hold off on that."

He turned to Potter. "Dave, you've been close enough to these crimes that you've already hit the ground running. I want you to stay in charge, and I want you to consider this your personal mission. Start with adding a veteran detective to work with Peoria here, both for extra legs and for appearances." He looked at Jaye. "Peoria, do you understand the why of that? You're still pretty green."

"Totally, sir."

Potter said, "I've already added a man, sir."

"Great. Call for as many uniforms as you need when you need them."

Jaye raised her hand slightly for attention. "Am I still lead on this?"

Davis looked at Potter. "Of course," Potter said. "Why wouldn't you be?"

Davis gave a dismissive look. I'll personally expect a progress report from you weekly until this bastard—or bastards—is dead or locked up.

"That's settled." Davis gave his you're-dismissed look.

Potter wanted to end the meeting with a light touch: "Do we get a reward when we solve this?"

Davis said, "Yeah, your reward will be you won't be transferred to the graveyard patrol shift down on the border. How's that for an incentive?" But because Jaye was sitting there wide-eyed, he added, "A joke. Potter here, and I go back."

The phone interrupted her review of the Jane Doe case notes. "Good morning, this is Detective Peoria." She always tried to make her phone manner friendlier than most cops'.

"This is Detective Lou Battino, Portsmouth, New Hampshire. Good morning to you. Uh, you had inquired some time back about one Lanny Pease, aka Lewis Price. In reading his file, I saw that you were told he was a rape suspect in Portsmouth the first week of November of last year." He paused, and Jaye heard papers rustle. "Well, I wanted to let you know we've learned his sighting at that time was a false report. We're satisfied he wasn't in this area at that time and hasn't been since."

"Any idea where he was?" Jaye asked.

"No idea. He could have been in San Diego for all we know. That's why I called."

"I appreciate that. I'd like to ask you something, Lou. How well do you know this Pease/Price guy?"

He laughed. "Brother Pease and I have had a close relationship. We know each other well, better than he would prefer."

"Do you think he's capable of murder? Of strangling women?"

The phone grew silent as he pondered. "I don't know. But I do know he wouldn't lose any sleep over it if he did."

"Thanks a lot, paisano." She used an Italian familiarity. "If I find him, I'll send him back to you as a gift when we're done with him."

"Don't do me any favors, paisana."

She leaned back in her chair and thought—Welcome back to the game, Lanny/Lewis.

She learned he had been released on his OR without posting bond from jail on the aggravated assault charge—How the hell did that happen? Jaye learned he had subsequently not shown up for a court date in December and now had a warrant issued for his arrest.

She went online to the "officer notification" website to put out a bulletin asking to be notified if he was picked up. She also walked down the hall to the patrol lieutenant and asked if he would personally put the word out that the stakes had now been raised from aggravated assault to suspicion of murder. He said he would have officers look in all the familiar places that would play host to men like Price.

First thing the next morning, Potter called Jaye and Tatum into his cubicle and closed the door. Oh-oh, each thought, a closed door. Potter leaned back in his swivel chair. "We've had a break about that anonymous letter you received, Jaye. We've identified the mysterious DNA on the paper."

Both were wide-eyed with curiosity. "Whose?" Jaye asked.

Potter's eyes swung between each but rested on Tatum. "The DNA belonged to Drew Tatum."

Each detective stared at the other, then at Potter. "What the hell?" Tatum said.

"The lab ran a bunch of routine tests through the department database and inadvertently included department employees, and *voila!* There it was."

Jaye's recall of receiving the letter kicked in, and her look was of exasperation. "I *told* you not to touch it."

He shook his head, shame-faced. "I didn't think I did."

"Well, apparently, you did," Potter said.

"You jerk," Jaye said, exasperated, but not angry. "Look at all the grief you caused me."

Tatum shrugged his shoulders. "Sorry."

"That's not all," Potter said. He was starting to enjoy this. "Tatum, you have to take a polygraph."

"What the hell are you talking about?"

"Department regs," Potter said, then smiled thinly, "which both of you know I'm an expert at the application of same. Anyway, the letter is considered a terrorist threat, and after 9-1-1, that's a serious matter. And since Tatum is not specifically involved in that case, he had no plausible reason for his DNA to be there, especially since he denied touching the letter."

"That's bullshit, Sarge," Tatum protested.

"Well, look at it from the department's viewpoint. You two might be having an affair, and the letter was a lover's revenge. Who knows?"

Jaye and Tatum stared straight ahead, not looking at each other, barely breathing.

"Anyway, it's also a CYA thing. Plus, we don't want rumors to start flying."

Jaye started giggling. "I love it. Maybe he *is* the real killer. I can involve the whole department; maybe sell chances for questions for the lie test. I could make some real money. We'll call it the Poly Fair."

"It's not funny," Tatum said.

"It's set up for tomorrow afternoon. You be here, Tatum."

All three stood up. "I don't want this to get around," Tatum said. But it did, of course. It was the cause of considerable hilarity. Frog down at the 10-7 even created a new drink called Truth Serum. It was made with cheap champagne and costly Drambuie. Might as well make a buck off Tatum's embarrassment.

When Tatum returned to homicide after passing his lie test, detectives had chipped in for a large flat cake that had written on it— 'We Don't Believe It.'

The search for Lewis Price had come up empty until a patrol officer named Tony Jefferson called and told her he had talked to a snitch who said he knew Price's whereabouts. He gave Jaye the fellow's contact information with the admonition to keep the snitch's identity a secret.

Jaye happily agreed and, the next morning, was dressed in what increasingly was her work outfit of a blouse and blue jeans.

No purse, minimal cosmetics. A light shirt-jacket partially concealed her firearm. For this snitch contact, she removed the pistol from her belt and put it in a waist pack. She drove to Hillcrest, the nominally gay quarter near downtown, and walked down an alley to an open area behind Whole Foods. She was to meet the snitch named Cottonmouth by the dumpster.

Cottonmouth—or 'Cottonmouf,' as he pronounced it—was a spindly black man of indeterminate age and needle tracks on his arms that showed where he invested his snitch money.

Without introduction, she said, "I'm looking for Lewis Price."

Cottonmouth wasn't going to sell his information easily. "I know where he's at. I want 100 dollars."

"In your dreams," she said. "Twenty, which is a good deal, provided you don't have any better offers." She was prepared for this, took a twenty from her pocket, and showed it to him. "This'll give you pleasant dreams tonight."

"How about tomorrow night, too?"

She pulled another twenty-dollar bill from her pocket. "This is it. Now, where is Price."

He reached for the two bills, but she pulled them back. "You know I'll deliver, but I'm not sure you will." Cottonmouth was fidgety. She knew he was hurting for a fix. That gave her a huge edge.

"Maybe a month ago, something like that, he said he was going to Phoenix to mule back some smack for one of the dealers downtown. I ain't seen or heard from him since."

"That it?"

"Why'd I hold back on you?" he said in a whine, eyeing the bills in her hand.

She gave him the money. "Okay, but your rep with the department is on the line, you know that."

She spoke to his back because he was already ten feet down the alley.

Jaye returned to headquarters and phoned a Phoenix detective she had met at a cops' rugby tournament when she first transferred into homicide. His name was Hector Munoz. After some brief catch-up chatter, she asked for help in locating Price/Pease.

"He's a bit of a snake," she said, "so he might have already slithered away. I'll email his ID info to you in about five minutes."

"The name has a ring to it. Let me get back to you."

Within the hour, Munoz was on the phone. "I've located your man, Pease, for you, Jaye."

"Great. Where's he at?"

"We've got him in custody, you might say. You're welcome to him."

"Well, of course, extradition…"

"No extradition necessary for a corpse. It seems the ambitious Mr. Pease tried running in a faster company than he could keep up with. He was screwing around with a cartel on drug sales, and the cartel, in turn, screwed around with him—using a screwdriver… Do you want his body?"

"Naw. Thanks, Hector. It's all yours."

The date Munoz gave her for Pease's demise was two days before Lila Brown was murdered. That didn't entirely remove him from suspicion of the Willows murder, but Price/Pease was not a serial killer, at least not in San Diego.

❧

Jaye laid out her papers before Potter like a winning poker hand. "I have the lab reports on the things I found in the La Brava Restaurant." She picked up a sheet. "The tablets that looked like aspirin? Guess what? They were lithium. To be specific, they were 450 mg of lithium carbonate."

"The stuff crazy people take, eh," Potter said.

"Actually, it's an antipsychotic agent for bipolar disorders," she said, teasing him with her new-found internet knowledge. "But we obviously don't know if the pills are connected to the killer. They were not the victims. Lithium was not in her system. However, the pills were shiny and clean, not dirty as you would expect on a floor for any time at all, and they were right under her body or within the chalk outline when I saw them. They were easy for the CSI to overlook. I don't want to make an issue of it. That place was as messy as a teenager's bedroom. They also checked the hypodermic syringes for prints. They'd been handled by more people than an airport doorknob."

"Jesus, I'll never get used to human stupidity," Potter said with a frown. "Sharing a needle is like lining up to die. If I ever get AIDS, I want it to be from sex."

"From what I've seen in this town, that's an available option."

"And about that lithium," Potter said, followed by an unimpressed grunt. "Considering the part of town and the number of wackadoodles hanging around that empty building, you might as well have found popcorn in a movie theater. I mean, you don't even know if the stuff was connected to the crime, and even if it was, can you guess how many people in that neighborhood alone take lithium?"

Jaye nodded. "I know all that, but someone dropped those tablets at the murder scene, and we know it wasn't the victim. It might have been the person we're looking for."

Potter moved on. "Anything develop on the citizen phone-ins the media's been promoting?"

"Art says nothing so far. It's been like trying to step on a shadow. Bunch of ex-wives and pissed-off neighbors turning-in people they love to hate," she said.

"What else do you have working?"

"We're looking at accessibility."

"Huh?"

"I read an FBI research paper that gave statistics that hypothesized that serial killers most often operate close to where they live or work."

"Hypothesized? Is that a word?"

"I'm proud to say it is," she said. "I could have said 'guessed,' but I wanted to impress you, Sarge."

"You frighten me."

"Moving right along," Jaye said. "The article said to look for likely types in the immediate area of the killings. So, a few days ago, I asked Art to canvass businesses in that area looking for employees with suspicious backgrounds. Nothing yet."

Potter rolled his eyes. "Well, I never had the FBI tell me how to do my job, so all I can say is just keep humping and hope for a break." Potter made restless moves and looked at his watch. "Speaking of breaks, I've got to help break in a new captain.

Captain Burton is transferring." He flashed an 'our-secret' grin at Jaye.

Jaye rose to leave, but as she approached the door, Potter cleared his throat and said, "By the way, it's good to have you back."

Jaye turned and smiled. "It's like I was never away." She hesitated. She wasn't good at this. "Uh, Dave, I'm sorry for the nasty things I said to you. It was the hurt talking."

He grinned. "Hah! That was nothing. You should have heard what a dame said to me Saturday night. What you said was like a lullaby." He put the humor aside. "But thanks. It's cool. Totally cool." This time, he hesitated. He wasn't good at this either. "All I remember is your comment about hassling Baker. You were right. You caused me to look in the mirror—Jaye." A cross look came over his face. "Damnit, go back to work, Peoria."

Potter called his detectives together and said, "All right, you studs and damsel—"

Jaye made a face and shook her head. "Jeeez, Sarge!"

"I'll bet I could earn a reward from HR for reporting that," Tatum said.

"Peoria here has put together a profile of our serial killer if that's what he is. I think she makes a lot of sense. Peoria, tell us what you got."

Jaye scooted her chair around so she was facing the four others. "Okay, guys. Here's what's happening. Art's continually talking to the FBI, and also to patrol cops in case they hit upon a suspect or helpful intelligence." She turned to Baker. "Art, anything to add to that?" Baker shook his head, and Jaye continued, "I'm doing a second go-around on the persons of interest I interviewed when all this started." Here's my guesstimate:

"I think he's under forty. An older man would be uncertain of the physical demands of strangulation.

"He's motivated, not by sex—there is no molestation of his victims—but by anger and the need to dominate and control. Both things tie to his method. Strangulation is an act of anger and domination, and interestingly, it's the most common form of murder for serial killers.

"People go overboard in labeling serial killers 'crazy.' Obviously, he has a sick soul and a major thinking aberration, but in most areas of his life, he's in a normal range. He could be anyone, even a detective." She stopped and looked at her colleagues. "Probably a detective."

Tatum pointed at Almaguer. They laughed, and she continued. "I think he's pretty well educated or at least bright—"

Tatum interrupted. "I withdraw my comment. It's obviously not Ignacio."

"Quiet," Almaguer said. "This is for the movie."

Jaye frowned, then continued. "He plans. He's not impulsive. All his crime scenes are in public places, but done when it's super safe from witnesses. He knows how to keep the killing areas evidence-free. He is not going to be some half-wit running around the homeless shelters on Imperial Avenue.

"One thing especially intrigues me. Why does he kill in the early morning hours? There's a danger in being the only one on the street at that hour. You stand out. I seriously doubt he's married because he would have to account for his weird hours to a wife. You can only sneak out of the house so many times. Maybe he has insomnia, and that's the only way he can get back to sleep. Maybe that's when he gets off work and does it on the way home."

"His choice of victims seems to be determined by their vulnerability and his opportunity to escape. He chooses homeless women because they're old, weak and alone. He's opportunistic and doesn't target a particular race or group; they are random: an older white woman, a young addict-hooker, and, I personally believe, an older black woman, Lila Brown. Once he kills, he walks away. He doesn't 'display' his victims. They are of no further use. Nothing personal, my dear. That's part of the signature.

"He prefers to live in the shadows, not as a creep, but as someone easy to ignore. He probably falls in the category of antisocial personality disorder. Without question, he's a psychopath. He has no concept of the pain of others. If you spent any time with him, he wouldn't be alarming, but he might make you ill at ease—like, this guy is a few degrees off true north.

"You've been doing some reading," Almaguer said.

"That's a good habit to develop, Ignacio," she said and waited for the snickers to fade. "Taken on balance, he's a pretty average, run-of-the-mill serial killer."

Almaguer said, "Well, from what you describe, we can narrow the suspects down to fifty thousand guys in San Diego."

"All we have to do is divvy them up. Twelve thousand apiece," Tatum said.

Potter frowned at the two jokesters. "Good job, Peoria. The more we get a sense of this guy, the more it becomes a real manhunt. My hunch is we're close enough that if the killer had heard this, it would make him nervous. I hope we get a chance to discuss it with him real soon."

"One final thing," Jaye said. "As they say on TV, full disclosure—everything I just said could be dead wrong."

Almaguer said, "Don't worry, we already had that in mind."

The meeting broke up in peals of laughter. A few minutes later, Almaguer walked over to Jaye's desk. "Great job. We've all got your back."

She smiled and shook her head hopelessly. "You guys…"

Chapter Fourteen

She had just settled at her own desk when Steve Ellski, a detective from sex crimes, approached. He was an easy-going veteran of twenty-some years who had discovered that if one moves with the flow, ulcers tend to relax and enjoy the ride. He was balding, pudgy, and his dry humor belied his manner. His quiet, shortcut-seeking competence had always impressed Jaye because he made a lot of arrests that stuck.

"Hi, Jaye, I've got something for you. I may have found a candidate for your suspects' club." He took out a small notebook. "Name's Sammy Clark, age twenty-three, works at that Chevron station out by the stadium. We pay him a visit occasionally, just to stay in touch."

"What about him, Steve?"

"For openers, he's been seen wienie wagging. The woman who reported it wouldn't press charges, but she ID'd him. When you see him, you'll understand why it's hard to mistake my man Sam for anyone else. He was kicked out of high school for what they called unacceptable conduct, but a cop who patrols the corridors—it was a tough school—said the guy wouldn't stop bothering girls. Nothing violent just had a lot of intimate thoughts he wanted to share with the young ladies."

"How about violence?"

Ellski thumbed through the papers. "Last year, he was identified and arrested for a rape in Fresno. There was serious choking involved. Didn't go to trial, but that doesn't mean he didn't do it. As you know, victims get cold feet.

"The reason he blips on our radar is he's a perpetual nuisance at the strip clubs. A couple of the girls complained that he's threatened them. Nothing to get him arrested for—yet. But he's on our watch list."

Jaye thanked him and said, "I haven't seen anything to suggest our killer is also a rapist, but there's always a chance he's gotten ambitious. Did you get prints and DNA on the Fresno case?"

"I did. No other hits on either."

"I'm surprised, from what you tell me."

"He's young. Give him a chance. Here's something else, and this is pretty weird," Ellski said. "When fun-loving Sammy was in high school, also in Fresno, he was arrested for torturing neighborhood cats. According to the animal control report, he had a regular animal dungeon in his garage. He even burned a Siamese. He was let off, provided he saw a shrink regularly."

"How would you describe him?"

"He's a scrawny little black guy with a grotesque, scarred face. His sister once got pissed and threw lye in his kisser. Looks like he fell face-first into a hot skillet. Nice family."

Jaye pursed her lips and thought out loud. "A woman disfigured him. Think that's reason to hate women enough to kill?"

"Don't know, never had lye thrown in my face," Ellski said with a chuckle. "Don Juan, he obviously ain't. Oh, and he lives on Imperial Avenue."

Jaye pushed a desk drawer shut and reached for her handbag. "I owe you one, Steve. Think I'll go get some gas."

Jaye stopped a few blocks away to phone the station and ask for Sammy Clark. When the man answering summoned him in a loud voice, Jaye disconnected. Within three minutes, she pulled into the station and stopped at the full-service island close to the work bay. A courteous young man approached and was told to fill it up and check under the hood. Jaye turned up the police radio and rolled down the window of the unmarked car so it could be heard inside the station.

The attendant, impressed, watched her as he pumped the gas. "You a police officer, ma'am?"

Jaye turned down the radio and left the car to stand by him while he checked the oil. "Yeah, I'm working those East Village killings. Have you heard any talk about them?"

The attendant, delighted at the invitation to be involved, said, "Yeah, ever since the newspaper did that big story. Do you think you'll get the guy?"

Jaye looked over the hood of the car and saw a man she

recognized as Sammy Clark watching from the nearby car-wash area. The lye-scars on his face looked as though a spider web had festered under the skin. Their eyes locked, and Jaye directed a brainwave toward the young black with the scrambled-egg face: Think about it and squirm sucker.

In a moment, he shifted his eyes and turned away. She returned to the attendant's question. "Will we solve it? You never know until the jury says guilty, but I can tell you this: We've got a suspect we're watching. We're closing in on him." Jaye gave the man her city gas credit card and drove away, certain that as she did, the attendant was repeating everything she said to his co-workers, including Sammy Clark. The bait was wiggling in the water.

Standing in the car wash bay, Sammy listened with trepidation to what Eddie said about his conversation with the lady cop. All cops made Sammy nervous. But he was interested in what she said about the East Village killings. Sammy had read every story about them and memorized the details. He had a professional interest in brutal crimes.

Jaye asked the patrol sergeant to have some of his black and whites drive slowly by each day and eyeball Sammy. Twice in the next few days, Jaye borrowed squad cars that needed gassing and stopped at the station, each time making a splashy display of her police persona and talking to attendants other than Sammy Clark about the case and how police were closing in on the unnamed suspect. When Sammy waited on her, she sat stonily silent behind the wheel and never took her baleful stare off him. He seemed nervous and would not look her in the eye. Finally, she decided he was spooked enough to turn the screws a little. On another visit, she spotted him across the station lot and yelled, "Hey, you." When he turned, she waved him over in a demanding manner. When he scurried over, she said, "Check my oil, will you?" Without taking his eyes off her, Clark reached down with his left hand and pulled the dipstick.

Left-handed. Love it, Jaye thought. "You're Sammy Clark, right?"

He reacted like the dipstick was a snake and pulled back from under the hood so fast he banged his head. "How you know that?"

"We know a lot of things, Sammy, and we're learning more all the time."

"I didn't do nothing wrong." Sweat glistened as it ran down his face, and his hands shook like a palsied old man's.

Jaye thought of a variety of ominous retorts but decided a steely-eyed silence was most effective. Tatum, sitting in the front seat, pitched-in with a glare of his own from behind the windshield. Sammy backed away to escape the scrutiny and started for the station almost at a trot.

"Hey!" Jaye shouted. He stopped as though stuck in wet tar and slowly swiveled his head back toward her.

"How about the oil?"

"It—it's o—kay."

As soon as she pulled away and turned a corner, Tatum broke up. Finally, he took a deep breath. "'How about the oil?' God, that was funny. He's changing his pants right now."

"He's a scumbag. Can you imagine torturing a cat? I had a Siamese once."

"Not to mention human women. Do you have the scent?" Tatum asked.

Jaye signaled to turn into the headquarters lot and talked while studying the side mirror. "He fits the signs: Background, opportunity, and he sure as hell acts guilty."

"What's next?" Tatum asked, and Jaye felt a tingle of pride that this respected colleague was interested in her judgment.

"Oh, I didn't tell you: his prints are arch pattern. It's game on until I learn otherwise."

Tatum leaned back in the passenger's seat and laughed softly. "Man, you can sure come on as one super bitch."

"Why, Drew, what a sweet thing to say."

A patrolman walking a handcuffed prisoner looked over in surprise as the two detectives burst into loud laughter.

Later that day, Jaye walked into the cafeteria and noticed Mike Palmer sitting alone with a cup of coffee. She stopped and stood by his table. "Well, hello, Mike."

He looked up and smiled. "Hey, Jaye, great to see you. You're looking terrific."

"You too, Mike." Unable to think of anything else to say for a long moment, she said, "Again, I want to thank you for your help on my cases."

"Anything new?"

"She smiled and shrugged. "Same old rat race. I just haven't been able to catch up with the rat yet."

"You will. Listen, this'll probably be the last time I see you."

Jaye's brow furrowed. "Oh? Is anything wrong?"

"No, but I'm leaving the department. Going to work for my father-in-law in Kansas." He said "Kansas" as though it were on Mars.

"Really?" Remembering how much he said he liked his work, Jaye looked at him closely. "Won't you miss this?"

He gave a what-the-hell look. "I guess it's time to make some real money. That's what I'm told, anyway."

"Hey, good luck, Mike," Jaye said, extending her hand.

Palmer took it and looked as though he wanted to talk more but said, "Thanks, same to you."

At the gas station, Sammy Clark was beginning to have nightmares about the white lady cop who seemed to be always staring at him. What did she know? Was she coming for him? He was frightened, and when that happened, he had trouble thinking. Why did people constantly push him? It made him angry. It made him want to strike back, to smash…destroy.

Sammy knew torment well. Always the littlest, ugliest, and dumbest, he was forced to keep to himself and found pleasure in causing pain. He didn't know why that was, and he tried to resist, but sometimes the urge was as compelling as a magnet. He felt shamed afterward, but even then, the thrill of the memory made his breath catch in excitement.

He thought of the first time. He had found a sparrow with a broken wing flopping on the sidewalk in front of his house. He had gently picked it up with the idea of nursing it back to health, but as he stroked it, he had almost accidentally plucked one of its feathers. Curious, he pulled another. A frenzy seemed to grab him then, and he held the bird on the ground and ripped one wing off and then the other. As he watched the dying creature flop on the ground, a feeling of sexual release flooded over him and provided a feeling so good it had to be repeated.

Sammy was not cruel for cruelty's sake, he just had needs. Those needs, like a narcotic, became more and more insistent, graduating from birds and cats to the hard stuff—to people. But he was trying to quit, he truly was, harder than he had ever tried anything.

Sammy was thinking about the lady cop when he looked up from the tire he was patching to see her standing a few feet away. He dropped the tire iron in shock and jumped back. Next to her was another plainclothes cop that he'd seen with her before. The woman was talking to Sammy's boss. Sammy saw them look at him and nod, and then she started walking toward him. Two uniformed cops were standing quietly a few yards away, watching. He thought about running. He considered grabbing the tire iron and smashing her haunting face. Instead, he stood dumbly and waited.

"Sammy Clark, we'd like you to come with us if you're willing." When he didn't answer, Jaye added, "We just want to talk. We'll bring you back. Your boss says it's okay." She reached for his arm, and he meekly let her guide him to the car.

In the police station, Sammy was taken to a small green room with harsh lights, no windows, and bare, except for a steel table and several armless office chairs. The lady and the other man fired questions at him from both sides, but he refused to say a word, staring first at the woman and then the man. The man was nicer. He seemed to take Sammy's side, arguing with the woman that the whole thing was a big mistake. However, the woman kept asking mean and insistent questions. After three hours of questioning, he even bought Sammy a Big Mac and fries over the woman's protests.

She looked down at him, unmoving, like a grim marble statue. Her voice was harsh and insistent. "C'mon, Sammy. Tell us what it's like to hurt things. Is there any difference between a cat and a woman? Do they scream the same way?"

"Hey, that's not fair," the man argued. "Sammy's here to help us. You've got no call to say that."

"Bullshit," the woman said bitterly. "He knows I'm right. Don't you, Sammy? How does it feel to have a woman's throat in your hands? Would you like to curl your fingers around my throat, Sammy? How about it? Would you get off on that?" She stalked out of the room and slammed the door behind her.

The man finally told Sammy his name, Detective Tatum. He turned to Sammy and shook his head sadly. "She can be a real bitch sometimes. I wish I could get her off your case, but as long as you don't answer the questions, she's gonna be on your ass."

Tatum glanced toward the door and then leaned closer to Sammy conspiratorially. "I shouldn't say this, pal, but I don't like to see anyone get fucked-over. Anyway, I'll deny it if you tell her I said it." He glanced again toward the closed door. "She's real close to the DA. Know what I mean?" He gave a what-ya-gonna-do shrug. "If she tells him to hang your ass, he might try it. That bitch is out to make her rep off poor bastards like you. Now, if you were to tell *me* everything that's true, then this'd be my case, and I could follow it all the way through. I tell you, buddy, in a situation like this, you need someone who understands. I guarantee, man, play ball with me, tell me the truth, and I'll see that you get a fair shake. Let's start with where you were and what you were doing on these dates. We call that an alibi, and I bet you have one." Tatum again recited the dates of the Willows and Jane Doe murders.

Sammy whined his answer. "Man, I don't know. Probably nothing. Do you remember where you were?" Sammy twisted his hands. "Man, I didn't kill no bitches. Just cats and things, man."

Tatum let his hands fall in resignation. "Shit, man, I tried. If they needle your ass, my conscience will be clean."

At that moment, Jaye stalked back into the room, and Tatum broke off the conversation. He said to the woman, "Detective Peoria, could I see you? I think I found some amelioration *and* exacerbation."

When Tatum returned, he was alone. "Look, Sammy," he said. "I've got to go off shift pretty quick. This is your last chance before I have to leave you alone with her." He motioned with his thumb toward the door. "How about it? You want to tell me anything?"

Sammy put his face in his hands and wept. The tears rolled over the alligator skin of his lye burns and dripped off his hands. "Oh, man, I did it."

Tatum turned to the tape recorder and repeated Sammy's name, the date, time, and location, and that it was a confession given by free will with no coercion. "How many did you kill, Sammy?"

"Two, man. Just like you all said."

"How'd you do it?"

"I choked them."

"Why did you kill them that way?"

Sammy saw women's faces in his mind and visualized the warm, calming sensation of feeling the life slide out of them. "I wanted to watch their eyes bug out and feel them die." He closed his eyes, and the images became even clearer.

"Did you know either of them?"

"I'd just seen them around the streets."

"Were they targeted victims?"

"Huh?"

"Did you want them specifically, or were they just handy?"

"Yeah, they was just the first I saw when I got the urge."

Sammy didn't mention the use of bleach to clean up. Tatum tried to get that out of him but was careful not to lead him into an answer. Sammy divulged an incriminating knowledge of the crimes; some answers were vague, a few others wrong, but it was enough.

Listening from the adjoining room through a hidden microphone, Jaye and Potter, who had joined her, hugged each other. He punched in the air and shouted, "Son of a bitch! Congratulations, Peoria." They listened some more, and he said, "Did you hear that? The ugly little mother knows the details. Man, oh, man, we've got him. We've locked-down got him. Would you believe the old good-cop, bad-cop routine? Oldest trick in the book."

Jaye was flushed with happiness and just smiled.

Tatum wrapped-up the confession into a tidy, air-tight package of self-incrimination. Sammy was put in a cell preparatory to formal charging, and various coming and going cops celebrated after work at the 10-7, with Jaye, the recipient of most of the praise.

Speaking over the whoops, Brian raised his beer. "Here's to Ms. Sherlock Holmes of San Diego. No criminal can rest easy as long as she is on the prowl for evil-doers." The three cops sitting around the table raised their glasses in unison. Brian's presence made Tatum accept that it was a game-over between him and Jaye. But that was okay. Always a new game to play.

"Aw, shucks, fellers," Jaye said in an exaggerated drawl, "I owe it all to affirmative action, God bless it."

Later, at her place, she and Brian changed into swimsuits and slipped away to her complex's spa.

Though it was well after 10:00 P.M. and the spa was dark and supposedly closed, they slipped a few inches at a time into the steaming water, acclimating their bodies to the momentary pain of 104 degrees.

"The manager would be pissed if he knew we were in here this late," Jaye said in a hushed voice.

"Piss on the manager then," Brian stage-whispered back. "I don't ruin his fun."

He opened a bottle of champagne that they shared without glasses. The champagne was cheap, but it bubbled like Moet and tasted like Mumms. As the bottle neared empty, their mood mellowed, and their guard lowered as thoughts crept onto the tongue from their hiding place in the brain.

"Is Jaye short for another name?" he asked, sort of aimlessly.

"No, it's just Jaye. It's my middle name."

"What's your first name?"

"If I told you, I'd have to kill you," she said with an impish grin. She turned sideways to face him. "Tell me some good war stories. Isn't that why men join the Rangers, to get good war stories?"

"Ah, you don't want to hear guys' drinking stories," he said.

"Don't forget, I'm sort of a guy, what with carrying a gun

and scandalously unladylike cussing." One question at a time, she coaxed the story out of Brian that he had kept hidden from everyone else but less successfully from himself—the memory of what happened on a hot August day in Iraq. Once he started, he couldn't stop. His voice slowed and lowered, and the smile vanished from Jaye's face. He was leading her into the secret room of his truth.

As Brian started unburdening his memory, Jaye closed her eyes and positioned her mind high above the desert scene as though in a movie. As he described what happened, she closed her eyes, scripted his words, and matched them to the drama in the desert below. She needed to place herself there, to see what he saw, hear what he heard, feel what he felt. She saw the village, saw him in the hide, and could see his tension and the sweat on his face. The pleas of his men took voice. She saw things go to hell.

They were still alive by the grace of God and clever camouflage.

The powerful binoculars made the half-mile distance disappear and brought Sgt. Brian Fogarty's eyes right to the edge of a homely Iraqi town called Kahlis. Through the heat shimmers and sun glare, he could see insurgents milling around the town square, sixty or seventy of them. They loosely carried AK-47s and a few RPGs. On a white Toyota pickup, he could see a mounted light machine gun.

He lowered the binocs and wiped the stinging sweat from his eyes. He took off his helmet and wrung out his sweatband. He glanced at the thermometer hanging on the canvas wall of the hide. The mercury was already beginning a red streak upward. Ninety-six degrees and only 10:00 A.M. He expected fifteen more degrees before the day was done.

Late August in the Sunni Triangle was not the best time for an outing.

Fogarty and two others from the 75th Ranger Regiment Special Troops Battalion had been attached to the 2nd Brigade, 4th Infantry Division. They were advance scouts for a counterinsurgency raid north of Baghdad called Operation Ivy Needle.

Spc. Eddie Washington and Cpl. Mike Howard sprawled in the broiling canvas confinement in the hills facing Khalis. The hide was a tent designed to look like a rock outcropping, of which there were many nearby.

The three were parachuted in on the other side of some small hills along with two large bags of equipment. They erected their hide/tent in darkness with exacting care to make it look just right.

They were looking for the expected arrival of a bandit group operating under the umbrella of the insurgency. In reality, they were thieves and murderers preying on innocent Iraqis and the occasional American they had the opportunity to kill.

The outlaws were a mixed bag of Sunnis and Shia, derisively called "Sushi." Their leader was Latif Hamid al-Kubayshat, a murderous psychopath turned loose by Saddam Hussein. He had lain low for a year until recently, taking advantage of the chaos following the American invasion.

The U.S. Army was planning to swoop in for the raid as soon as Fogarty told them the gang had arrived as a tip had predicted.

They were now here.

Fogarty turned the watch over to Howard and flopped down on the sand, and closed his eyes. In minutes, Howard's voice woke him.

"Sarge, Sarge." The tone of it brought Fogarty instantly to the corporal's side, who handed him the binoculars. "Look, fifteen degrees left, 200 meters out."

Fogarty swung his head and saw a small dog sniffing its way in their direction, followed by a girl of about eight.

"That fucking dog is gonna find us, for sure," Howard said, shaking his head. "That'll bring the girl." He looked expectantly at Fogarty, who said nothing but kept his eyes on the dog and girl.

"We gonna take her out? She'll find us, absofuckinglutely," Washington said in a harsh whisper.

"If she sees us, we got to. No choice," Howard said, still keeping his eyes on Fogarty.

Washington said, "Could we maybe just grab and hold her?"

"That's not practical," Howard said. "Ain't no room in here. We ain't babysitters."

"Let's cool if for the moment," Fogarty said. "We don't know what's happening."

"We gotta make a plan, Sarge," Howard said. "If it happens, I say we got to do it. We gotta think of the mission."

Kneeling behind them, Washington said, "Me, too. No choice."

Fogarty didn't lower the binoculars. "Let me think."

"About what?" Howard challenged. We—have—no—choice!"

Fogarty could feel Washington nodding behind him. "I vote with Mike."

He turned to face both of them. "There's no vote. It's my call. My job."

"If she finds us, I can pull her in and do the job," Howard said. Then he shuddered and whispered to himself. "My God. What a nightmare."

Fogarty saw the girl trying to keep up with the dog about fifty meters distant.

He turned to both men. "If we kill her, she'll be missed, and they'll start searching."

"But not right away," Washington said.

"We don't know that."

"If we let her go, she'll bring the whole mob down on us," Howard said.

Fogarty shook his head. "We don't know that either. We don't know if she'll say anything. We don't know if she'd be believed."

Howard spoke in an even voice. "Brian, you're responsible for the mission. You're responsible for three lives. You know what has to be done." He took out his knife.

Fogarty turned back to the small opening to see the panting face of a yellow mongrel. Ten meters back was the girl looking curiously at the tent that, up close, was obviously not made of rock.

Howard tensed and edged forward. In moments, the three men saw a pretty, young, brown face with black eyes wide with fear.

Howard lunged. Fogarty threw his arm out, disregarding the knife. "Let her go," he shouted. "That's an order."

Howard stared at him. Washington shook his head.

The girl screamed and turned and ran for home.

For an hour, the men waited and hoped that was the end of it.

Suddenly, Fogarty saw movement that slowly emerged as a skirmish line of about fifty men walked toward them, slowly getting larger. He picked up the radio and shouted into it, that converted his words into an encoded burst.

"Extract now. Extract now. Under direct attack. I repeat. Extract now. Direct attack."

The three grabbed the radio and water jugs, then checked their weapons. Fogarty and Howard had M-16 rifles, Washington a SAW light machine gun. They grabbed all the ammunition they could handle and scrambled out of the tent and behind what scant cover they could find.

The Iraqis had grown to twice the size and coming closer, still at a slow walk, uncertain if what the girl said was true.

Fogarty called out. "We don't have much ammo. Open fire at 100 meters." He again radioed his plea and waited. But not for long. He shouted over to his two men: "They're coming. Hold on."

An RPG round exploded the abandoned hide. Scraps of canvas, MRE meals, rocks, and sand flew high in the air.

The bullets came. The "crack, crack" around the men's heads reminded them that death was nearer than rescue. They kept up a measured fire, not knowing how long their limited ammunition would have to last.

The insurgents attacking them, however, were unaccustomed to their targets fighting back, especially with the accuracy of these three as they saw several of their comrades clumped among the weeds and sand. Their firing slowed and lost accuracy as they quickly shot and ducked.

After a half-hour, Fogarty heard the clump-clump of approaching helicopters. Emerging over a rise was an Apache attack chopper whose Gatling gun sent the insurgents scurrying for cover that didn't exist. A Black Hawk settled a short distance away.

Fogarty grabbed his rifle and radio and started for safety at a hunched-over run. He saw Washington doing the same, but

Howard wasn't moving. Fogarty stopped and ran to the corporal. He saw he had been gut-shot and was barely conscious. With the help of crewmen, they got Howard onto the floor of the Black Hawk and swooped into the air.

There was no medic on the flight, so Fogarty could only grasp Howard's hand and try to talk him into holding on. Finally, a half-conscious Howard looked up at Fogarty and said only three faltering words before fading out: "You were wrong."

❧

Fogarty jumped to attention as the colonel entered the room and sat behind his desk. His body language made it clear this was going to be quick and final. "Sergeant Fogarty, I've read your report on the incident on the Kahlis operation and the death of Corporal Howard. I've also interviewed Specialist Washington. I'm confident I have a clear picture of what happened.

"The issue is whether your actions were correct in letting the young female escape or should you have terminated her to save your command."

"With all respect, sir, we don't terminate children, we murder them."

The colonel looked up sharply but did not react except to clear his throat. "I'll overlook your impertinence considering the stress you've been under."

He looked down at his notes. "I've gone over all the details; I'm familiar with the alternatives of the situation, so there's no point in re-arguing them."

He leaned back in his chair. "This is a close call; I don't know the answer, and I don't think a formal inquiry would find differently. Moreover, you're a good soldier. I respect the Bronze Star you earned." He looked at his file. "I see you're a psychologist."

"I've earned a master's degree in the army."

The colonel studied him. "Hmmm. I've never known a combat man who was a shrink." He slapped the desk and stood up, leaning forward. "Well, for certain, you can't return to your unit. Many of the soldiers would resent you for what happened to Cpl. Howard and the choice you made. I also don't think you should command men in combat again. Consequently, you are being transferred stateside, where you will be processed with an honorable discharge with the thanks of your government."

He walked around the desk and shook hands with Fogarty. "You are a brave man, but find something else to do."

As Brian finished the story, he looked closely at Jaye to gauge her reaction. It was a kind smile.

"After that, I committed to psychology. You can speculate as to why." Tiny beads of sweat were on his hairline. It may have been from the spa's heat. He glanced at Jaye for a reaction.

Jaye had listened quietly and then said, "Did you do the right thing? That's not for me to say. You have to sort it out and make your peace with it over time."

She partially rose out of the water to lean over and kiss him on the forehead. "You're a good man. I respect your heart. That's the only thing I understand."

They stared upward silently at the stars for a while, then Jaye said something.

"I can't hear you," Brian said softly across the spa. "Come over here."

Jaye moved quietly through the steam until she was beside him. Their hot bodies touched, and she whispered, "I forgot what I was going to say."

"Well, stay right here until you remember it."

They lapsed into a time-ticking silence, savoring each other's closeness and the mysteries of their own thoughts. Actually, not thoughts, but inarticulate emotions that lacked words, but each with a directed drive that spoke for itself.

Jaye moved closer until their legs were touching.

He reached out. In only a moment, the straps were slipped off her shoulders, and he felt the soft buoyancy of her breasts in the water. He wasn't aware of his hands moving, but the suit peeled smoothly down her midriff, then past her soft, smooth buttocks, and she gracefully stepped out of it. His own suit was easier. She ripped it off in seconds.

It happened by itself, some sort of hormonal auto-pilot. She was straddling him, groping to guide him in. Then he was there. One hand touched a soft breast and passion-swollen nipple. The other hand held her tightly around the back.

She moved sensuously at first, then rapidly, then with an urgent pounding. Their mouths and exploring tongues pressed together. Soft moans and labored breath mingled frantically.

It was over quickly, and it wasn't graceful, but it was perfect.

With passion sated, their kisses turned soft and tender, and somehow that seemed even sexier. They each thought of remarking about how wonderful it had been, but the words seemed flat and pointless.

"If the manager comes by, I'm going to say you lured me in here," he whispered.

"Oh, yeah? What're you going to say when I start screaming?" They hugged and laughed defiantly—not against the manager's broken rules, but against the life they each were convinced had tried to deny them this.

"You know, it's only going to get better."

"Whooo," she half-whistled. "If that happens, it'll have to be something Danielle Steel would write about."

As they were getting out, Brian said, "I hope you're on the pill."

"No worries," she said, turning her back.

After they dressed and when he was at the door to leave, she said, "I like you. I do-do-do like you."

"Friendship is the finest expression of love," he said.

She languidly leaned forward and brushed her lips against his, and he touched her arm lightly. It was innocent and lasted only a moment, but to both of them, the touch existed beyond that, the way a bright light leaves a lingering aura in the eyes. She pulled back, and their parting glance met for an instant.

The door closed, and both were alone.

Chapter Fifteen

Potter's squad was playing host to a visiting cop from Barstow, a small city in the Mohave Desert. The fellow was in charge of starting a two-cop homicide squad and was in San Diego to pick up pointers.

Tatum and Jaye were telling him about a visit the two of them were about to undertake to Marvin Winters, a murder suspect. It was a chance for the two of them to put on a little show for the small-towner.

Tatum said, "He's a teacher's aide at an elementary school, or was. They fired him. Four years ago, his wife disappeared. He wants to forget her, but we don't. We just want to go over his story for about the umpteenth time. He won't come to us, so we go to him. This brother has issues, you might say. It's Almaguer's case, so we're going in as fresh faces. Ignacio says he's a good-sized fat guy."

"It'll be the usual shtick," Jaye said. "We tell him his voluntary presence is requested down at headquarters to answer some routine questions, just to clear up some details. However, we don't arrest him because to make an arrest, we've got to have a better reason then we have, then jump through all the Miranda hoops, and safeguard his rights, and all that jazz." Jaye turned to the visiting cop, whose name was Ed Conover. "Of course, you certainly know how that goes down, Ed."

Tatum grinned. "Then, when he gets to the station, accompanied by these two tight-lipped, sorry-faced detectives, he's uptight, scared, and feeling alone. His pucker valve is shut tighter than a Yale lock."

Jaye chuckled. "Then who's there to greet him but this smiling, understanding, nice Mr. Almaguer who puts his hand on poor Winters' shoulder, gets him a cup of coffee, and says he's sure they can clear up this 'minor confusion' if they just talk about it, just one more time."

Tatum nodded. "And they talk, and they talk. They send out for Burger Kings with fries and a shake, then they talk some more, right up to the time Winters signs a confession."

"And we all live happily ever after," she said, "except for the aforementioned Mr. Winters, who is just beginning his journey through the Slough of Despond."

Tatum looked at her curiously. "Where?"

"Slough of Despond. Pilgrim's Progress. Sophomore lit. I did well," she said in an exaggerated preen.

❧

Tatum leaned close to Jaye and looked out the passenger window. "This is Brookhaven. Do you see the number?" he asked.

Jaye was quite aware of Tatum's closeness, as he intended. "This is 1132, so 1138 is probably the next house… Yeah, there, the gray one with blue shutters." Jaye reached into the back seat. "If I'm going in there, I'm wearing my duty belt. The guy is maybe—probably—a murderer." She strapped the heavy belt over her jeans.

"Ah, just stand behind me. I'll protect you," Tatum said, needling.

"I trust pepper spray more than you."

Tatum parked directly in front of the house. Jaye reported their location to dispatch. Tatum led the way, looking like a real estate agent or a Jehovah's Witness peddling the Watchtower.

With Jaye standing at his shoulder, Tatum rang the bell. In moments, it was jerked open, and the detectives stared aghast, first at the man, then at each other. Somehow, the image Almaguer conveyed of Marvin Winters, teacher's aide, had not prepared them for this angry-looking man of six-five and about 280 well-muscled pounds.

Tatum cleared his throat. "Are you Marvin Winters?"

"Yeah."

"We're police officers. May we come in?"

The man grunted and stood aside for them to enter. Once inside, Tatum gave their names and said: "We're still a little confused about your wife's disappearance. Just a few details. We'd like to close the case out. You can be a big help if you'll come down to police headquarters." Tatum shrugged innocently. "Just a few final questions."

The man's eyes widened with anxiety. He was primed. "What?"

Tatum was ill at ease. "Uh, we can talk about it down there."

Winters' face flushed, and his muscles tensed. "I'm not going to jail," he shouted.

Tatum held up his hands. "No one said any—"

The veins in Winters' neck stood like twine on a package. His eyes swung wildly from Jaye to Tatum. Both could tell that his stability was a frayed rope holding up an anvil, but they faced a classic cop's dilemma: The man's in his own house, he's not officially wanted, so you can't pull a gun just because he's upset. You wait.

With a roar, Winters snapped. He grabbed Tatum by the lapels and shook him like a ventriloquist's dummy. He slammed him down to the carpet and straddled him, shouting over and over, "You son of a bitch, you're not taking me to jail, you're not taking me to jail." He grasped Tatum around the neck with both hands and began to choke. His language became incoherent, and slobber dripped from his lips onto Tatum's chest, face, and hair. Tatum's face began to turn red, and he kicked his legs like a fish in a rowboat.

Jaye watched in momentary shock as the attack on Tatum took place, but in seconds she reached for the walkie-talkie in her purse and cried, "Code 3. Jesus! Code 3 cover NOW!" She gave the address, then dropped the walkie-talkie and reached for her gun. Even though Tatum's face was changing from red to purple with the giant's hands continuing to bear down, she couldn't bring herself to shoot a berserk man. She almost used the gun to club Winters but then remembered: If you don't use a gun for shooting, keep it out of sight. She dropped the butt of the gun back into its holster and, caught up in the excitement, jumped onto Winters' broad back.

While Jaye yanked at his hair as hard as she could, Winters tried to throw her off by shaking his back, which bounced her around like a rodeo rider, but she gritted her teeth and hung on. Finally, Winters swung a wicked elbow back and caught her squarely above the left eye. Jaye flew off his back and landed on her shoulder with a painful grunt. Winters ignored Jaye and resumed trying to strangle Tatum.

Her pain masked by adrenaline, Jaye removed her Taser and pointed it at Winters' back. But just as she pulled the trigger, Winters shifted, and the two electrified prongs sank into Tatum's thigh. His scream came out as more of a squawk that dwindled to a moan. The jolt was akin to sticking his whole body into a light socket. It turned his body and brain into electrified mush momentarily. His desperate twitching tore him loose from Winters' grip.

With Tatum gasping spread-eagled on the floor, Winters turned his attention to Jaye and started to rise, glaring at her. She pulled her pepper spray canister and sprayed him full in the face. He screamed and put both hands to his eyes. Shortly, however, he shook off the stinging and took a step toward Jaye. She sprayed him again. She was into it.

"I've got more in here, you bastard. Come on!" she shouted. "I'd rather spray you than shoot you, but I can do that, too."

Patrol officers burst through the door with guns drawn and tackled Winters. One threw an arm lock around his neck, trying for a sleeper hold, a move that was officially prohibited but was known to be used in desperate straits. Jaye felt like cheering him on but, at the moment, didn't remember how.

The two men lay on the floor, straining against each other. The officer was putting all the pressure he could muster against the carotid artery while Winters was trying to pull free. As Jaye stumbled around the room trying to clear the blood from her eyes, Winters' grip slowly loosened, his eyes became glassy, and finally, he collapsed in the officer's arms. Two others handcuffed his wrists behind him and sat him in a corner as he roused.

Tatum recovered onto one elbow and took his first look at Jaye. Her face was covered with blood from the cut, and she blinked furiously trying to clear her vision. "Holy shit," he muttered. He pulled the Taser prongs from his thigh and scrambled to his feet. He took out his handkerchief and pressed it against the cut while she leaned against him for support.

As a half-dozen officers milled about, Tatum switched hands, holding the handkerchief against Jaye's forehead, and fished out his badge. "I'm Tatum, homicide." He used his foot to nudge Winters, who was just starting to groan himself back to awareness. "The son of a bitch assaulted a police officer—make that two. Book him on a 241(c) and notify Detective Almaguer in homicide he's in custody. This could work out for the better."

Jaye said, "Oh, yeah? Look at my face! Does that look 'for the better'?"

A patrolman helped Winters to his feet and led him out the door. Tatum watched him leave and said, "Jesus. He's big enough to eat hay." He then looked at his bloody handkerchief and Jaye's face and turned to another cop. "Check the kitchen for some paper towels. Wet them. I need something for a compress."

An overweight sergeant, still puffing from the run-up to the house, was told loudly about Tatum being electrified by Taser. The officers filling the room chuckled, and some laughed out loud. One who knew Tatum said, "Hey, Sparky, walk over and touch that TV and see if it turns on." The sergeant said, "Tatum, that was a major bowel bubbler. You're getting too old for this shit."

"Nah, Matt," Tatum said with a weak grin, "this was just a little workout. I thrive on this stuff. I've got another one scheduled later this week."

Turning to Jaye, who was sitting and holding the wet towels in her eye, he unloaded, "Why the hell'd you Taser me? You were supposed to get him!"

She'd had enough. "Dammit, he moved! Why the hell'd you not control him? That other cop did. I could've done better than that."

Tatum looked around to see the uniforms enjoying the scene. He heard one cop say, "Tatum's steaming like a dog turd in December."

Tatum knew he was beaten and laughed. "Oh, the hell with it." He patted her on the back.

"Who's the lady?" the sergeant asked admiringly.

"This is no lady," Tatum said, kidding. "This is the notorious Jaye Peoria, a public menace with a Taser."

The sergeant turned to Jaye with a look of respect. "Oh, you're the one who buried that jerk, Burton. He's now a commando in records, and the rest of us are safe from him." The sergeant took a closer look at Jaye's wound, which was beginning to swell and discolor. "You'll be okay. Any cut above the eye bleeds like hell. Capillaries. How'd it happen?"

"She couldn't stay out of the way," Tatum said.

Jaye twisted her head. "I heard that. Next time, I'll just stand back and enjoy."

Tatum grinned. "I was getting ready to put a move on him when you interfered."

A nearby patrol officer teased Jaye. "We were late to your party because the call was 'Code 3, Jesus.' We didn't realize the call was for us."

Jaye laughed. "At that moment, I was asking for help from him, not you."

Tatum drove Jaye to the hospital emergency room, where five stitches closed the eyebrow laceration. When Jaye walked out to the waiting area, Tatum made a low whistle and said, "I'm impressed. That's a shiner a schoolyard bully could be proud of giving."

Jaye gingerly touched her eye, which was buried in puffy rainbow colors. The eyeball itself was bloodshot with jagged streaks of red. "I know. Isn't it beautiful? Easter Sunday is coming up. I'll have to find a matching hat to be seen in church like this."

"Church? I always considered you a heathen."

"Only around you, Tatum."

He winked. "With that supercharge you gave me, I gotta be a real dynamo in the sack."

"That'd be a shock."

Jaye felt like a circus performer trying to juggle the balls of her four-case load. Uppermost in her mind were the two strangulation cases, Edna Willows and Mandy Martin. She spent hours reviewing those files, looking for possible leads missed or for fresh insights that the material might give her. She also repeatedly called Art Baker close to the nuisance level to see what he'd found. His answer was a consistent, "Nothing."

On the Willows murder, the only person with even a remote idea of what happened that night was Henry Gunnison, the night clerk at the Bird of Paradise motel. She read his comments about seeing a disturbance in an alley across the street that night, based on Almaguer's brief interview on the morning of the crime.

She saw that Gunnison had not had a follow-up interview. Time to change that. She also realized he lived in a low-income hotel known for a guest book filled with nasty characters. She called over to Tatum, "Hey, you want to take a ride?"

Jaye watched the street numbers to confirm the address of the sagging three-story building squeezed between a thrift store and a sandwich shop that seemed to have corralled the remaining Formica in San Diego. The faded sign said "Oceania Hotel." It was a long-closed dump that probably started downhill about the end of World War II.

The door opened to a stairway that was about twenty feet wide. In its day, it must have been majestic, but now it was creaky, dusty, and a little spooky, even for cops. Tatum said, "I expect to see Dracula at the head of the stairs."

"Don't worry, it's not a full moon."

It was now a residence for down-and-outers and for those who spent much of their money on John Barleycorn but who could still afford the 400-dollar robbery rent per month for a dingy single room, bath down the hall. It was Henry Gunnison's home.

Gunnison was an angry little man, especially when forced to be sober. He was early old at fifty-three, his testament to liquid living. He was angry about having to force the booze his system craved past an angry liver. He was angry about his ulcers, baldness, loneliness, and the starvation salary of a flophouse clerk. Deep though his anger was, it was distributed democratically to the whole world.

He was also a possible witness to the murder of Edna Willows. At least, he claimed to witness two figures tussling across the street in the place, and at the time, she was killed.

With Tatum standing off to the side, Jaye knocked on the door with the outline of number fifteen, where a brass number had once hung.

Gunnison peered around the edge of a cracked door. He wore a rumpled flannel shirt around a toothpick body. At 3:00 P.M., he had sleep in his eyes, booze on his breath, and anger on his face.

The two cops flashed badges. "Mr. Gunnison, I'm Detective Peoria. This is Detective Tatum. We'd like to ask you about last November fifth." He looked blank. She added, "That was the night a woman was murdered in the alley across the street from your work."

Gunnison stared at Jaye's eye. "That's a beaut. Who gave you that, a fugitive wienie wagger?" He laughed, overjoyed by Jaye's black eye and his wit. Then he saw the small recorder in her hand. His mirth faded, and the anger returned. "Hey, you recording this?"

"Yes, I am."

Tatum leaned forward. "Any reason she shouldn't?"

"I already told a cop what I saw. Go away. I work nights. I got to sleep." He started to close the door, but Jaye put her foot in it.

"That's not going to happen, sir. You're under arrest."

Suddenly, he was wide awake as handcuffs appeared in Tatum's hands. "Huh? Wha'd I do?"

"There is an outstanding warrant on you for public urination. It's not your first offense. It could mean jail time."

"Going to jail for street pissing? Who'd I hurt? Would you prefer I pissed my pants?"

"That might be against good manners, but it wouldn't be against the law. Come out, sir, and put your hands behind your back. Don't make us come in there."

"Uh, can we talk about it?"

Jaye looked with dramatic uncertainty at Tatum. He frowned but reluctantly nodded while giving squint-eyes to Gunnison.

She put the cuffs away, biting her lip to keep from smiling. "That's what we came here to do, sir."

Gunnison repeated the same story he told Almaguer on the late morning of the murder. He said he was waiting to have coffee with the janitor, Eddie Lee, in the front office of the Bird of Paradise when he noticed a scuffle in the dark alley across the street.

"Like I told your man before, I watched for a minute or so. The one who went down seemed to fall kinda funny."

"Did Mr. Lee see it also?"

"No, he was just coming on duty. I told him about it, though. You gotta talk to him 'cause I ain't putting words in anyone's mouth when it comes to cops."

"What time was that?" Jaye asked.

"It were 2:40. When he gets there, I remember Eddie saying, 'Shit, Hank'—they all call me that—"

Tatum couldn't resist: "Shit, Hank? They call you that?"

Gunnison sneered at Tatum. "Very funny, asshole."

Jaye frowned at Tatum but had to bite her lip again. "Go on, sir."

"So Eddie says, 'You better set that clock back if'n the boss comes in.'—The boss did that sometimes, sneaky like—That was my job, you see, keeping the clock straight."

"What was the time on the clock when you did that?"

"I remember that, and so did Eddie 'cause he remarked on it: 2:45."

"What did you set it to?" Tatum asked.

Gunnison cocked his head, exasperated at such a dumb question. "Why, an hour earlier. Are you listening or just being the clown?" He shook his head. "Duh!" He continued. "I was late doing it 'cause I had to deal with a ruckus in one of the rooms."

Jaye said, "How much have you had to drink today?"

"Two beers."

Tatum said, "Jesus, don't you guys ever drink anything but two beers?"

Jaye said, "So, let me get this straight: You saw the struggle in the alley directly across the street at 2:40 A.M., but that was

still daylight-saving time. Correct? And after you saw that disturbance, five minutes later, you turned the clock back one hour to
1:45 A.M. standard time. Correct?"

"That's what I just said. You don't pay attention either."

Jaye pushed ahead. "And when asked by the detective later
that morning, you told him the incident happened at 2:40 A.M.
However, you did not say the 2:40 was daylight savings time and
that it was, in fact, 1:40 A.M. standard time. Correct?"

"Christ, you want me to write it down?"

"I want everyone to be absolutely clear on this. You did not
tell him you only set the clock back after you saw the struggle
across the street?"

"I don't tell cops nothin' I don't have to. I told him what the
clock said. The shorter the conversation, the better, if you ask
me." He looked at the detectives hopefully. "Uh, does this square
me on the street-pissin' beef?"

Jaye looked at Tatum. "What do you think, detective? Shall
we let him walk?"

Tatum pursed his lips indecisively. "We should take him in,
detective, but he cooperated… I'm just not sure… Hell, why not?
But only for now. Consider it probation. I'm going to put out an
APB for the patrol to watch him."

Jaye gave him both of their cards. "Stay in touch with us, Mr.
Gunnison. Don't make us come looking for you if we want more."

Walking back to their car, Tatum casually said, "You know,
it's just about quitting time." He looked sideways at Jaye.

"Nice try, lover boy, but it ain't gonna happen."

Chapter Sixteen

After staring at the wall for an hour, alternately angry and feeling sorry for himself, the shock of what he had just learned began to wear off. Brian realized that the one thing he didn't want at the moment was to be alone. He could think of only one person he wanted to be with. He grabbed his cell phone, punched in a number, and waited hopefully while it rang.

"Hello, Detective Peoria."

"Jaye, this is Brian. Can you get away for a little while? I need to talk."

"From the sound of your voice, you need CPR. What's wrong?"

"Can you get away?"

"Uh, sure, I guess so. Where you at?"

Since Jaye was on duty, she wouldn't go into a restaurant or bar, so the two started walking in the neighborhood of his half-way house. Brian told her everything about leaving a highly-paid job at San Diego Utilities and the move to New Hope. Finally, he told her what was bothering him—Maureen was having an affair.

"How do you know?"

"Some detective work of my own. And it's with a good friend of mine—used to be a friend."

Jaye was a good listener, interrupting only a few times with questions. When he had finished, she said, "Well, you and Maureen are split. She's entitled to her own life… So, what do you do now?"

"God, who knows? I've screwed up everything so far. Maybe I'll do nothing and see how that works."

"Doing nothing is doing something," Jaye said.

He grimaced. "Come on, that's the kind of thing I'm supposed to say." He walked a few steps and then said, "That's not all that bothers me. It's the betrayal. Being a cuckold is about as emasculating as it gets for a man."

"Oh, don't get so melodramatic."

He stopped and faced her. "That's a nasty thing to say."

"You're also whining. It doesn't flatter you."

He stood back, shocked. "No one's ever said that to me."

"You're not the first person to ever feel self-pity. … Look, Brian. I know you're hurt, but people get hurt and get over it. You know that. That's probably what you tell your patients. Follow me for a day, and you'll see some real pain."

"That's a bit patronizing."

"It's the truth."

"Thanks a lot," he said dryly.

She tensed. "I'm trying to help you. And don't talk to me that way."

"Huh? What'd I say?"

"I just don't like to be spoken to in that tone. It reminds me of my ex."

"Well, I'm not your ex-husband."

"And I'm not Maureen."

He looked at her with a twinge of resentment. "Considering the horseshit that's been dumped on me today, can't you give a little slack?"

"I'm happy to be here for you, but don't take your problems out on me. I have no intention of being shot by friendly fire."

They walked quietly for a few minutes as the tension slowly swirled down the drain.

In an effort to change the subject, Jaye said, "Ever since I was a kid, this poor part of town seemed different, like there was something bad in the air. I don't know, I can't explain it."

"You can't?" He stopped in the middle of the sidewalk and raised his head to sniff the air. "What do you smell?"

She breathed deeply. "Nothing."

"Concentrate. It's the smell of poverty: Burned oil from worn-out cars, cheap food frying in lard, trash fires in empty lots, and dust. I'll bet you didn't know dust has a smell, did you?"

"Can't say I ever thought about it."

"These people down here don't get to grow flowers and damned seldom get to smell them."

They continued walking and fell silent. As they rounded a

corner, Brian almost walked into a middle-aged woman who could not have been as old as she looked. She was dressed in cast-off clothing and mumbled to herself as her eyes wandered aimlessly. As they moved past her, Brian said, "Do you see that woman?"

"Who is she?"

"By name, I don't know, but generally, she and others like her have become my work."

Jaye swung her eyes from Brian to the woman and back. "I think anyone would feel sympathy for her."

"Sympathy? What's sympathy? Is it decent clothes? Is it medical treatment? Is sympathy a roof over her head? I'll tell you what it is. Sympathy is a salve most people put on their conscience to keep it from hurting and as an excuse not to help."

Jaye looked at him with mild irritation. "A lot of people care about others."

"He laughed sarcastically. "Right. So long as they belong to the same country club."

"Stop it, Brian. Within recent months I've seen two women like that murdered. You're feeling resentful toward life, and you're taking it out on me." She stopped and faced him. "This is going nowhere. I'm going back to work. You don't need me to help you feel sorry for yourself."

An hour later, he emailed only one word: "Sorry."

She replied, "Me, too."

Another hour later, Brian phoned. "As they say in the movies—Thanks, I needed that." Her little laugh put him at ease. "I guess since Maureen has a boyfriend, there's no point in keeping me from being your boyfriend, assuming, of course, that you don't reject the burden. What I'm getting around to saying is I want you to meet Traci. She's a precocious seven-year-old. You two'll get along great, considering you're a precocious thirty-two-year-old."

Jaye's chuckle encouraged him to go further. "I'm taking Traci to Legoland this Saturday. Care to make it a threesome?"

"Love to. I'm a big kid in theme parks."

When they picked up Jaye on Saturday, Traci was a bit stand-offish in a wait-and-see manner. Jaye chose to sit in the back seat with the child, and the two were quickly laughing together as new friends. While eating hot dogs, Traci asked her, "You're a policeman, have you ever shot anybody?"

Jaye winced toward Brian. "There's that question." Then to Traci, "No, dear. My job is to help people and to keep bad people from shooting them."

While Traci was on the mini-train of Fun Town, Brian and Jaye watched silently. Finally, Brian said solemnly, "Maureen might have cancer. All the tests aren't done yet."

Jaye wanted to say she didn't need to know that; she didn't want to know that. Maureen was in his life, not hers. Instead, she reminded herself—keep your mouth shut. She simply said, "I'm sorry."

After a long afternoon, Jaye and Traci held hands, and she gently guided the sleepy child into the back seat. She quietly said to Brian, "What a lovely child."

"She dropped in from heaven," he said.

When Brian stopped to drop Jaye off, Traci woke up and said, "If you're daddy's girlfriend, are you going to be my second mommy, like Uncle Ralph is my second daddy?"

"I'm going to be your first friend, sweetheart."

The tender moment was ruined when she glanced at Brian and saw the stricken look on his face.

Several days later, Potter and his crew were sitting in his office, still high on the euphoria of the Clark arrest and gloating over its details.

From out of left field, where he sometimes played, Baker said, "It occurred to me last night that when you die, so does everybody else."

Jaye and Tatum looked at each other with quizzical "What the hell did he just say?" glances. Potter, though, nodded with a self-satisfied grin. "I get it, Art. That's pretty deep."

The telephone rang, and Potter answered it, then stood up

and motioned to Jaye. "They want you and me over at the DA's office."

"All right!" she said. "The wheels of justice are turning."

When Jaye and Potter walked into the DA's conference room, a tense mood saturated it like an Oklahoma dust storm and instantly put them on alert. Facing them across a conference table were District Attorney Edward Baudino and the new captain, whose responsibilities included homicide. Sitting at the far end as though to avoid contamination was a cold-eyed black man with an open attaché case in a burnt-orange three-piece suit. His name was the verbal tag team of Herman Sherman. He prided himself that the police department's institutional blood pressure went up every time he appeared. None of the men rose when Jaye and Potter entered.

Baudino introduced Sherman as retained by the Social Justice League of San Diego. The cops and the lawyer eyed each other without speaking.

Baudino said, "Mr. Sherman has something to say."

Sherman cleared his throat and started in a deep, gravelly voice. "All I want from you two is my client, Mr. Samuel C. Clark. I want him released with apologies."

Instead of replying, Jaye and Potter looked apprehensively at the DA. Sherman continued, "Mr. Clark is being held on the strength of a bogus, coerced confession. He is a victim of police racism, brutality, duplicity, and false arrest, an offense for which the courts have been known to award generous relief."

Jaye's face turned red. "He's the victim of nothing except his urge to strangle women. He confessed, didn't he?" She spoke angrily but with an edge of fear in her voice.

"That confession was honky jive; just shit you planted in his mind on stuff everyone read in the newspapers, including Mr. Clark." Sherman, though Ivy League educated, found it effective to lapse in and out of the ghetto language when arguing with whites. It reminded them that he was different and suggested an unknown, ominous power. He took a sheet of paper from his briefcase and slid it across the table to Jaye, who barely glanced at it. "That paper, Miss Peoria, gives a documented alibi for both occasions on which the murders in question were committed. Mr. Clark was under constant observation at the home for young men operated by Blessed Jesus Baptist Church. It's a dormitory-style establishment that serves the needs of disoriented youths like Mr. Clark, who have suffered the afflictions of white racism. The home he lives in has a strict curfew, and I can prove that Mr. Clark was in the building every night in compliance with that curfew."

Jaye shook her head disbelievingly. "It can't be. He never said anything about an alibi. We asked several—"

Sherman slammed the palm of his hand loudly against the table. "Asked? My ass. Browbeat, coerced, threatened, you mean. You motherfuckers make me sick."

"That's enough, counselor," Baudino said sharply.

Sherman glanced at the DA to gauge his anger, then toned down. "You think it's cool to take a poor, dull-witted, oppressed, underprivileged young brother and put him through the medieval inquisition you call interrogation, and then you express amazement when he gets so addled he can't remember his name, let alone an alibi. Sheeet." He contemptuously held the E's like a swimmer holding his breath. "The young brother is a martyr."

Potter spoke with clenched teeth. "Martyr, my ass." He angrily pointed his finger at Sherman. "Listen, counselor." He said the noun like a disease. "This Mr. Clark of yours got his Miranda and was given every protection of due process. This "brother" of yours you're so eager to turn loose is nothing but a slimy torturer, everything from cats to—I don't know what all. If he's innocent, fine. I wish the hell he'd said what you've told us to save everyone a lot of trouble. But you can't come in here and accuse us of brutality for trying to find the murderer of a black woman."

"If Mr. Clark had been white, would you have bothered to ask his name, not to mention taking him in?"

Potter's face reddened, and he held his fingers up and snapped them angrily. "Like this. And fuck you for asking."

Baudino said, "Okay, okay."

Sherman started to say something, but Potter added, "And I also won't apologize for not treating that sleazy little creep like visiting royalty. I'll be damned if I'm going to let you Mau-Mau me."

Baudino held up his hands before Sherman could make his angry response. "Gentlemen, gentlemen, cool down. What we want here is justice, not conflicting lectures in sociology." He turned to the lawyer. "Mr. Sherman, I trust you will be satisfied with the freedom of your client just as soon as we verify his alibi."

"I also demand an apology for his treatment."

Baudino looked at the captain, at Jaye, and then at Potter and shook his head. "No, sir, you won't get that. I won't slap hard-working cops in the face for trying to protect the public."

Outside, Jaye leaned against Potter and groaned softly.

Potter gently pushed her away. "Goddamnit, don't start that. Go find a killer."

Chapter Seventeen

The man finished the last page, slammed the book shut, and stared at the title: Serial Killer: The Mind of the Monster.

"Fuck him," he said, raging at the author. "That asshole doesn't know anything about a guy like me. They're just trying to score a buck, these writers and shrinks. And the cops, they just want to sound like they know something about it, but they sure as hell don't. It's all bullshit to fool the idiots who read their crap. They claim I'm crazy. Yeah, sure, I am. Don't they wish?"

He tossed the book away from him as he scoffed at the public perception of serial killers' mental instability. However, he devoured every new edition of the DSM manual of mental disorders, looking for descriptions that might fit men like him.

He was talking aloud to himself alone in his home. That was something he did a lot because he obviously couldn't share this huge part of his life with any other person.

He put the book in the box with a half-dozen similar titles and pushed it back under the bed. Like everyone who performs to a public audience, he was curious about how his work was received. Since he dared not keep press clippings of his achievements, these books would have to do.

However, every book he read tried to explain how he and others like him thought and felt. And every book was wrong. Not even close. He wanted to set the record straight, if only for his own consumption.

He went to his hiding place, reflexively looking right and left, though no one else was near. In a nook behind a beam, he took out a plastic box that contained a small recorder and miniature tapes. He used an analog device because digital recordings, regardless of how or where they're downloaded, seem to always be retrievable by an expert. You can hide or destroy a tape.

He had started making an audio journal so he could enjoy his own recollections. The taping had now extended to well over a dozen hours. He would sometimes sit and listen to himself describing his adventures and rejoice at his cleverness and daring. He was careful not to reveal the identity of any victim and to obscure the crime's details, just in case the police were to find his tapes. He would just say he was making notes for a novel he intended to write.

He was smart, all right, even though he was still cursing himself for writing that stupid letter to the detective. Stupid, definitely. He wouldn't break his pattern again. Certainly, he'd love to watch that bitch croak, and if he ever got the chance…

He inserted a fresh tape. He touched the small red button that said "rec" and started:

Tape number eight: What do all those losers out there know of me? I'm as normal as the best men, far more normal than most. I probably seem to be a pretty average guy. I hardly drink at all. I don't smoke. I don't even gamble. I'm not racist or bigoted. I never tortured an animal, set fire to a building, was abused by my parents, or did anything as a child that wasn't normal.

I like baseball. I went to a half-dozen Padres games last year. I enjoy Christmas, getting gifts for my parents, office parties, and all. I give to charity, some. I don't harass pretty women. In fact, they make me ill at ease, but there's nothing wrong with that.

You look at me, and you think here's Joe Average, going about his humdrum daily life, doing all the things that boring people do. But I'm not that. Noooo fucking way! I'm not average. I'm way above average. You think I like people, but I don't—hell no, I don't.

I make myself seem at ease with guys who laugh and joke and slap each other on the back, and I flirt with girls. I used to want to like people, but they didn't seem to like me. Oh, they don't say anything, but I can tell. So, I just gave up. Piss on them. They're obviously jealous. I left them far behind.

He continued talking in an unemotional monotone, getting closer to the grievance that had become the touchstone of his being. The grievance was the reason hatred became hot lava in his mind, its fingers of fire erupting higher as his mind tore open the memories that he could never hide from.

His resentment inevitably smashed head-on into the physical deficiency that ruined his life and made him a human viper because of the abuse he had taken. It had its beginnings in middle school; it wasn't too bad then, but it was the harbinger of what was to come.

High school. Goddamned high school. Boys bullied me in locker rooms and showers. They made crude jokes and humiliated me in front of other students, so the whole school, especially the girls, knew about my problem, my curse. My whole body burned with humiliation when I saw the sniggers and the smirks as I passed them in the corridors.

And then there were the women. When I tried to be the lover they expected and I desperately desired, they would look at me in shock and either regard me with sympathy or ridicule. God damn them. I don't want their sympathy, and I'll kill them for their ridicule.

When people don't understand you, they think being different is bad. In my case, it was great, and naturally, the people around me didn't appreciate that. In high school, I was sent to a shrink who talked to me enough times that he figured he couldn't get any more money out of my parents. After all that, he came to the idiotic conclusion that I had an "acute antisocial personality disorder" and that I should be watched carefully. I found his diagnosis in my mother's dresser drawer. Betrayed! Even by my parents.

As these words tumbled into the recorder, his lips compressed, and his voice trembled. His teeth clenched, the veins in his neck corded, and his fist tightened on the arm of the chair. The hatred boiled as he screamed into the microphone.

GOD DAMN THEM! I'LL KILL THEM ALL!

Moments later, his temper subsided, but not the underlying fury that caused it. All he had left from the shambles those tormentors had made of his life was revenge. He had to make do with outsmarting the stupid cops who flailed around trying to catch him. Their humiliation was one of the few joys in his life. But it wasn't enough.

I remind myself of these things because I don't want to forget why I hate and why I seek vengeance—righteous vengeance.

Women. My favorite subject, but not in a way they would enjoy. They need a more— "dramatic," shall we say?—" treatment than cops. To be honest, I used to yearn to be loved and desired, but all I got was ridicule and rejection. I wanted their admiration and the "best" I ever got was pity. Nothing is worse than pity. I make them pay for every hang-dog look that I adopted as a mask to cover their laughter. They sensed I was different; they just didn't know different meant better.

I get my revenge, yes, oh, yes. The only way my outrage stops boiling is when I put my hands around their skinny necks and feel the warm, smooth, rubbery flesh compress beneath my thumbs and see their eyes go from shock to fright and then fade into death, like the dimmer on a light bulb.

As I feel their bodies go limp, they become all the females who rejected me for something I could not control, that I was born with.

The cops are my playthings. Ha! Here's how I screw up their minds. I choose my victims from women that society has trashed and thrown away. When their bodies are found, there's always a bit of a fuss, but no one truly cares. Soon, the politicians and the press lost interest. Then, the investigation becomes short and half-hearted. That's a part of my brilliance. People, in their ignorance, might say those miserable creatures haven't done me any harm. However, others like them have, so they have to be the stand-in bitches. They'll do.

I know what I am, and I know what the so-called experts and shrinks think I am. They think I'm a monster. Well, their aim is off. The real monsters are those who made a normal life out of reach for me. They and the society that stood by and enjoyed the spectacle while I was being tormented. They're all paying for it now. Their chickens have come home to roost. It sounds like I see myself as some sort of avenging angel. I can do better than that. I'm an avenging devil.

The idiot "experts" claim that people like me are sociopathic and that we have no feelings for other people. Well, that's not true. I have a feeling that jumps off the charts. It's called hate.

Just like a drug addict can't describe the euphoria of his high, I can't describe the feeling I get when my mission is accomplished, and some worthless bitch is lying dead at my feet. It makes my senses come alive. I feel like a king. A cat on a prowl. It turns that lump of hate in my chest into a marshmallow. It's called being the best at what I do, the absolute very best, and there's no feeling like it in the world.

I don't mean to get too detailed about my work, but the enjoyment is in two parts. The first, like I said, is when I get the emotional release from finishing the job. The second is when I see the relatives, especially the mothers, and the sisters, and the daughters of what they call the "victim," blubbering away on TV, and then the cops saying they're going to do this, and they're going to do that; of course, nothing they do ever works. So then, after a "decent" passage of time, they forget about the victim and about me, and I just start planning another adventure.

FUCKKKKKKK THEM ALL!!!!!!!!!!!!! DIE!!!!!!!!!!!

I don't care about what people say or write. They can kiss my ass. They don't know me. They don't know what people have done to me. I didn't start out this way. They made me who I am. The thing is, I've found a life, a purpose, that's exciting and fulfilling. It's become my thing.

I even date women once in a while to see if I can maybe somehow feel the things that other guys feel. Those few dates either ended with her not inviting me in and not taking my calls later, or if we had sex, she started out all clinging but then pulled back like I had some sort of disease.

What is it about females? I study them. I sometimes try to be nice to them, but they look right through me, or they look away like I'm some kind of—that word again—monster. They always make me feel little. I hate them all. I hate them so much it ties my guts into knots.

When I'm down, maybe even depressed, the only thing I can turn to is what I call my great adventure, where I become a lethal, sinewy, pouncing man of darkness. No one can out-think me or catch me because I cover all my bases. I stay ahead of them at every turn. I'M THE WINNER!! That's the one thing in my life that ree-lee makes me come alive, that turns me loose, where I reign supreme. I know that sounds like bragging, but it's true.

The police, the politicians, and the idiots on TV say I'm evil and twisted. Well, if that's true, well, thanks for the compliment. I wasn't born that way, I was made that way. I can't speak for others who are like me because I don't know any of them. But if they were tormented the way I was, then more power to them. Like me, whatever they became was caused by others. They are my brothers.

Sometimes, all that's left is hatred. And if that's the way it is, then that's the way it is. You have to make the most of it.

He clicked the recorder off and ejected the tape. There would be more adventures. He would have to buy more tapes.

A receptionist came to the squad room door and said, "Jaye, there's a Mr. Spiller here to see you."

Jaye was stunned. Ben? What's he doing here? Confused and a little shocked, Jaye made her way to the public waiting area to see Ben sitting and leafing through a two-day-old newspaper. He jumped to his feet when she appeared.

"Hello, Jaye. Long time." He started to hug, but seeing no reaction from her instead extended his hand. She took it and said, "Ben, what are you doing here?"

"I decided to come and have coffee with the woman I used to sleep with." His grin vanished when he saw her icy reaction to that rehearsed line.

"Well, okay," was all she could think to say, and she led him to the cafeteria. When they were seated, she waited for him to speak.

"Well, let me bring you up to date. My business is doing exceedingly well. Janet and I have two children, you may have heard. A boy, Jason, he's five, and a girl, Darla—that's Janet's mother's name—she's three. The kids are doing great."

"That's nice," Jaye said.

"What's new with you?"

She spread her arms. "This is it. This is who I am and what I have. Homicide. I'm happy."

"You look funny with that gun on your hip."

"If there's anything funny about me, it's not this pistol," she said flatly.

"Oh, I was just joking."

Ben fixed a look on a far wall. "Uh, Janet and I have decided to call it quits. We're still friends, but we just drifted apart. It's a common story these days."

"I'm quite aware."

Her aloofness was not what he expected. Given that she was just a cop, and he was fast-tracking it to becoming rich, he figured she'd be eager to reignite the old flame. It just needed some thawing. Give her a chance to realize they could pick up where they left off.

"Just for old time's sake, I thought it'd be nice to have dinner together. Talk about the happy days we had. You know, catch up. How about Donovan's Steak

House?" He had picked perhaps the swankiest restaurant in San Diego. "Eight o'clock. I'll pick you up. How about it?"

Jaye stared at him for a long moment. Good God, she thought, where did he suddenly come from? She felt a churning and a longing, but she wasn't going to relinquish control over whatever this was leading to.

"I can do that, I guess. I'm free tonight. However, I'll meet you there."

Jaye had time to get her hair and nails done and pressed her best dress, which happened to be the only outstanding dress she owned. She took a small vial of Joy perfume by Jean Patou and touched it behind her ears, on her neck, and on her wrists. Sparingly. She intended to make this ridiculously expensive bottle last twenty years.

She left her car at the valet and walked into the posh steakhouse. Ben was already seated in a booth off to the side, and before him was an opened, chilled bottle of 100-dollar Aubert's Chardonnay. She slid into the booth, and he reached across and took her hand, and kissed it. "It's like we slipped back to when we were drinking Gallo and eating at Jack in the Box."

Through the appetizer and salad, he talked about his business, his children, and how Janet grew distant from their relationship. Jaye heard the words, but her mind was elsewhere, a dozen places, anywhere but here, listening to the man who had deprived her forever of a great part of life that it was her right to claim. And in all his self-centered braggadocio, he had not uttered one word of apology or remorse, nor did he ask about her. She almost told him there was someone else, but that was none of his business.

Jaye angrily gulped the rest of her wine and said, "You've talked about everything except the fifth of August."

He was mystified. "What…?"

"Of course, you don't remember. That's the day you made me less of a woman."

Jaye reached for her purse, took out two 100-dollar bills, put them on the table, and stood up.

"What's this?"

"I'm leaving, Ben. I don't want to see you again."

He picked up the bills and tried to hand them to her. "You don't have to do this."

"I can afford it now, Ben…I hope you find happiness." She then added, with a sharper edge, "And enjoy your children. Goodbye."

She took two steps, then suddenly turned around as tears streamed through her makeup. "Remember this, Ben. The past always catches up to the future."

When she got home, and the anger had seeped out of her system, she was on the downer that usually follows dissipated strife. She logged on to check her emails. At the top was one from Brian. It only said: "You're a detective: Love's Labour's Lost, 4.3.12."

It took her about a half-hour to figure out he was referring to act-scene-line. She had an old text of Shakespeare's plays. She leafed to the reference and read: "By heaven, I do love, and it hath taught me to rhyme and to be melancholy."

She emailed a reply: "Ahhhh."

Potter rested his elbows on the desk and rubbed the back of his neck. With a deep sigh, he looked up at Jaye sitting across from him. "This sure the hell is frustrating. Not that I can't handle dead ends; I've seen so many in my day that sometimes I think about moving into a cul de sac just to feel more at home. What makes this case so tough is the publicity, those damned reporters snooping around and asking why we haven't done our job and solved it yesterday."

"The press has backed off lately since they finished trashing us after the Sammy Clark thing," Jaye said.

"Yeah, but only until the next killing. Then, they'll buzz around like flies at a barbeque…the self-important bastards."

"Maybe there won't be another."

"And if wishes were horses, beggars would ride," he said and rubbed a big hand across his face. "Christ, why wouldn't he kill again? He apparently enjoys it, and it's working for him. He doesn't seem to have to worry about us. So why stop now?"

"I feel like I'm batting with two strikes. It's discouraging," Jaye said.

"In this game, you get all the strikes you need. He, on the other hand, will eventually strike out."

Jaye made an exaggerated growling sound and ground her teeth. "Damn it, Sarge, sometimes I think this thing is—is cursed." Jaye pounded the side of her fist against the desktop. "Like that Sammy Clark fiasco. Jeez, I thought I would die when that smart-ass, insulting lawyer hit us with that alibi. The pompous jerk." Potter said, "At this point, we have to try to be patient. It's funny how these things can turn out. I've seen them where you sweat out the scientific approach for months and get nothing, then you grab some average-looking guy for running a red light, and he confesses to being your killer. Just relax, keep a clear head, and ask yourself what more can we do."

"Nothing. I feel like a chicken chasing a bug."

"You think the chicken has problems? Think how the bug feels…Let's go over the case again."

"Okay, Sarge, we've been over this a dozen times, but here goes again," Jaye said, as she ticked off on her fingers all the things that had been done in the investigation. "There, see? We've tried everything that's made sense and a few that didn't."

"In that case," Potter said, "we start all over and do them again."

Jaye nodded. "Fine with me."

"Okay, then let's do it. Tell me where you're at."

Jaye went to her desk to get her files and returned. She once again recited details about the crimes, the guessed profile of the killer, and the investigative steps undertaken.

"Art and I have tracked all men who've been arrested in the county for abusing women the last three years, especially if strangulation to any degree is involved. As you know, I had a couple of likelies, but they didn't pan out.

"Art has done regular checks with ViCAP and, again, nothing. However, there's been a development that could be something I'm not sure about. There's a guy that I looked at on the Willows murder. He had a perfect alibi, we thought, but that's falling apart."

"How's that?"

"His name is Mark Joseph. He works at the Eagle Mountain Casino east of town."

Potter said, "I've been to that one. Ka-ching! The Indians finally found a treaty they could win."

Jaye hid her impatience at the interruption. "He's only been in town since last February. He is an arch fingerprint and is left-handed; actually, ambidextrous. That matches what we've learned. His only history we know of is from a girlfriend who said he almost choked her out.

"But here's the thing: On the early morning of the Willows murder, we were led to believe he was in a car accident at the exact time that the motel clerk saw the crime developing. But check this out, Sarge—It was November fifth, and the morning clocks were supposed to turn back at 2:00 A.M., But Gunnison didn't do it, so he gave us daylight savings time, 2:40 A.M., but in reality, it was 1:40 A.M. standard time. Joseph's car accident was standard time, 2:20 A.M. So the accident would have been 40 minutes after the murder, plenty of time for him to do it and drive away."

Potter had calculated the time as she talked. "I get it," he said. "We first thought he didn't have time to kill her, but then we realized he did. So, what's next?"

Jaye reminded him there was no killer's DNA on either Edna Willows or Jane Doe 18-2, so Joseph's DNA would be of no value to get a match.

Jaye had come to the part that might be a hard sell. "All we have are the lithium tablets." She raised the palm of her hand. "And before you say anything, Sarge, I know it's a reach. However, they were under her body, and they didn't look like they'd been on the floor long. I'd like to find out if lithium is a drug Joseph takes."

Potter shook his head doubtfully. "If you did find that out, it wouldn't mean anything. Plus, you'd have to search his house, and no judge would approve a search warrant on such a slim reason."

She nodded. "I realize that, but it might be a valuable building block if a case against him materializes."

He clasped his hands and thought for a long moment, then he nodded in agreement. "We could search his garbage, maybe get an empty bottle or some drug instructions for lithium, something of that sort. As you know, the law considers garbage to be abandoned property, so we're free to seize it." He chortled. "Plus, there's one thing about it that sort of amuses me."

"What's that?"

"You'll be the one to go through the garbage."

All Jaye could hope for—and she did, earnestly—was that he would not kill again before she put a case together against him. But every time she thought that, a yellow light flashed in her mind—Jaye, she warned herself, you don't know he's the killer, not for certain. You've jumped on that bandwagon before. And a gut feeling won't get you an arrest warrant.

Jaye learned the garbage in Joseph's neighborhood was collected on Wednesday mornings, normally about 9:00 A.M. She asked the third-shift patrol to drive by about 4:00 A.M. so Joseph wouldn't see them and check his container on the type of bags he used.

She got an email from a patrol officer the next Wednesday morning saying the container in front of Joseph's house was a type furnished by the collection company that could be hydraulically lifted into the truck. More important, Joseph's garbage was in two single white kitchen plastic bags with a red tie.

Jaye purchased the same type of bags and started collecting her garbage in them. On Tuesdays, she took two filled bags to work with her and dropped them off at the patrol desk. These were given to a patrol officer to put in place of the bags he removed in pre-dawn Wednesday, just in case Joseph added something to the container. The Joseph garbage was then held in the headquarters garage for her to come down and don rubber gloves to search—ick!—among the coffee grounds, bacon grease, and whatever else might be there.

Jaye was troubled that while she was hung up on garbage, Joseph was free to maybe kill again. She knew there was no evidence to take to a judge to authorize a GPS tracker to the underside of his car, and neither was the budget available to put a tail on him, which would demand the around-the-clock commitment of several cars.

For an hour each Wednesday morning, Jaye spread out Joseph's garbage on a table in a remote corner of the garage. Baker stood by as a witness to whatever she might find. It was a distasteful job for about ten minutes, then it just became a job. She spread out coffee grounds, used tissues, and used whatever orange juice cartons and other refuse of the type found in every kitchen. She was amazed at how much stuff could be crammed into one household plastic bag.

It was on the second Wednesday that she recognized a small opaque plastic bottle with prescription information on it. It was from a pharmacy near Joseph's home. The Rx was for 450 mg of lithium carbonate. The prescribing psychiatrist was Walter Redding, M.D., in San Diego.

Jaye held the bottle aloft like a trophy, and her voice rang out: "God is good!"

Later that next day, Jaye called at the office of Dr. Redding. After a twenty-minute heel-cooling in his waiting room, she watched a patient exit his inner office and go to the door and knock. He opened the door and, mystified, said, "What can I do for you?"

Jaye held her badge low so it wouldn't be noticed by other patients. Redding asked her to come in and closed the door behind her.

"What can I do for you, officer?"

Jaye took out a tape recorder and put it on the edge of his desk. He asked, "Is that necessary?"

She said, "Yes, sir." Then she told him that a patient of his, Mark Joseph, was a person of interest to the police department and she would like to ask him some questions.

"I never said he was a patient of mine."

"Doctor, we have an empty bottle of 450 milligrams of lithium recently prescribed by you and made out to him."

"You know my counseling of any patient is confidential."

Jaye nodded. "Yes, doctor. I am aware of that legal protection. However, we both are aware of the legal obligation to report to the police any information that you happen upon in those sessions that might represent a danger to the public. I would like to ask you if you have any such information about Mark Joseph."

Redding absently picked up a pencil and began tapping it. He thought deeply. Finally, he said, "I want it understood that what I am about to say is only in compliance with the legal obligation you refer to."

"Noted," she said.

"Mr. Joseph has been my patient for eight months. He is bipolar, as I am sure you have surmised. His condition is satisfactorily managed by medication. I see no direct correlation between his bipolar disorder and any behavior that would be unlawful. To say otherwise is simply conjecture, mind you. In fact, that condition, as studied by my profession, is no more violent than the public at large." He paused. "However, I have seen manifestations of deep antipathy toward women in him. I don't know the cause of it. He says he has had no pernicious interactions with women, either in growing up or as an adult, occupationally or socially. My treatment of him gives me no direct reason to think he would be a danger to the public. That is all I am prepared to say."

"As a youth, did he ever torture animals?"

Redding was startled by the question. "It never came up. However, I understand what the question represents, and it deeply troubles me."

"Troubled that I asked it?"

"That, too."

Jaye put her notebook away, then made a show of pushing the recorder stop button. She gazed steadily at Redding. "Doctor, the recorder is off, and I'd like to ask you in deep personal confidence this question: Are we correct in thinking that Mark Joseph could be a dangerous man?"

He stood and shook her hand, then said, "I trust you understand that psychiatry is a science, but there are things we don't understand, and some of them are deep and dark. Evil is not scientific, but it's real."

Chapter Eighteen

She had a pocket full of circumstantial evidence but no proof. But she'd take what was offered and try to gather more.

She called the CHP to learn the name of the towing company that removed Joseph's car following the accident that he was involved in the morning of Edna Willows' murder. She was given the name of Martinez Towing Company in National City. She drove to that storage lot and asked for the manager.

The one question she had was whether they note the gas level when they bring in a car.

"We sure do," the manager said. "Ever since some joker accused us of siphoning his tank. Stupid idiot."

She asked him to look at the paperwork on Joseph's car that night. He did and told her the gas level was one-quarter full.

Something else to put in her circumstantial bag. No one would start a long trip across the desert late at night with less than a full tank. Mark Joseph had no intention of driving to Las Vegas. He was going home after murdering Edna Willows.

Mark Joseph was one stranger Jaye wanted to get to know. Other than words on paper and a brief interview, he was unknown to her. As a police officer, doors to public records were open to her that would be locked to the citizenry. All it took were a few hours on the telephone and internet with directories at her elbow to fit some pieces into his puzzle.

He was born in 1983 in the small town of Belvidere, Illinois. She called the chief of police of that town and asked for any information he had on Joseph. The chief opened online arrest records and said his name didn't appear but that Jaye should call Carl Swanson, the retired assistant principal of the local high school, saying that if Swanson knew anything, he'd be happy to talk about it. "In fact, don't try to stop him."

Jaye reached Swanson on the first ring. He turned out to be a garrulous retiree overjoyed to hear his phone ring. He didn't have to dig too deeply into his memory bank. "Mark Joseph? Oh, yeah. He graduated, let's see…in, uh, 2001." He gave the zero the old-style pronunciation—aught one— Yeah, '01. He was an odd duck with few friends. Come to think of it, he had no friends, at least that I was aware of. He was just sort of 'there.' That's about all I can tell you."

"Thank you, Mr. Swanson, is there—"

"Wait a moment. You'll have to forgive my memory. It has a mind of its own." He chuckled at his well-used pun. "I recall the school counselor had several sessions with his parents. Of course, she didn't tell anyone what it was about. I was under the impression they got him some help of some kind. Now, whether it took or not, I cannot say."

"Did you know his parents?"

"Did I know them? Make that "do." Ed and Mary Alice Joseph are fine, upstanding people, church people. Got some health problems. Become a little reclusive in the last few years. He's also a Rotarian, yes, sir. They had just the one child, Mark."

After high school, Joseph enrolled in college at nearby Northern Illinois University. Jaye reached the chief of the campus police, Stuart Harmison.

"I know who you're talking about," the chief said. "We were well shed off that one." Joseph had been a third-year accounting major in good standing who abruptly his classes and withdrew from school. The chief explained why.

"We had two complaints of stalking from women students. As I recall, one was in 2003—let me double-check…Yeah, '03. The other was in the following year. I interviewed both girls in depth. And I'll tell you, they were spooked. Neither wanted to file charges, though, and I didn't press them on it—I'm not sure I did the right thing. That's a hard position to be in: You want to respect the victims' wishes, but then again…I just don't know. Joseph was a creepy guy. If I heard he went from here and did some bad stuff, it'd bother me a lot. Anyway, the dean of students and I called him in and told him to shake the dust of this university from his heels fast, or he'd be talking to the county prosecutor. That's the last we heard of him."

Groping for something helpful, Jaye asked if he were aware of any strangulation murders in the area.

The chief thought for a moment, then said, "A while back, maybe a dozen years or so, there was a killing like that in Rockford, just a few miles from here. As I recall, it was strangulation."

"Do you remember a victim's name?"

"Sorry, I don't."

"Thank you for your help, chief," Jaye said.

"Uh, detective—Jaye, isn't it? Tell me, Jaye, what'd he do?"

"If I told you what he's being investigated for, chief, it'd bother you a lot."

Jaye phoned the lieutenant in charge of homicide at Rockford. He put her on hold to look up the information she s. He confirmed the murder in 2008 of a victim named Karen Walker, age twenty-seven. The case seemed to offer several similarities, including strangulation and the use of bleach.

The victim was also a social outcast, an alcoholic, what the lieutenant called a common drunk. "She was awfully young to sink that low that fast," he said. The case was unsolved and transferred to a cold case. At Jaye's request, he said he would copy the file and send it to her.

The lieutenant explained that the department had not entered the case in ViCAP. The database was but a few years old at the time and frequently overlooked by smaller departments, he explained. "That would not happen today."

She asked if a Belvidere man, Mark Joseph, was interviewed in the case.

She heard the rustling of paper. "I don't see his name. I never heard of him, and he's not in our computer."

Jaye bold-faced the name Karen Walker on her computer list.

Jaye and Baker tracked Joseph's job-hopping through the years until he arrived in San Diego in February, nine months before the Willows murder. Joseph was an accountant who had worked for casinos around the country. The sole police problem he had, other than in college, and the Bonnie Fletcher complaint in San Diego, was a harassment complaint from a woman in Seattle, which was dismissed.

Art Baker ran Joseph's fingerprints through the national database. Nothing showed up.

Neither was there DNA under his name. His DNA had never been collected. Jaye even had the lab try to take DNA from his fingerprints on the assault booking. However, they got nothing.

Jaye checked for unsolved murders of women in areas where he had lived at the time of his residence. There were three. She exchanged investigation data with each department, but nothing developed. None seemed to fit the killer's M.O.

Jaye closed the file and turned off her computer. She rubbed her eyes, feeling good about her progress but feeling sullied by the man she had been exposed to.

"Mark Joseph, maybe you're our killer, maybe not, but you are a son of a bitch," she muttered.

Sitting nearby, Baker said, "What?"

"Nothing, Art."

Jaye happened to mention to Brian that her thirty-third birthday was coming up two Fridays hence, and she would have the day off. Brian nodded but said nothing. Three days later, Brian handed her two envelopes, saying they were an early birthday present.

"Oh, you didn't have to do that," she said, using the requisite words. She put the envelopes on the table.

"Go ahead." He gestured to the table. "Open them."

"Now?" She picked up the first envelope and opened it to two tickets. She read what was written on them with curiosity. "What is a Nabucco?"

"He's a guy. It's an opera by Verdi. Opening night. Those seats are in the dress circle."

Jaye blinked in bewilderment and opened the second envelope. It was a $300 gift certificate to Neiman Markus, the department store for those who don't have to ask prices. She was surprised and wasn't sure what to say, so she just looked at him.

Finally, she said, "What in the world?"

"If you're going to be the most beautiful woman there, you have to look the part. That's for the perfect dress for the opera. But I have to warn you, you can't wear a gun on your hip that night."

She looked again at the gift certificate. "This is too much."

"It's not enough for you."

"Oh, shut up," she mock-scolded. She felt her eyes moisten. "Oh, my."

That Saturday, she walked past the unfamiliar chic stores of Fashion Valley and into Neiman Markus. She passed the clearance rack without stopping and into a section she would never think of going near. She found the perfect blue cocktail dress for 190 dollars and a pair of shoes for sixty dollars. She took the balance of the gift and bought Brian a twenty-five-dollar tie.

Opening night at Civic Theatre made her as proud as she had ever felt. Walking on the arm of Brian in his tuxedo, she said, "I feel like everyone is admiring this beautiful dress."

"I doubt it's the dress."

She was mesmerized by the lavish, resplendent set of the 6th century B.C. Babylon. The thought crossed her mind—If any place looked like that in real life, I'd move there. In the third act, she heard the "Chorus of the Hebrew Slaves." The soft music and the gentle singing were a psalm that carried her over billows of bliss.

They had a sublime dinner at the Top of the Market on the harbor. Afterward, she got a glimpse at the bill and gulped. They returned to her place and relaxed on a CD of Nabucco she had bought in advance. Jaye brought a beer to Brian, lounging on the couch with his tie draped over his shoulders. She sat next to him, and he put his arm around her. She said, "I felt divine tonight."

"You showed divine taste in the dress you chose."

"No, no," she said. "I felt divine because I was with you."

Brian said in almost a whisper, "'Love, whose month is ever May.'"

She raised her head from his shoulder. "What?"

"'Love, whose month is ever May.'"

The quizzical look did not leave her face.

"Those are words of Mr. Shakespeare to say that when I am with you, December becomes springtime. You are a spring breeze that gentles my spirit."

She returned her head to his shoulder. "We've only known each other a short time. It's amazing."

"You are amazing," he said softly. His words were a blanket of warmth, but they also gave her a chill because there was no longer room to evade what he had to be told. Jaye arose from his shoulder and said those most ominous words between a man and woman: "We need to talk."

She moved to the far end of the sofa so that if he wanted to leave, she would not be in his way. She began. "I haven't told you much about my marriage. It's not what I like to talk about. When I think too much about the kind of man Ben was, I turn it back on me, and I ask myself: What is about you that attracted you to such a man?

"He had one attractive quality for me as a girl struggling to become an adult—he promised to lift me out of the ditch that was my early life. He was selfish and domineering, but nothing in my upbringing told me that wasn't normal."

She made a swipe at the tears that filled her eyes. "In the last year of our marriage, I became pregnant. I thought having a baby would strengthen our marriage." Her voice took on a momentary harsh edge. "Hah!" She used a tissue to touch her nose.

"The idea of a cozy little family made me happy. Ben agreed, or so he claimed. However, when I was far along in my second trimester, he changed his mind. I think that was right about the time he decided to dump me. He demanded I get an abortion. I refused. Even then, I thought I was too far along. It made him angry. I have nothing against family planning. Earlier, I would have done as he asked, but it was too late. Everyone told me that.

"He became more belligerent about it, almost threatening. Finally, near the end of my sixth month, he said if I didn't do it, he would divorce me. I was scared. I went to doctors in San Diego, and none would do it that late. He kept hammering on me, telling me it would be safe—I was too weak to resist him. I was still a dumb, scared kid. Cornered, I gave in.

"He took me to Tijuana to get it done—and they botched it. They aborted my little girl...the fetus was a girl. But they also scarred my uterus. It caused a condition called Asherman's syndrome that sometimes results in infertility. In me, it did." She started to cry. He handed her his handkerchief.

"Later, I realized he just didn't want a child because he didn't want to be saddled with support payments. He was already in a hot affair and was planning to divorce me. When he walked out on me, he left me with bills and remorse. I was able to pay off the bills."

She looked at him with uncertainty. "Brian, I can never have children. What haunts me is remembering you saying that you wanted a sister or brother for Traci. Well, I can't give you that."

He moved over to where she sat and gently pulled her head down to his lap. He stroked her hair and face. He said nothing for minutes. Then he spoke, still stroking her hair. "Every person is injured in some way, including you and me. Be grateful that each of us now has someone to lean on."

"Thank you. I love you."

"If I were my own psychologist giving love advice to myself, I would warn me about rebounding. But then, I would answer myself—You're right, but you're also wrong because I know how I feel." Brian turned to Jaye. "And this is how I feel— I came upon you late, but I came upon you, and it was not too late."

She brushed aside tears. "Ahhhhh."

He gave her a playful slap on the butt. "This new dress is getting wrinkled. I think you should take it off."

Chapter Nineteen

The spring night was balmy in San Diego, as mellow as Kentucky bourbon. The man was walking on an empty side street off Imperial Avenue, moving languidly. But this man had one. He was hunting. He sized up a figure shuffling along the dark sidewalk. The hunt was about over.

It was unknown why seventy-two-year-old Maria Estaban ended up homeless on these streets. She had forgotten the reason herself. What she did know was that San Diego was a decided upgrade over her native Tijuana. On this side of the border, she had soup kitchens and free medical care for her arthritis, and even a warm bed on occasion. Life being relative, she was content.

He was a professional at this, an achievement of considerable self-esteem. Edna Willows was his showcase, done with artistry. He knew her name from the newspaper, a story he read many times. He always worked his will on his "subjects" and outwitted the police. Always. Of all who practiced his calling, he was un-equaled. He felt guilty that he had forgotten his latex gloves at the Willows event, but the bleach covered any prints he might have left. However, working barehanded, if only for that one time, gave him a more intimate sense of the event.

He considered himself the nonpareil, the champion. He was Ali taunting Frazier, the slugger glaring at the rookie pitcher. He was Manolete caping the bull. He followed the achievements of his peers, and when they were caught, he game-planned what went wrong.

He was a sociopath. He had accepted it and considered it a strength, a tactical advantage. He did not feel human empathy. He did not love, but neither did he hate, at least not personally. The women he killed meant nothing to him. If he went to a romantic movie, it might as well be a boring travelogue. If his emotions were charted like an EKG, he would be flat-lined. He knew he was different, but he believed that meant superior.

What made his blood rush was achieving what he was about to do.

The man closed the distance at a normal pace to about ten feet, then slowed to maintain the separation. The street was empty. He saw a storage lot just ahead with no lighting and heavy equipment for cover—an Elysian field for a killer. That was where he would stage the event.

But even as he plotted his attack, he wasn't bringing his normal energy to the job. Earlier, the usual anticipation had hummed like a tuning fork in his mind. Ah, the excitement, the risk, the exhilaration…

But that was then. Now, he just felt blah. The mood had passed. That happened on rare occasions like this. There was no point in killing this old woman just to pad his record.

Maria heard the steps and turned around. He gave a short wave and said, "Have a nice evening." He turned and crossed the street, then went to his car to go home and watch Netflix. First, he had to stop for a few groceries. He was almost out of milk.

Maria Estaban would see the sunrise.

Jaye, Baker, and Potter sat in his office, letting their coffee get cold. They were silent and discouraged, trying to think but not having a lot to think about. Jaye's mind was an echo chamber of doubts. They had run out of space on the Joseph trail. Potter considered him no more than a person of interest. Baker was a little more intrigued, but Jaye believed he was the logical suspect.

The strength of Jaye's opinion bothered Potter. When a detective's focus becomes too narrow, other suspects can slip by like ships in a fog. However, he said nothing, just watched.

Baker didn't lighten the mood. "This thing's given me a cauliflower ear. I've been living on the phone. There've been a lot of strangulations, but the M.O. falls apart after that. I've made myself a pest with ViCAP, but there's nothing there that helps, and they're looking at the whole country. The street interviews by our cops have been a big nothing. The public suggestions are so bizarre I'm tempted to make some of them suspects."

Jaye said, "I'd relax more if we had a tail on this guy, Joseph. Who knows when the next killing will happen?"

Potter shook his head. "No way would the department approve that. Staff surveillance is damned expensive, and you don't have near enough on him."

"I know, I know, I'm just saying…"

"You're obsessed, Peoria."

"I feel like a drunk stumbling around in clown shoes. Maybe I'm not the right person to be lead on this," Jaye said in a moment of self-pity.

"Oh, shut up," Potter said. "Tell you what, when you're stuck in a tunnel, dig yourself out. Why don't you go back and review all your suspects?"

"I've gone over that file a hundred times," she said.

"Then start on the next hundred." Potter clapped his hands. "Go get 'em. You're not going to find a murderer moping around here—not unless you screw this thing up, and then it might be me." He turned pastorly. "Remember, failure is just practice for success."

Jaye laughed and started toward the door. "Did you just make that up?"

He became theatrically defensive. "Of course I did."

"I'd love to give you a polygraph on that."

"Get your ass out of here."

"That's what I like about your enlightened management style: subtle motivation."

Jaye worked through lunch and into the late afternoon, again reading documents that she had almost committed to memory. Near the bottom was the lab report on Jane Doe 18-2. In all that had been going on, she had just read it once. She opened it and hoped there might be something there she and Baker had overlooked. She read through it and almost went to the next document in the file. However, something she read—or didn't read—struck her as odd. She went through it again… Strange. She put the paper down and thought about it: If a woman is having the life choked out of her, she's going to fight and claw for life. She'll reach around to try to rip the hands off her throat, maybe resulting in her assailant's DNA being under her fingernails. However, the lab report had no reference to a fingernail scraping for DNA evidence.

Jaye hurriedly called a lab supervisor that she knew, Edith Mitchell. She told her about the missing part of the report, and a suddenly tense supervisor said she would get right back to her.

Thirty minutes later, a contrite Wilson called. "My god, Jaye. I've never been so embarrassed." In a sad voice, she told Jaye that a rookie technician had forgotten to scrap 18-2's fingernails, and no one caught the omission.

Jaye accepted the apology and commiserated, then thanked her for the help, and ended the call. However, it was followed by a moment of panic. Was the body gone? She knew that Edna Willows, being an identified but unclaimed body not held by police, was cremated, and her ashes spread at sea. Lila Brown's body was released to her family for burial. But what about Jane Doe? Was she cremated, too?

She picked up the phone and asked for a meeting with Dr. Racklin.

The next morning, Jaye waited for a half-hour before Racklin could break free to see her. Walking into the room, the old doctor's eyes lit up in recognition. "Ah, yes, the only detective I'd take home to Mother." He shook her hand. "Being an old man means I can get away with saying such things. Now, what can I do for you, my dear?"

Jaye nervously asked the whereabouts of the body of Jane Doe 18-2. Racklin went to a cabinet and leafed through the files. Finally, he lifted one and studied the contents, humming as he worked. He turned to Jaye and said, "Buried."

"Excuse me?"

He sat down next to her. "When a body is unidentified, we anticipate that someone will eventually claim it and perhaps want to take the body back home for burial, as so often happens. That's why we don't cremate those corpses. She's in Mt. Hope cemetery."

Jaye explained the problem of the omitted fingernail scraping and the possibility that vital evidence might be locked in that coffin.

"That is disturbing," he said. "Here we have a strangling, and there's no indication that fingernails were examined." Racklin glanced at his own fingernails. "It's axiomatic that a woman being choked would start clawing at her assailant. And if that were the case, it's possible that fragments of the attacker's skin, hair, or blood would be lodged under the nails."

"I know that, and it's freaking me out," Jaye said. She also told herself— "Axiomatic"—a new word to look up.

"You made a nice catch, my dear. The question is, What do we do now?" he said.

"Based on your experience, what are the chances of finding evidence under her fingernails? My concern is that bleach might have been used on her fingers to erase DNA."

He shrugged. "We can't control that. But even if bleach weren't used, any scrapings we get might not be of value, DNA-wise. However, forensic pathology is not a guessing game. The only way to know for certain is to look."

"I was hoping you would say that," she said.

"Yes, an exhumation. What you discovered is an unturned stone. We need to look under it."

"That would mean a court order, doctor."

"That's what courts are for, young lady, to give orders. Be aware that judges tend to jealously guard the sleep of the dead." He paused. "As I believe they should. Anyway, we'll have to see the DA."

Jaye groaned, then saw him looking at her quizzically. "Don't mind me. Just a few days ago, I had an unhappy encounter in his office. He won't be happy to see me for a while."

"Well, that's where we have to go, so no point delaying it."

District Attorney Baudino agreed to see them immediately, and when Jaye walked in, he gave her a wide smile. "Well, well, another visit so soon? All we need is attorney Sherman, and we can have a reunion."

Jaye grimaced. "That's one reunion I'd like to miss. By the way, Mr. Baudino, thanks for backing us up on the Sammy Clark thing."

He dismissed it with a wave. "No problem. Timidity never solved a crime, and we know you sometimes have to play hardball." He looked toward Racklin. "Doc, how are you?"

Racklin shook hands and said, "Fine, Ed, except we need a favor."

Baudino's politician's smile split his face. "You mean this isn't a social visit? What can I do for you?"

After Racklin finished explaining, Baudino had a pensive look, the smile was gone. "Pretty thin reason. Superior court judges tend to be more protective of the dead than the living. It can be tougher to get an exhumation order than a search warrant. It's the sort of thing that 'offends the conscience of the court.' But give me a few hours to see what I can do."

Jaye spent the rest of the day sorting files and catching up on paperwork, and glancing at the phone every few minutes. More than once, she had to start a task all over again because her mind had wandered over to the courthouse where an assistant district attorney was arguing for the exhumation order. A few minutes before five, her phone rang, and it was to her ear in an instant. "Jaye Peoria."

"Jaye, this is Dr. Racklin. Guess what?"

"I'm afraid to."

"We got the order. They're going to dig early tomorrow morning. Be in my office first thing, and we'll see if we've wasted everyone's time."

Jaye accompanied Racklin into the autopsy room the next morning. Alongside was Marilyn Noguchi from the crime lab, who had also worked on the Willows case.

The corpse had already been laid on a steel examination table. The simple wooden coffin waited in a corner with the lid ajar.

As the pathologist busied himself with preparations, Jaye approached the body with the awe of the living toward the dead. She had not been in this business long enough to become jaded.

Sadness enveloped Jaye's spirit because she was looking at a wasted, tragic life and also at the dread that, in time, this would be her: all alone and soon to be forgotten.

The body's light brown hair had been combed, and she was

wearing a blue shift provided by the mortuary. There was an unpleasant sweet, pungent smell of beginning decay that rose above the body like ozone. The flesh had turned the color of the blue-white stone, causing her to almost resemble a statue brought in for repairs. Her eyes were closed, as in sleep. On her face were splotches of green and black. Those were fungi attacking the soft flesh. Racklin came silently up to Jaye's side. "Pondering eternity? That's what people do, standing here as you are." He appraised the corpse. "She was buried in dry, higher ground. That's why she still looks preserved." He gave Jaye an apologetic look. "I hope I don't sound crass. In here, that's shop talk. But we do not lose respect for what was once a living, breathing human.

"There is something…violating…about disturbing a grave. I know it makes no sense, but when it comes to death, we're not terribly logical."

Jaye asked why the cheeks were puffy, almost like a squirrel with jaws full of acorns.

Racklin said, "We remove upper and lower jaws for future identification. The attendants filled the jaws with cotton this morning."

"Why go to that effort?"

The pathologist thought for a long moment. "It's hard to explain. Maybe it's a way of saying to the spirit of this murdered young woman—You've been abused your whole life. We will give you this gesture of respect. It's not a religious thing, it's a feeling thing."

Noguchi said, "But doctor, she's dead."

He smiled gently at her. "But we are not."

His voice turned more businesslike. "Well, time to go to work." It was Noguchi's job. She put on latex gloves, picked up the body's left hand, and peered at the fingernails one at a time with a powerful magnifying glass. The nails were easier to work with because as the skin dried, it shrank, leaving much more nail surface. Noguchi took a knife and scraped the underside. Nothing. Finger after finger. Nothing. After several minutes, she put the hand down and said, "Clean." She went around the table and did the same to the right hand. When she reached the index finger, she scratched underneath the nail, which let several dark flecks loosened by the blade fall onto a sheet of white paper. She did the same with the middle finger, again getting some residue. She returned the hand to the side of the body. "Thank God morticians don't clean the nails in these cheap funerals."

"What'd you get?" Jaye asked, looking into the paper where the tiny items lay.

"The DNA folks will have to tell us that." She picked up a test tube and, oh-so-carefully, bent the paper and funneled the matter into it. She sealed the tube with a rubber plug and attached an adhesive label that said, "Jane Doe 18-2" with the date and Racklin's name. He filled out a form that detailed what he had done. "You are now in the chain of custody of evidence," he said.

"Yes, sir, I'm aware of that," Noguchi said.

He smiled. "I know that you know that, but I have to say it." He looked at the corpse. "Meantime, I'll send her back to where she belongs."

The two women thanked him and headed for the door, but Jaye turned around when she heard him say in a muted voice, "Sorry, we had to do that, my dear." When Jaye realized he wasn't talking to her, she quietly closed the door behind her.

Grant Barstow, an outgoing bear of a man, had started as a high school chemistry teacher where he tried introducing football players, punkers, and dropouts-in-training to the mysteries of the microscope. He soon realized he would have a better chance of selling a time-share in Des Moines. After six years of this, his favorite reading became the help-wanted ads, and it wasn't long before he joined the crime lab of the San Diego Police Department.

Eleven years and a Ph.D. later, Barstow had risen to chief scientist of DNA, the keeper of the latest hi-tech toy.

Barstow had just finished shop talk with his counterpart in Boston when a woman, alongside Marilyn Noguchi, came into his area of the lab. He recognized her from her photo in the news. She thrust out her hand. "I'm Jaye Peoria from homicide."

He rose, and they shook hands. "You're our first celebrity.

Maybe we should capture your handprint in plaster, sort of our variation of that Hollywood sidewalk."

"Celebrity?"

"I've seen you on television more than Jay Leno."

"Oh, you mean the Dark Street Assassin crap. Well, that's my fifteen minutes, I suppose. I would have settled for fifteen seconds."

He looked at the container Noguchi was holding. "Is this what I think it is?"

Jaye nodded at the test tube kit as Noguchi handed it to him. "I hope you can rush it. I believe a killer's name is hidden in this DNA."

"We'll see," he said. "But, if bleach was poured on her fingers, as I was told…in other words, don't get carried away with hope."

She shrugged. "Understood."

Barstow accepted the item, then filled out a chain-of-custody form, signed it, and gave it to Jaye. "I like what you're doing, and this'll go to the top of the pile. And I assure you, it's a big pile."

"How soon?"

"We have an equipment malfunction that should get fixed in a few days. I'll have it in maybe a week, I hope." Then, he excused himself and carried the kit toward the DNA lab.

Jaye was excited to tell Potter of the finger scrapings taken from the corpse of Jane Doe, that is, until his reaction deflated her spirit because he wasn't that impressed.

"I hope you're right, but we'll see what the lab finds if anything. I keep telling you, Peoria, you have to get off that high-low roller coaster. Let's wait and see. I know you want the evidence— if there is any— to nail this Joseph guy. There are a lot of buts and howevers to deal with first."

He didn't even smile when she suggested an electronic tracker be put on Joseph's car. She was prepared for his reaction.

"Sarge, I know the evidence is not that strong yet, but other women could be in danger today, tonight."

"The evidence is 'not strong,' you say." He shook his head.

"I'd say it's thin, almost nonexistent. If you want an electronic tracker put on his car, you've got to get a court order. No judge is going to sign such an order on what you've got here."

"I think Joseph's the one," she insisted.

"Oh, so he's the one, is he? You mean like Lewis Price and that pathetic little bastard with the barbed wire face—"

"You mean Sammie Clark."

"Him, too."

"Sarge, I never said they were the ones. I just said they were suspicious."

A wide smile spread over his face. "Peoria, don't try to out-bullshit a world-class bullshitter." His face became more kindly. "Look, I know I'm being tough on you, but that's my job."

She fought back her own smile and affected a forlorn pout. "Let's just try, Sarge? Huh? Please?"

The next morning a buoyant Jaye and unenthused Potter were in the county building, explaining to DA Baudino why the tracker was necessary. The DA was also skeptical. "I'll try, but it's thin."

"That was my word, thin," Potter said, nodding.

"I've come to hate that word," Jaye said.

"Well, our best shot to get a warrant would be with Judge Hugasian. But I'm telling you, it's a reach."

"Thank you, Mr. Baudino," Jaye said sweetly.

"Well, Hugasian's the closest thing in this county to Roy Bean, that Old West hanging judge—don't repeat that I said that. He's more open to this sort of thing. But I'm telling you again, it's a reach."

As they stood to leave, Baudino teased Jaye. "I might have to go on part-time if I didn't have you giving me work."

Hugasian was in his chambers waiting to reconvene court after the lunch break. He faced Baudino, Potter, and Jaye across his desk. "Let's make this fast. I've got to get into court." He scanned Baudino's appeal for a warrant to put a tracker on Mark Joseph's car. He put it down and said, "Is this all you've got? And you want a warrant for a full month? Uh-uh."

Baudino said, "Judge, a tracker would be minimally intrusive. I think—"

"No."

Baudino and Potter were half out of their chairs to leave when Jaye said, "Your honor, we in homicide believe this man killed two women and maybe three in just a matter of months. We have tissue evidence from the victim we exhumed that's being analyzed as fast as possible—and, by the way, thank you for signing that exhumation order. We should know soon if we have usable DNA. We're confident we will.

"Could you please just give us two weeks of the tracker? I'd never forgive myself if Joseph killed again while we wait." She summoned forth her most sincere, pleading smile.

Hugasian rose and removed his robe from a hangar. As he put it on, he said, "I've got a trial waiting." He looked at Jaye. "Ten days, not a day more. Get the paperwork to me. Good day to you all."

As they walked out, Potter uttered an incredulous chuckle. "You are one slick conniver, Peoria. You could sweet-talk a dog off a sausage."

At about 11:00 P.M. that night, an unmarked car drove slowly through the casino parking area and pulled in close to a particular car in the employees' lot. A man got out of the passenger side and sauntered over to the car, and checked the license plate. He looked around and saw no people nearby. He dropped to one knee and took out a device about the size of a cigarette pack. He flicked a switch to activate it and reached under the car, where a powerful magnet grabbed the steel of the frame. The man got back into the waiting car and left. Time elapsed: forty-five seconds. Tracker attached.

For a week and a half, the tracker would be constantly monitored, with special attention given to the hours between midnight and dawn. If it showed the car was moving, the built-in GPS would reveal the movement and location to the monitor. If Joseph moved from his house, in the pre-dawn hours especially, a car would follow for a few blocks and then pass him off to another car to avoid tipping that he was being tracked.

For five days and nights, the tracking device magnetized to the frame of Joseph's car reported his comings and goings, mostly to shopping centers and other activities common to ordinary citizens doing routine business. However, in the time period Jaye was most interested in, the early morning hours between midnight and six, he didn't move from his house. At first, she was disappointed, but then she thought twice—that's a good thing.

Her angst was familiar to department veterans. Jaye was on a mission. Nothing is more frustrating, even maddening, to a cop than to know—absolutely know—who did the crime but not have the proof to arrest.

However, to cops who had been around the block many times, that zealotry could turn into myopia that blocks off other alternatives and other suspects and might even allow the guilty to get away with their crime, not to mention driving the cop to drink.

At the end of a week, she heard from Barstow, who told her that the DNA from Jane Doe's fingernails had yielded two contributors. One was Jane Doe; the other was of an unidentified person. He said the lab had run it through CODIS, the FBI database, and no hits came back.

"What I can give you, Jaye, is a killer with no name. That's going to be your job. Good luck."

Jaye hung up the phone and leaned back in thought. She needed to get a sample of Joseph's DNA. She wished they had not destroyed the garbage she had gone through. That surely would have his DNA on things he had handled—Wait a minute! The lithium prescription bottle she recovered from the evidence room. She called Barstow, who said he would send a tech over to bring it back to the lab. "We can tell you in short order if it has DNA on it."

It wasn't until late the next morning that Barstow called. Jaye answered on the first ring.

"Hi, Jaye. Bad news. That bottle had been handled by so many people it was impossible to get DNA that made any sense off it. Maybe you could have a cop he doesn't know follow him and retrieve a restaurant cup, a spoon he's eaten from, or maybe a cigarette butt. Any of those would work."

"Damn! The problem is, Grant, my tracker court order runs out in three days. I just don't have time."

"Hmmm. Let me think." After a long pause, he said, "There is something I read about that might work. Let's talk. Can you come over here?"

She was out the door in sixty seconds.

Chapter Twenty

J aye finished scrubbing her right hand with distilled water and let it air dry. She twisted around to face Marilyn Noguchi in the back seat. She had requested that Noguchi, who had become a pal, be assigned to the job. "So you think this will work, huh?" Jaye asked.

"My boss heard of it being done before, but you never know," Noguchi said. "We're going to find out."

Almaguer pulled up in front of Mark Joseph's house. "I'm eager to meet your new boyfriend, Mr. Joseph," he kidded Jaye. "I may have the two of you over to the house."

The two detectives exited the car while Noguchi remained in the back seat. They approached the front door, and Jaye rang the bell with her left hand.

After a long wait, the door opened a few inches. "Yeah?" came the surly challenge.

Jaye smiled sweetly. "Mr. Joseph, you'll remember me, Detective Peoria." She gestured to her smiling partner. "This is Detective Almaguer. We have some good news for you. May we come in?"

The door opened, and he stepped back to let them enter, then stared at them with narrowed eyes.

Jaye said, "Thank you. We're here pursuant to a new department policy suggested by the police commission. We are directed to inform people we've considered possible suspects in serious cases that they no longer are. The directive was the result of complaints from people left hanging with no explanation."

"You mean you're going to lay off me and forget that BS about killing some woman? For real?"

Almaguer said, "Yes, sir. For real."

Jaye added, "You are no longer a person of interest. I think this new policy is a good step forward to better community relations."

Joseph's mood softened. "Well, okay. Thanks."

Both detectives took advantage of their entry to learn the house's layout. Jaye looked around and said, "This looks like one of those California bungalows built before World War II. It's a classic."

Almaguer said, "I was raised in one of these. Two bedrooms, one bath, right? But the garage is new."

Jaye said, "We'll be going. Sorry to bother you, Mr. Joseph, but we felt we owed you a visit." She extended her right hand, and he reached out to shake it. She held his a little longer than normal but then turned and followed Almaguer out the door.

Almaguer drove around the corner and pulled over. Jaye extended her right hand into the back seat, where Noguchi was ready with swabs to wipe the palm of her hand. When finished, she put the swabs in a DNA kit.

Almaguer pulled away from the curb and said, "Man, you are one polished bullshitter. I should take lessons from you for when I come home after midnight."

Jaye was elated at how well her ruse worked. "I figure, if he's innocent, no harm done. If he's guilty, then screw him. I don't owe him the truth. I owe those women justice."

"We just have to hope this works," Noguchi said.

They dropped Noguchi and her swab kit off at the crime lab, where Barstow signed his own chain-of-possession form and then was handed the swabs. He gave it the highest priority for analysis. If the swab contained DNA, he could tell Jaye if she had identified a serial killer.

"My equipment is now humming. I'll have this in two days, but don't tell anyone I can do it."

She and Almaguer drove back to headquarters. Everything was done except the waiting. Jaye got no work done the next two days except shuffle papers and stare at the phone.

The tracker warrant had expired, but Jaye was able to cajole the department into assigning a patrol officer in an unmarked car to follow Joseph home from work and then watch his house until dawn. It was done on overtime, so she was only promised three nights of coverage. Even so, the captain was not happy with the damage done to his budget.

On the morning of the third day, the phone rang. There was no second ring: "Good morning, Detective Peoria," she said.

"It is, indeed," Barstow said merrily. "We've got a match. The DNA under Jane Doe's fingernails and the DNA from Mark Joseph off your hand are identical. Go get him. He's your killer."

The emotion of preparing a raid or a major arrest is like the jitters before a big game: the camaraderie of those milling about the staging yard, the danger they might face, the excitement of the chase, the heady scent of expected success.

Jaye was right in the middle of it. It was her show. The arrest warrant for murder had Mark Joseph's name on it. She had proudly taken it to the DA's office to be put into the system.

The arrest would follow standard procedure: When possible, make the apprehension in daylight, in an area that minimizes the chance for him to reach weapons and represents the least possible risk to bystanders. Joseph was a mystery as to what danger he might pose. He had no known history of firearms, and his victims were helpless women. But—and it was an ominous but—he was a violent killer.

His house was decided upon as the safest place to take him down. However, it was important to get him outside; no one knew what he had stashed inside. Surveillance had established he left the house for work at 2:00 P.M. without fail. Routinely, he went from the house, through the open breezeway, into the garage, and departed. His practice was to swing around in front of the garage and then back in his SUV, primed for a quick getaway.

The house was built as a farmhouse years ago and now sat on the backside of a large lot with a long, sloping driveway of perhaps 100 feet.

Two uniforms and Tatum would be stationed on the side of the garage, not visible from the house. Two patrol cars would be out of sight down the block, one in each direction, ready to chase if necessary. Jaye would be in an unmarked sedan across the street. Her car had tinted windows that allowed visibility only through her side. When Joseph went through the breezeway to the garage, the men on the blind side would respond to her signal and rush into the garage and arrest him before he got into his car.

Since his vehicle was pointed outward, a truck with a heavy barrier grill used for pushing was also sitting across the street. It would drive up next to the garage door to block his exit if necessary. If, by chance, he walked out into his yard or to the mailbox, the takedown would be even easier. All of this would be activated by Jaye with an alert through her hand radio.

That was the plan. Uh-huh…

Everyone was in position at 1:30. Now, what remained was the wait as the clock crawled toward 2 P.M. Jaye saw a shadow pass the front window of his house; maybe a shadow, maybe him.

It was 1:50, ten minutes to go. Suddenly, she was jarred alert to see Joseph pass through the breezeway and enter the garage. She quickly signaled the others and jumped out of her car.

The cops on the side were confused only momentarily, but it cost valuable seconds. The cop driving the unfamiliar truck was outside the vehicle making a mechanical check. When he got the signal, he frantically jumped into the cab. The truck roared awake and started to slowly move toward the driveway.

Jaye stepped onto the sideyard grass, pistol in hand.

Just as he inserted the Chevy Suburban ignition key, Joseph spotted the three cops enter through the breezeway. He gunned the car and shattered the thin wood of the garage door. As he slammed his way out, the truck had not yet entered the driveway.

Violent death does not approach in slow motion. It doesn't sneak. It's a cat's spring.

Joseph's Suburban started down the long driveway on a clear path to the street. But before it gathered speed, Joseph began to steer toward Jaye, standing ten feet off the driveway on the grass. She saw his face. His eyes were looking into her eyes. His look was flat and without feeling. Later, she wonders if that was the look his victims saw.

The large vehicle was a metal beast bearing down on her. Its roar was a growl. The grill was a devouring mouth. No time to jump clear. Her instinct processed faster than her mind. Her neurons realized what would only reach her mind minutes later. They told her she was about to die.

She swung her pistol into a shooter's stance and leveled it at the windshield. Training put her mind on autopilot. Her aim was deliberate, but her trigger was fast. She knew the glass would deflect and make a bullet's path erratic and reduce velocity. She had to fire for overkill.

Eight shots, Tatum later said he counted. The windshield spider-webbed. Joseph slumped forward as the big car veered toward the oncoming truck and smashed into its heavy grill. The engine died, too.

One of the officers ran up to the car and looked inside. He turned away, stunned. "Wow," he said.

Jaye started to shake. Tears rolled down her cheeks. She made no attempt to hide them. Tatum ran up, took the Glock from her hand, and enclosed her in his arms.

One of the officers put out the call. Doors in the neighborhood crept open, and people edged out onto driveways, content to watch from a distance in stunned silence.

Sirens sounded from every direction. Squad cars filled the street, and uniforms surrounded her. But Jaye was alone.

When the scene was cleaned up, they discovered fifteen-hundred dollars in cash, a pistol, and a fake passport in the Suburban. They were hidden in a bag under the seat, stashed there, ready to run.

Joseph wanted to escape, so why didn't he just keep going? Maybe his compulsion took over—another woman to kill, and one he especially wanted to kill, the one who had bedeviled him. It was later theorized that he was attempting "suicide by cop," although Jaye didn't believe that for a moment.

Standard protocol locked into place. Jaye surrendered her firearm and was placed on desk duty to await a department hearing and also the DA's judgment on the shooting. There were obligatory questions about the extent of the danger to her life posed by Joseph's action. However, the trajectory of his vehicle toward where Jaye was standing satisfied even anti-police activists that she fired in self-defense. Her exoneration from the DA's office happened in record time.

While that was happening, Jaye took a week off to just walk the beach, sleep late, do a little morbid thinking about what she had done, and then shake that off.

Potter took charge. After the autopsy, Joseph's ashes were shipped back to his parents in Illinois. At their request, his brain was given to the FBI for medical study.

Potter organized a complete shakedown of Joseph's house. The searchers found a jacket in his closet with a dark spot on the sleeve. A DNA test showed it to be a small splash of Lila Brown's blood. Jaye was right. Brown was victim number two. They also found a hidden stack of newspapers, each of which had a write-up of one of the three killings. Three half-gallons of oxidized bleach and a box of latex gloves were in the laundry area.

They found Joseph's secret audio tape stash. They hoped the tapes would reveal the identities of more victims, but they were only generalized boastings. After analysis, a copy was given to the FBI's ViCAP database, another for psychiatric study, and yet another was passed hand-to-hand around the department. It became a frequent source of fascination and morbid amusement.

Baker came across a rental-space key to a local storage location. When they gained entry and went through the stack of items, they found a lockbox near the bottom and forced it open. Inside was a trove of his trophies. They found Edna Willows' shoe and Lila Brown's bracelet. But that wasn't all. Also in the box were items that couldn't be placed: a wedding ring, a woman's empty wallet, another single shoe, and a cosmetic case. There was also a purse-size photo album bearing the initials "K.W." It contained the smiling faces of a family who would never have guessed their images had become the keepsake of a psychopath. Detectives calculated that six women had died to fill his box of morbid souvenirs. At least.

It became Baker's job to track down families of victims who once owned the items. Over the following weeks, he was successful only with the photo album. It was identified by the mother of Karen Walker of Rockford, Illinois. Local police returned it to her. Jaye sometimes thought of how it must have torn her spirit to be handed all that was left of her daughter.

"Closure," as it's called, is a feel-good myth. Heartbreak cannot be erased or shut like a door. Time alone can lull it to sleep.

Jaye became a media shooting star in San Diego. However, her public acclaim for taking down Joseph was brief because any police shooting, no matter how justified or even heroic, makes politicians and the press nervous. She quietly went back to her job.

She had tired of reporters slobbering over her. She said to Brian, "I'm tired of this BS. I'm not Annie Oakley or Calamity Jane. I'm just a cop, and all I want is to go back to being one without this baloney."

No one said much at work. Death—anybody's—was not a comfortable thing to cheer. However, though not much was spoken, the looks were there. Admiration didn't require speeches. Respect was apparent in the eyes. She would never again be who she was, and that would take some getting used to.

Jaye had no nightmares or second guesses about shooting Mark Joseph to death. But that didn't mean taking a human life did not exact a personal price. No, she wasn't smitten with guilt or "Why me?" entreaties to God. But, there were times when she again saw Joseph's face the instant he aimed the vehicle at her. She didn't see hate in his eyes, only deadness. She had thought he would enjoy killing, but now she wasn't sure. It was too complex. Someday she'd like to understand it.

How all this changed Jaye was hard for her to comprehend. She didn't have anger, regret, or guilt, though she vowed she would never gloat about taking his life. She still laughed and loved. The change was hidden within her: the realization that simplicity was gone, and she could never again be a light-hearted woman. She had added a new weight to her life, and wasn't sure what it was, and didn't know how long she would have to carry it.

She had learned much about her chosen career in the months she struggled to find the killer of the East Village women: the frustration of stumbling and the disappointment of being doubted.

Most of all, she learned that the taste of success is never as savory as expected and never as long-lasting.

And she was fine with that.

Brian's profession was counseling people and helping them cross rivers safely in their lives. Wisely, he said little to Jaye. For the time being, he backed off and let her explore her depths for whatever she could find. Plenty of talk would come later. Over time, the silence ended, and her smile returned as he knew it would. He just made sure he was there within reach.

The time then came to sit her down to prepare for another river to cross. "Jaye, you know I love you, but I have bad news…"

Her face took on a guarded "oh-oh" look, and Brian saw her stiffen.

He reached for her hand. "Yesterday, Maureen called and asked me to come over. When I got there, she had been crying. She hugged me like I was a lifeline. We talked."

Brian stopped and exhaled to steady himself. His voice quavered. "All the illness she's been experiencing has…." He shook his head as though to clear it. "Maureen has stage-four pancreatic cancer."

Jaye breathed her shock. "Oh."

Brian nodded sadly. "That is the worst kind. The worst. People don't recover from that. The doctors give her a year at the outside."

"I'm so sorry. Poor woman, poor Traci. What are you going to do?"

"I have to move back. She's alone, and there's Traci. I have to do it." He saw the look on Jaye's face. "It's platonic, of course. I hope to see you from time to time."

Jaye wanted to feel empathy, but the instinct did battle with selfishness, and that bothered her. She wanted to be big of heart, like Brian, but her own memory of loss and the fear of rejection was quicksand that threatened to suck her down.

However, at that moment, she chose to look in her inward mirror. There she saw trust she didn't know she had.

"Will you be back?"
"Believe me, I will be. We will be Traci and I."
She believed. "And I will be here."

Chapter Twenty-One

She had never figured Mark Joseph out. That used to bother her, but she learned over time that some things in life, especially dark things, never fill out the puzzle. Shrinks and crime experts claim to understand a lot about serial killers, but they don't, not to the degree they claim. Mark Joseph was one of those secretive vipers that slither among humans and then disappear down a hole.

At least a hundred people asked her why Joseph killed those women, and to each, she gave the same honest answer—I have no idea.

She regretted never having had the chance to confront the killer. She'd have liked to see his face when he heard her single question— "Why?" She wouldn't get an answer because he wouldn't have one to give, but the question might stay with him.

She sometimes thought of his victims. They had nothing, and all they wanted was to hold on to their finger grip on life. But he denied them that.

The young addict-hooker named Jane Doe, 18-2, remained unidentified in her small plot in Mt. Hope cemetery. Jaye kept the picture in her memory of the young woman lying dead on that steel table but having the identity of her killer under her fingernails.

"I wish she could at least have her own name," Jaye once said to her partner as they drove by the cemetery.

Before she could turn loose the memories of the Joseph case, there was something remaining to be done, something that had grown in her mind from an idea to a desire and then to an obligation, as she gained in wisdom and compassion.

It was time to take a trip.

Karen Walker was a twenty-seven-year-old alcoholic in Rockford, Illinois, an hour and a half west of Chicago's O'Hare Airport. Despite being the largest city in that part of the state, it was quiet and conservative and just fifteen miles west of the Joseph family home in Belvidere.

Rockford was not a place to be tolerant of a woman prone to turning into a street drunk at the opening of a vodka bottle. More than once, police picked Karen Walker up from a doorway and took her to the drunk tank.

Karen was found dead in an alley on a frigid night just before Christmas 2008. The assumption was that booze had won another battle. However, the autopsy showed she had been strangled. And though the state crime lab was called in, no fingerprints or DNA were found. All that was discovered were traces of bleach on her skin and extensive bleach stains on her clothes, which her mother said had never been there.

For ten years, Karen Walker's killer was unknown until police found her mini photo album in Joseph's storage lockbox. It was identified by her mother.

Joseph had also killed Karen.

When Jaye picked up her rental at the airport, she opened the GPS and typed in 348 Rock River Lane, Rockford, then pulled out into traffic. After driving seventy-five miles, she pulled up to a narrow, fake-brick house with a 1940s look. "Here goes," she muttered and parked the car.

The door was answered by a woman appearing to be in her mid-seventies wearing a housecoat, though it was 2 P.M. She was thin and gray and looked resigned to life. "Yes?" she asked.

"Good afternoon, ma'am. My name is Jaye Peoria. I'm a police detective from San Diego, California. I apologize for showing up unannounced. May I come in?"

The woman hesitated.

Jaye said, "It's about your daughter, Karen."

Marian Walker pushed open the screen door and led Jaye to an old couch, lumpy but clean. Marian looked at Jaye expectantly, maybe hoping she brought something to make her feel better, although she had no idea what that could be. All Jaye had to offer were answers and maybe a little peace of mind.

Jaye broke the ice by saying, "You may not remember me, but I phoned you with news about Karen's killer."

The woman nodded, which meant either yes, or I don't care.

Jaye wasted little time on amenities. This was not a social call. She told Marian how San Diego police had cornered Karen's killer, Mark Joseph, and that he had murdered several women. "I won't go into the details of how we track criminals or why the trail led to this man. But after a great deal of careful work, we cornered the man who killed your Karen. Of course, I know you are aware of that." Jaye swallowed hard and looked at Marian for a reaction.

Nothing. Marian returned her stare for long moments, then said, "It's been a long time, ten years. I would see that man's face in my mind, day and night. I didn't know what he looked like, but I created a face for him. It was not an ugly face because then he would become just a monster. In my mind, he was an ordinary man who was filled with evil, but I had no idea how the evil got there.

"It was strange. When I was shown his picture, he looked like I imagined. They told me he could be personable when he wanted, but it had to be an act. From what I heard, he could sit right where you are and sell me a vacuum cleaner. I think I'd prefer him being a monster so everyone could have seen him coming and run. I wish Karen could have run."

"Tell me about Karen," Jaye said gently.

Marian pushed herself up off the couch and went to a table across the room. She brought back a framed color photo of Karen, a happy girl of average looks. Also lying on the table was the same small album recovered from Joseph's morbid stash. Jaye didn't remark on it.

"Her high school graduation picture. She was an only child." She looked down at the picture in her hand. "That was a happy day. There weren't many after that."

She returned the photo to the table and walked back to the couch. "Karen had a weakness for drink, just like her father, who drank himself to death. There was no help for either of them. I guess she inherited something." She added, a bit defensively, "My folks weren't drinkers."

"I'm sorry, Mrs. Walker—Marian, if I may."

Tears welled in Marian's eyes and were soon followed by Jaye's. "Not as sorry as I am." Then she quickly spoke again and raised her palm to Jaye. "Oh, I didn't say that to be mean. No, not at all."

Jaye shook her head. "Not to worry."

"Sometimes, sitting in that chair over by her picture, I think given more time, she could have straightened up, but in my heart, I know that probably wasn't true. She was too far gone in the bottle... You know what I wish most often?" She didn't wait for Jaye to answer. "I wish I could've had five more minutes with her to tell her that I was sorry for the hurtful things I said to her and that I loved her, no matter what."

Jaye groped for the right words. "Marian, the man who killed her, I'm sure he could have sold you that vacuum cleaner, and you were also right—he was filled with evil."

"Who was this man, this Mark Joseph? Why would he want to kill my Karen?" Marian asked. "His parents live in a town not far from here. They're known to be good folk. I would never blame them for a second. I know they're suffering, too."

Jaye took a paper from her purse and unfolded it. "This is a copy of some words we found in Joseph's house. They're written in his hand and with a circle around them in an angry scrawl. I'll read it to you: 'There is love in me the likes of which you've never seen. There is a rage in me, the likes of which should never escape. If I am not satisfied with the one, I will indulge the other.'"

"Mark Joseph said that?"

"We found out those are words an author wrote for the Frankenstein monster. Joseph took them as his own."

"What does that mean?" Marian said.

Jaye pursed her lips, pondering. "I think it means that love was a mystery to him, but hate wasn't. Who knows? He took the answer with him if he even knew it."

Jaye re-folded the paper and returned it to her purse, then

leaned toward the older woman. "Marian, I came here to answer your questions as best I can and to tell you that I pray for Karen's soul and for all the others." She reached out and touched the woman's thin hand and papery skin. "I understand goodness, but I'm still learning about evil. It's more complicated."

Marian asked, "Do you have a daughter."

Jaye smiled. "I hope to."

"Keep her close."

"I will, every hour of every day," Jaye said.

They walked together to the door. Marian said, "I know Mark Joseph is dead, but I wasn't told the details of how it happened."

Their eyes met. Jaye said, "I killed him."

Returning to O'Hare on Interstate 90, Jaye saw the exit signs approaching Belvidere and debated what to do. With a surge of resolve, she pulled off the last exit to the town and typed in another address. She followed it to a small frame house in an older neighborhood. She pulled up across the street and looked at it with more sadness than curiosity.

She knew this was the home of Mark Joseph's parents. She sat there staring at the house where he had lived and let her mind absorb whatever passed through it. Scenes flashed by as if in PowerPoint, taking her in many directions. Gradually it settled on her that Mark Joseph remained a presence in her life and would never go away. She had never thought of it in just that way, but she accepted it.

After a few minutes, she watched a bent old man come to the front window and look out. That must be Ed Joseph, she thought, and the figure moving behind him must be Mary Alice. Then he closed the drapes.

The old couple were now alone with their memories in a darkened home, as they were every night. Mark became again a sweet boy bundled up in new school clothes, scared about starting kindergarten, unable to sleep because the tooth fairy was due. And questions... Was it something we did? Did one of us pass on an evil gene?...

Alone in the car, Jaye's thoughts formed silent words. "I wish
you peace, Ed and Mary Alice. Your son killed innocent people,
but he also killed part of you. I'm sorry for you. I'm sorry for
them. And in a way I don't understand, I'm sorry for him. I'm
sorry for us all."

She started the car and drove away.

www.ingramcontent.com/pod-product-compliance
Lightning Source LLC
Chambersburg PA
CBHW061803190726

48289CB00007B/2057